U0119145

READING DRILLS FOR THE NEW TOEIC® TEST

編者：Institute of Foreign Study
譯者：柯乃瑜・葉韋利

眾文圖書股份有限公司

TOEIC® is a registered trademark of Educational Testing Service (ETS).
This publication is not endorsed or approved by ETS.

前言

當 The Japan Times 出版社建議我將 NEW TOEIC 長篇文章閱讀的準備方法寫成一本書時，我立刻覺得這個建議非常好。雖然市面上有很多關於英文長篇文章閱讀的參考書籍，但是卻沒有任何一本考慮到美國人的文章是以段落爲理論基礎，因此就缺少了詳細解說段落閱讀理論的書籍。在美國，英文文章的寫作有明確的規則，只要了解這些規則，就能提高閱讀的效率。ETS (Educational Testing Service) 製作的各種英文測驗，更是嚴格遵守段落閱讀理論。因此若能事先熟悉段落閱讀理論，除了能順利因應 NEW TOEIC、TOEFL iBT 等測驗，還能增進英文寫作與閱讀的效率。

本書將詳細解說這套段落閱讀理論，客觀評估 NEW TOEIC 的方向，並從宏觀的角度找尋因應之道。2006 年開始，TOEIC 和 TOEFL 的試題內容有所變動，TOEFL iBT 的閱讀部分變得更接近於 GMAT 和 GRE 的程度；NEW TOEIC 則增加了詢問全文主旨的問題，這在 TOEFL iBT 中幾乎不會出現。若要順利回答這些詢問主旨的問題，就得先了解段落閱讀理論。基本上段落閱讀理論是各種測驗的共同形式，但因爲每一種測驗的方向不同，所以在準備上就有明顯的差異。本書將比較 ETS 所製作的各種測驗，解說 NEW TOEIC 的獨特規則，來幫助讀者提升閱讀能力。

目前已經知道，若要製作閱讀測驗的模擬試題，就必須遵照既定的段落閱讀理論。很幸運的是，Institute of Foreign Study 長期致力於分析 ETS 的試題，並致力於製作原創的模擬試題，經由 Donald Miller 老師和其他成員的努力，才能編輯出這本忠實呈現出 NEW TOEIC 閱讀題型的模擬試題。

如果沒有這些了解我想法的成員來通力合作的話，是無法完成這本書的。本書以淺白易懂的方式解說，即使是中學生也能迅速了解這套段落閱讀理論。此外，本書提供質、量兼具的模擬試題，讓考生直接將目標設定成「閱讀測驗滿分」。我衷心希望本書對讀者的幫助，除了直接反映在 NEW TOEIC 的考試成績上，更能爲希望熟悉英文文章的讀者開啓另一扇窗。

Institute of Foreign Study 學院院長　中野正夫

TOEIC 簡介

TOEIC 的起源及現況

TOEIC（Test of English for International Communication，多益測驗）最早是由日本企業委託 ETS（Educational Testing Service，美國教育測驗服務社）所設計的一項英語能力測驗，用來評估英語非母語者的商務英語溝通能力，目前已發展成爲一項國際性的英語能力認證考試。TOEIC 成績爲目前企業組織、教育機構及政府單位在求才任用及內部考核時最常參考的標準，全球每年約有 700 萬人次報考，而台灣每年也約有 20 萬的報考人次。TOEIC 旨在測驗受測者實際的英語溝通能力，故測驗內容除了著重日常的生活英語，也相當重視商務職場上的英語溝通能力。

測驗形式

TOEIC 目前爲紙筆測驗，測驗形式分爲聽力與閱讀兩大類，共 200 題選擇題，測驗時間爲兩小時。考生要特別注意，TOEIC 的聽力測驗，不只是美式英語的口音，可能會有來自英國、澳洲、加拿大的各國口音。

I. 聽力測驗

聽力測驗分爲四大部分，共 100 題單選題，測驗時間爲 45 分鐘。

Part 1：照片描述（10 題）

邊看試題冊上的照片，邊聽取播放的四個選項，從中選出最符合照片內容的選項。

Part 2：應答問題（30 題）

聆聽播放的問題及其對應的三個答案選項，然後選出最符合問題的選項。

Part 3：簡短對話（30 題）

聽取 A-B-A-B 或 A-B-A 的兩人對話，閱讀試題冊上的問題及四個答案選項，然後選出最符合問題的選項。每段對話會有三個問題。

Part 4：簡短獨白（30 題）

聽取一段廣播、新聞報導或天氣預報，並閱讀試題冊上的問題及四個答案選項，然後選出最符合問題的選項。每段獨白會有三個問題。

II. 閱讀測驗

閱讀測驗分爲三大部分，共 100 題單選題，測驗時間爲 75 分鐘。

Part 5：單句填空（40 題）

閱讀一句英文短句，句中有一處空格，從四個答案選項中，選出一個最符合句子空白處的選項，以完成一個完整的句子。

Part 6：短文填空（12 題）

閱讀一篇短文，內容可能是一封電子郵件、一份說明書或一篇廣告，其中會有三個空白處，然後從空白處下的四個選項中，選出一個最適合填入空白處的字彙或片語。共有四篇短文，12 個問題。

Part 7：閱讀測驗（48 題）

包括單篇文章測驗（28 題）及雙篇文章測驗（20 題）。單篇文章爲一篇文章搭配二至五個問題；雙篇文章爲兩篇有關聯性的文章搭配五個問題。文章取自報紙或雜誌的短篇報導、廣告、公告或商業文件。

■ TOEIC 計分方式

考生用鉛筆在電腦答案卷上作答（需自備 2B 鉛筆及橡皮擦）。分數由答對的題數決定，答錯不倒扣。將兩大類（聽力類、閱讀類）答對題數轉換成分數，每大類分數範圍在 5 到 495 分之間。兩大類加起來即爲總分，範圍在 10 到 990 分之間。成績單將於考試完約 15 個工作天後寄發。

■ TOEIC 成績與英語能力對照

TOEIC 成績	英語能力	證書顏色
905~990	對任何主題的談話都能清楚地理解，可運用正式及非正式的語言進行溝通。英語能力已相當接近英語爲母語者，能親自主持以英語進行的會議。	金色 (860~990)
785~900	對於各種專業、社交甚至抽象的談話都能大致理解。在會議的討論中表達流暢，除非過於緊張，用英語進行溝通時少有停頓及遲疑的情況。	藍色 (730~855)
605~780	在熟悉的主題下，能了解及進行基本對話，故可應付例行性的業務會議。仍侷限於使用簡單且常見的字彙及句型。	綠色 (470~725)
405~600	可以主動進行簡單的對話，對話的內容也不侷限於日常生活場景。已經可以從事須使用簡單英語的相關工作。	棕色 (220~465)
255~400	能理解日常生活中特定場合的簡單對話，可用簡單英語表達詢問、打招呼及自我介紹等。	
10~250	能說出日期及時間等簡單的字彙，以及背誦簡單的句子，但尚無法自行造句進行溝通。	橘色 (10~215)

TOEIC 口說與寫作測驗

TOEIC 測驗於 2008 年 9 月開始實施口說與寫作測驗，考生可自行選擇是否加考這部分測驗。TOEIC 口說與寫作測驗的施測方式不同於聽力與閱讀測驗的紙筆測驗，所採用的是電腦網路測驗 (internet-based test, iBT) 的形式。

口說與寫作測驗的測驗時間約為 80 分鐘。

I. 口說測驗

口說測驗共有 11 題，包括六種測驗內容，測驗時間約 20 分鐘。

測驗內容	說明
Read a text aloud （朗讀）（兩題）	朗讀一段英文短文
Describe a picture （描述照片）（一題）	根據電腦螢幕上的照片，詳細描述照片內容
Respond to questions （回答問題）（三題）	根據題目設定的情境，回答與日常生活有關的問題
Respond to questions using information provided （根據題目資料應答）（三題）	根據題目設定的情境及提供的資料，回答問題
Propose a solution （提出解決方案）（一題）	根據題目設定的情境，針對問題點提出對策或解決方案
Express an opinion （陳述意見）（一題）	根據題目指定的議題陳述意見並提出理由

II. 寫作測驗

寫作測驗共有八題，包括三種測驗內容，測驗時間約 60 分鐘。

測驗內容	說明
Write a sentence based on a picture（描述照片）（五題）	使用題目指定的兩個單字或片語，造出一句符合照片內容的句子
Respond to a written request（回覆書面要求）（兩題）	讀取一封 25 ～ 50 字的電子郵件，並依據其內容回覆
Write an opinion（陳述意見）（一題）	根據題目指定的議題，陳述意見並提出理由及例子作爲佐證

■ TOEIC 報考步驟

1. 上台灣 TOEIC 官方網站 (http://www.toeic.com.tw) 查看並選擇考試日期。
2. 報名並繳費。可選擇網路報名、通訊報名或現場報名（詳情請參閱台灣 TOEIC 官方網站）。
3. 考試當天務必攜帶有效身分證件，並自備 2B 鉛筆及橡皮擦。
4. 考試後約 15 個工作天後寄發成績單。

■ 進一步資訊

有關 TOEIC 考試日期、地點或申請證書等相關資訊，可以親自向忠欣股份有限公司查詢（電話：02-2701-7333，網址：http://www.toeic.com.tw）。

本書使用方法

本書希望能幫助考生以最理想的方式學習長篇英文閱讀，以便能在 NEW TOEIC 測驗中拿到至少 900 分，甚至滿分 990 分的成績。

一般來說，只要時間足夠，NEW TOEIC 的閱讀測驗幾乎都能答對。也就是說，NEW TOEIC 是一種時間因素占有相當重要地位的限時測驗。因此，如果想要以接近滿分或以滿分爲目標，就必須提高反射作答的比例，也就是說，提高一看到題目就能立刻作答的比例。然而，當然也有一些題目是無法反射作答的，只能用消去法逐一刪除個別選項。對於那些無法反射作答的題目，如果不想辦法積極應付的話，終究還是無法拿到滿分的。因此，本書將題目分成反射作答型和花費時間型兩種，並提出不同的因應策略。以下就是本書的具體使用方法。

1 首先，必須了解段落閱讀理論，此爲 ETS 製作試題的基礎。在第一章裡會詳細介紹這套理論，在此只需要掌握住這套理論的重點即可，無須死背，因爲往後的第二～五章中，這套理論會反覆地應用在試題解說上。了解這套理論後，自然能看出可以反射作答的題目。

2 接下來，試著練習做試題。做試題時，步驟如下：
從題目開始閱讀 → 找到題目所指的段落 → 精讀該段落後判斷正確答案
應該要熟悉上述的作答模式，而不是讀完整篇文章後才開始看題目。

3 記錄每篇試題所需的作答時間。眞正的重點在於，即使遇到 NEW TOEIC 中難度較高或不懂的單字也要做完所有的題目。若遇到不會的單字，覺得較花時間時，就直接閱讀「解題技巧」的說明，確認作答的順序。所有反射作答的題目都詳述了相同的解題方式。

4 每篇試題都會標示出理想的作答時間，然而一開始時不用太在意。每次練習時如果都能詳細閱讀「解題技巧」，自然而然就會接近理想的作答時間了。

5 做本書的第一遍試題練習時，切記千萬不要試圖去了解整篇文章。因爲 NEW TOEIC 的出題特色就在於，不用確實理解整篇文章的內容就能答對所有的題目。相反的，必須訓練自己能找到題目在文章中的關鍵部分，並培養以理解重點來判斷是否爲正確答案的能力。
注意：由於 NEW TOEIC 沒有單字考題，所以背誦英文單字未必能直接反映在分數上。

6 以這套方法將所有的試題做完一遍、讀過解答後，可以進一步將本書當作強化英文閱讀能力、提升英文字彙量的教材。換句話說，試題做第一遍時並不需要精讀全文或鑽研單字，可以等到做第二遍時再加以研究和學習。這套方法是 Institute of Foreign Study 這 31 年來教導學生在比 TOEIC 難上 2 ～ 3 倍的 TOEFL CBT 閱讀測驗裡拿滿分的方法。

7 練習第二遍時，請將學習重心放在培養基礎的閱讀能力上，而不是在閱讀技巧上。在這個階段，最重要的工作就是，將英文原文和中文翻譯對照閱讀，這比只讀如何解題還重要。此外，務必要精讀，它的效果遠勝於只了解題目的解題技巧。本書對於準備 NEW TOEIC 閱讀測驗的考生來說，是一本極有效的教材；對於準備 TOEFL iBT、大學考試等的長篇英文文章的考生而言，也非常適用。

拿到 NEW TOEIC 閱讀測驗滿分的能力、迅速累積英文字彙量的能力、掌握一切長篇英文文章的能力，這三種能力互有關聯，但實際上卻得倚賴不同的技巧才能獲得。舉例來說，有的考生在 NEW TOEIC 的閱讀測驗中拿到滿分，但在 TOEFL iBT 的閱讀測驗中只拿到 80% 的分數，有的甚至在 GMAT 的閱讀測驗中拿不到一半的分數。由此可知，還是要掌握各種測驗的命題方向加強訓練才行。在閱讀本書內容時，如果能確實應用上述七個方法，不但可以收到最大的學習效果，也能獲得本段一開頭所說的這三種能力。

CONTENTS

Chapter 1

Tips for Part 7

Part 7 滿分策略

NEW TOEIC® TEST

■ TOEIC 測驗 Part 7「閱讀測驗」的特色

TOEIC 測驗在 2006 年 5 月重新修訂。分析新修訂的 TOEIC 測驗之後，可以歸納出 Part 7「閱讀測驗」的命題方向有下列幾種特色：

I. 100 題中 Part 7「閱讀測驗」占 48 題

TOEIC 的閱讀部分總共有 100 題，其中 Part 7「閱讀測驗」占了 48 題，其餘的 52 題爲文法填空題。閱讀部分的作答時間爲 75 分鐘，也就是說平均一題只有 45 秒的時間可以作答。

II. 有雙篇文章的題型

Part 7「閱讀測驗」分成單篇文章 (single passage) 和雙篇文章 (double passage) 兩種題型。單篇文章的題型是一篇文章搭配二至四個題目，雙篇文章的題型通常是兩篇文章搭配五個題目。

III. 以 5W1H 和詢問理由的題目為主

題目多是以 Why, What 爲首的問題，其他和 Where, Which, Who, How 相關的題目也十分常見。雖然 TOEIC 的 Why 類型考題不會像在 TOEFL iBT 中出現得那麼頻繁，但也算是出題頻率很高的類型。

IV. 不會出現單字題

TOEIC 幾乎不曾出現只考單字字義的題目，這部分和 TOEFL 有很大的差別。由此可知，準備 TOEIC 的閱讀測驗時，如果只有在英文單字上下功夫，學習效果並不顯著。包括本書在內，一般精確掌握住 TOEIC 閱讀難易度的題庫，都是透過詳細的英文解析與考題練習，來幫助考生提升字彙能力。

V. 問主旨或主題的題目增多

TOEIC 的題目大多是問整篇文章的主旨或主題。雖然 TOEFL CBT 同樣是從整篇文章來命題，但是這一類的題目已經不會出現在 TOEFL iBT 了。因此，問主旨或主題的題目往後將成爲 TOEIC 閱讀測驗的一大特色。

VI. 文章內容和題目的順序幾乎一致

TOEIC 閱讀測驗的文章內容和題目的順序通常會呈現一致的關係。題目依序作答時，文章的對應部分也會依序順下來，需要往回找尋內容作答的題目大概只會出現一題而已。基本上，只要閱讀文章的開頭部分就能回答第一個題目。

VII. 題目的關鍵字以同義字或相關字的形式出現在文章中

難度高的題目有一個特色，就是題目裡的關鍵字，在文章中常常會以同義字或相關字的形式出現，因此在作答時會比較花費時間。由此可知，做 TOEIC 的閱讀測驗時，不能只專注在單字上，還要對內容加以融會貫通才行。

▩ 作答時間的掌握

只要作答的時間充足，TOEIC 的 Part 7「閱讀測驗」都應該能拿滿分，然而，大多數的考生都認爲「時間不夠」。與文法塡空題部分一樣，作答時間不夠的最主要原因在於，可以反射作答的題目，與只能用消去法逐一刪除個別選項的題目，這兩種類型的題目巧妙穿插。面對這種狀況，如果想要提升作答速度就必須反覆訓練，加強反射解題的能力。此外，題目數量從原先 100 題中的 40 題增爲 48 題後，閱讀測驗就更需要迅速作答的技巧了。簡單來說，對於作答時間的掌握比起以往來得更加重要。

ETS (Educational Testing Service) 製作的長篇閱讀文章題，最主要的是針對 GMAT 測驗，此爲申請美國企管研究所 (MBA) 前必須報考的考試。接著是針對法學院的 LAST 測驗與其他研究所的 GRE 測驗。另外還有針對外國人申請美國大學時，必須報考的 TOEFL 測驗。雖然 TOEIC 也是由 ETS 出題，但是相較於前幾個評斷考生英文學術性文章閱讀能力的測驗來說，TOEIC 閱讀部分的考題主要在測試考生的日常商用英語溝通能力，同時也測試考生的英文閱讀能力。

然而，只要是由 ETS 出題的考試，大致上都有一個共同點，那就是不用讀完整篇文章就能迅速且正確地作答。簡單來說，只要能找到題目與文章相對應的部分，就能直接作答，其中以 TOEIC 測驗最具代表性。至於要如何達成「不用讀完整篇文章也能迅速且正確地作答」，最好的方式就是徹底了解段落閱讀理論。只要徹底了解這套理論，就能在瞬間鎖定文章的出題部分，並迅速判斷出選項的敘述是否正確。接下來就針對這套理論詳細說明。

■ 段落閱讀理論與應用

I. 理論

段落指的就是文章的每一段。段落閱讀理論是由美國的學術機構建立的，目的在教導美國人寫出簡潔明瞭、清楚易懂而且不會讓人誤解的文章。由於美國是一個民族大熔爐，各個民族的思考方式不同，因此必須要有一套統一的文章書寫規範，這也讓英文寫作展現出嚴謹及標準化。

半數的美國人在大學得花兩個學期的時間，徹底接受段落閱讀理論的訓練。如果沒有取得這門課程的學分，一般來說是無法取得大學學位的。在學會這套段落閱讀理論之後，美國人才得以寫出比較理想的英文。

由此可知，如果能先了解這套段落閱讀理論，那麼閱讀文章時將能更有效地掌握內容。這是因爲當初建立這套段落閱讀理論的出發點，除了要讓撰寫者能寫出好文章外，也要讓閱讀的人更容易理解文章。因此，美國的一切正式文書都依這套理論的規則書寫，但因亞洲人較少有機會可以學習到這套理論，所以在這裡就先簡單介紹一下。

Rule 1

文章的第一段稱爲引言段 (introductory paragraph)，必須在這一段的一開頭就寫出主旨，又稱作主題句 (topic sentence)。GMAT 和 TOEFL iBT 常會刻意不在第一段寫出主旨，而將第二段設成引言段，然而這並不會出現在 TOEIC 閱讀測驗中。

Rule 2

敘述各項與主旨有關的要素時，每一項要素都必須在不同的段落陳述。舉例來說，主旨是「日本料理」時，關東地區和關西地區的料理必須在不同的段落陳述。唯有當文章只有一個段落時，才可以忽略這項規則。注意，在 TOEIC 測驗中，每一個段落的主旨都設定得很清楚，因此很容易作答。

Rule 3

文章除了一個整體主旨外，每個段落還會有各自的主旨，基本上一定會出現在每個段落的開頭。

Rule 4

文章的最後一段一定要寫出整篇文章的結論。GMAT 有時候會出現例外，刻意不在文章的結尾敘述結論，但是這一類的文章並不會出現在 TOEIC 或 TOEFL 中。此外，因爲題目常常會引用長篇文章的部分內容，所以不會用沒有結論、立場未明的文章來出題。

Rule 5

結論必須與文章的整體主旨有關，換句話說，整體主旨會包含在結論的內容當中。此外，結論也可以出現在文章的開頭，當作主旨（在 ETS 的作文題中以這種方式寫作比較容易得分）。換言之，只有結論可以同時出現在文章的開頭和結尾，最多出現兩次，並不會發生結論在文章的開頭出現過，在結尾就省略掉的情形。

Rule 6

每個段落的個別主旨不能重複出現。舉例來說，先出現一個敘述關東料理的段落後，下一個段落就不能再出現敘述關東料理的內容，否則就會違反規則。若要在同一個主旨的情況下更換段落，則段落之間必須出現一個可以顯示不同主題要素的連接詞。

Rule 7

開頭段落裡可以放入題旨句 (thesis statement)。題旨句將主旨的論述一步一步地寫出來。例如說，「日本料理博大精深，不同的地區發展出各別的風格。我將區域特性分成北海道、關東、關西等地區說明。」在這樣的敘述中，「將區域特性分成北海道、關東、關西等地區說明」就是題旨句，而前面部分「日本料理博大精深」就是主旨。如果將這些敘述用記號表示，如以 X 表示主旨、A 表示北海道、B 表示關東、C 表示關西的話，畫成簡圖就如右頁所示。

段落 1

X
X= (A, B, C)

段落 2

A
A1: A 的相關特色等
A2: 相同

段落 3

B
B1: B 的相關特色等
B2: 相同

段落 4

C
C1: C 的相關特色等
C2: 相同

段落 5

結論（包含 X）

上面是典型的文章架構，雖然不是永遠一成不變，但卻是學習英文作文的基本形式。

II. 應用

段落 1

X ＝日本料理
X ＝（A ＝北海道、B ＝關東、
C ＝關西）

段落 2

A ＝北海道
A1：A 的相關特色等，如螃蟹料理。
A2：相同，如鮭魚卵料理。

段落 3

B ＝關東
B1：B 的相關特色等，如江戶前壽司。
B2：相同，如淺草海苔料理。

段落 4

C ＝關西
C1：C 的相關特色等，如大阪燒。
C2：相同，如章魚燒丸子。

段落 5

結論（包含日本料理）

接著，請試著將這套理論應用在解題上吧。如上圖所示，主旨 A（北海道）在段落 2 敘述，而不是在段落 1 敘述。基本上不可以出現重複敘述 A 的內容配置與架構，如 A → B → A。因此，如果在題目中看到了 A、A1、A2 的單字，這一題的對應內容只會出現在段落 2 中。此外，假設在選項中出現了 B、C 的單字或內容，例如淺草海苔料理、章魚燒丸子的話，在這個內容關於北海道的題目中，就可以自動假設該選項是錯誤的，因爲淺草海苔料理和章魚燒丸子的內容應該不會出現在只有敘述北海道的段落 2 中（如果段落 2 出現了敘述北海道以外的內容，就違反了 Rule 6）。

由此可知，對於與 A 相關的題目，即使未能清楚掌握到敘述 A 之段落 2 以外的單字和內容，大致上還是可以選出正確答案。以這個例子為例，即使不知道淺草海苔料理或章魚燒丸子的意思，只要知道沒有出現在段落 2，就一定不是正確答案。從這個角度來看，即使遇到不會的英文單字，其實也不必過度擔心。

現在就從第二章開始，試著用這套段落閱讀理論來實際解題吧。

Chapter 2

E-mail・Letter

電子郵件・書信

NEW TOEIC® TEST

From: Living Well Sports (billing@livingwell.com)

To: John Russel & Associates

Subject: Cancellation of membership

Your cancellation request was processed on 1/19/2009. Since Living Well does not prorate fees, we will not be refunding the unused portion of your membership contract. You can continue to use Living Well's facilities until April 1, 2009, since you have paid up until that date.

We will, however, keep your account open for the rest of the year, so if you change your mind and decide you would like to reactivate your full membership at Living Well, simply click the "renew membership" link on our homepage well-sports.com, or visit your local Living Well Sports and Fitness Center.

If you have any further questions about your account or Living Well, please reply to this e-mail. We recommend that you print this e-mail as confirmation of your request to cancel your full membership.

We look forward to assisting you with your future health and fitness goals with our improved and expanded services, facilities, and sporting goods.

Thank you,

The Living Well Customer Service Team

1. What does this e-mail confirm?
   (A) An order has been shipped.
   (B) A service has been discontinued.
   (C) A membership has been canceled.
   (D) A membership has been reactivated.

C

2. How can customers reactivate their membership?
   (A) By calling the sports club
   (B) By replying to this e-mail before January 19, 2009
   (C) By visiting their local branch of the sports club
   (D) By sending a new payment before April 1, 2009

D

associate 合夥人
prorate 按比例分配
refund 退还
portion of 部份
contract 合約.
account 帳號
the rest of 最後
reactivate 重啟
recommand 建議
print 列印
assist 協助.

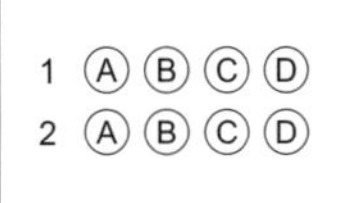

寄件者：健康生活運動 (billing@livingwell.com)
收件者：約翰．羅素與合夥人
主旨：取消會員資格

已經於 2009 年 1 月 19 日受理您的會員取消申請。由於健康生活的會員費用沒有按照比例分配，您會員合約中尚未使用的部分將無法按照比例退還。到 2009 年 4 月 1 日前，您都可以繼續使用健康生活的設施，因為您的會員費用已預付到該日期。

不過我們仍舊會將您的帳號保留到年底。如果您改變主意，決定重新啓用您在健康生活的完整會員資格，只要到我們 well-sports.com 的首頁上按下「續約」的連結，或是就近到您所在當地的健康生活運動與健身中心即可。

如果您對於您的帳號或健康生活有任何疑問，敬請回覆這封電子郵件。我們建議您將這封電子郵件列印出來，作為您要求取消完整會員資格的確認。

未來我們期待能以更佳且擴增的服務、設施、運動用品，協助您達成您的健康與健身目標。

謝謝您。

健康生活客服小組

題目中譯

1. 這封電子郵件要確認什麼？
   (A) 訂單已經寄出。
   (B) 服務已經終止。
   (C) **會員資格已經取消**。
   (D) 會員資格已經重新啓用。

2. 顧客要如何重新啓用他們的會員資格？
   (A) 打電話給運動俱樂部
   (B) 在 2009 年 1 月 19 日前回覆這封電子郵件
   (C) **造訪運動俱樂部在當地的分店**
   (D) 在 2009 年 4 月 1 日前寄出款項

解題技巧

答案 (C)

遇到這類問電子郵件內容的題目，首先要確認 Subject:（主旨）。通常 Subject: 就是答案。

答案 (C)

這題的重點就在於迅速從文章中找到題目裡的 reactivate。雖然在第一段的內容中確認要取消 (cancellation) 俱樂部的會員資格，但接下來的第二段裡有 however。換句話說，敘述內容是和 cancel 相反的 reactivate。

註解

process (v.) 處理
prorate fees 按比例分配費用
reactivate (v.) 使恢復活動

From: Dearborn Parks and Recreation Department
To: Softball 1-B Team Sponsors
Subject: League Dues and Uniform Payment

We are almost in April, and I am sure everyone is looking forward to getting out and having some fun on the diamond again this year. Before we do so, however, I need to address the issue of outstanding payments. I still have not received diamond use rental dues from 6 of the 8 teams in 1-B. I would urge those of you who still need to provide signed contracts and uniform payments to forward them to me as soon as possible. All uniforms have been ordered and should arrive by May 1.

It is important that all contracts be signed and returned, and all payments brought up to date, so as to avoid depleting the Parks and Recreation Department budget from these outstanding costs. The uniform fees were included in your payment plans, and team members cannot be issued uniforms until their sponsors have turned in their checks.

Please contact me as soon as possible to discuss your outstanding balances on your accounts. If I do not hear back from you by April 15, I will assume that your team has decided not to take part in the league this year, and will have to cancel your team's uniform order.

Many thanks,

Jamie McGregor
Dearborn Parks and Recreation Department

1. What does this e-mail request?
   (A) Payment for park rental and uniform fees
   (B) Information on this year's uniform designs
   (C) Rental information for uniforms
   (D) This year's softball league schedule

2. What should be sent to the writer of this e-mail?
   (A) Uniform designs
   (B) Payment plans
   (C) Team information
   (D) Signed contracts

3. Who would be the recipient of this e-mail?
   (A) Players on softball teams in League 1-B
   (B) Uniform manufacturers
   (C) Companies sponsoring softball teams
   (D) Dearborn Parks and Recreation Department workers

1 Ⓐ Ⓑ Ⓒ Ⓓ
2 Ⓐ Ⓑ Ⓒ Ⓓ
3 Ⓐ Ⓑ Ⓒ Ⓓ

原文中譯

寄件者：迪爾本球場與娛樂部門
收件者：壘球 1-B 球隊贊助商
主旨：聯盟會費與制服款項

即將進入 4 月，相信各位都很期待今年再次上場好好表現一番。不過在這之前，我必須先處理未付款項的問題。我一直還沒收到 1-B 八隊球隊中其中六隊的球場租用費。我想促請那些還沒交出已簽訂之合約與制服款項的贊助商盡快交給我。制服已經訂了，預計 5 月 1 日之前送達。

所有的合約都必須簽好並交回，所有的款項也都必須如期支付，這很重要，如此才能避免這些未付款項耗盡球場與娛樂部門的預算。制服費用包含在貴贊助商的付款計畫內，所以除非贊助商繳交支票，否則隊員將無法領取制服。

請盡速與我聯絡，以便討論貴贊助商的未付款項。如果 4 月 15 日以前還沒有收到貴贊助商的消息，我將認定貴贊助商的球隊決定今年不加入聯盟，接著會將貴贊助商球隊的制服訂單取消。

萬分感謝。

迪爾本球場與娛樂部門
傑米・麥奎格

題目中譯

1. 這封電子郵件有什麼要求？

(A) **支付球場租金與制服費用**
(B) 今年制服設計的資料
(C) 制服的租用消息
(D) 今年壘球聯盟的行程

2. 應該要寄什麼給這位電子郵件的寄件者？

(A) 制服設計
(B) 付款計畫
(C) 球隊消息
(D) **簽好的合約**

3. 這封電子郵件的收件者是誰？

(A) 1-B 聯盟壘球隊的球員
(B) 制服廠商
(C) **贊助壘球隊的公司**
(D) 迪爾本球場與娛樂部門的員工

解題技巧

答案 (A)

閱讀文章前，從 Subject: 一欄就可以知道內容是有關請款事宜。(A)、(B)、(C) 裡都有 uniform 這個單字，但是提到付款的只有 (A)。

答案 (D)

首先先找到第一段第五行 forward 這個字，重點是要了解 send = forward。雖然 urge ... to forward 的關係有點難分辨，但只要知道 forward them 的 forward 是動詞，就回答得出來。

答案 (C)

電子郵件的收件者就在第二行的 To: 之後，很容易看出正確答案。結果只要看這封電子郵件一開頭的前三行和文章的第一段就能回答這三個題目。

註解

due (n.) 會費
outstanding (adj.) 未償付的
deplete (v.) 用盡
recipient (n.) 接受者

P.O. Box 51924, Waterfront
Cape Town 8002
South Africa

July 7, 2008

William Bradford
Park Manager
P.O. Box 61190
Marshalltown 2091
South Africa

Dear Mr. Bradford:

I visited Hallows Lake and had a wonderful time on the weekend of July 4. The park management does an excellent job of keeping the park in tip-top condition. While I was there, I could not help but notice that there was a big, open space. On the National Parks website, it indicates that this facility does not accommodate large groups.

I am inquiring as to whether or not a wedding could be hosted in this locale. I believe that the space is large enough to hold a party of about 150 people. I have a client who is interested in having a wedding there at the end of October. We understand the need for eco-friendliness and can assure you that we will leave the area cleaner than how we found it.

Hallows Lake is a beautiful park and I understand the need to keep it that way. I have been charmed by its beauty ever since I first visited it as a child, and think it's a perfect match to celebrate a special event. Please let me know whether or not the park will accommodate this request.

Thank you for your time.

Sincerely,

Lauren Tai
Wedding Planner

1. What is the purpose of this letter?
   - (A) To report a violation
   - (B) To ask for an extension
   - (C) To explain an opinion
   - (D) To request permission

2. When did Ms. Tai first visit the park?
   - (A) The first weekend of July
   - (B) When she was a child
   - (C) On July 7, 2008
   - (D) At the end of October

3. What guarantee does Ms. Tai provide?
   - (A) That they'll clean up for themselves
   - (B) That they will fill all seats at the wedding
   - (C) That her group is large enough
   - (D) That she will find new customers

1 Ⓐ Ⓑ Ⓒ Ⓓ
2 Ⓐ Ⓑ Ⓒ Ⓓ
3 Ⓐ Ⓑ Ⓒ Ⓓ

原文中譯

南非開普敦 8002
濱水區郵政信箱第 51924 號

2008 年 7 月 7 日

2091 南非馬歇爾城
郵政信箱第 61190 號
公園經理
威廉 · 布萊德佛

布萊德佛先生您好：

7 月 4 日那個週末我造訪了哈羅斯湖區，度過了非常美好的時光。公園管理處非常盡心，將園區維持在最好的狀態。我在那裡時不禁注意到那裡有個很大的開放空間。國家公園的網站上寫明，這個場地無法容納大型團體。

我想詢問是否能在這個公園裡舉辦婚禮。我相信這個場地足以容納 150 人的團體。我有位客戶 10 月底時想在那裡舉辦婚禮。我們了解生態保護的重要性，並可以向您保證我們一定會把場地整理得比原先還乾淨。

哈羅斯湖區是個非常漂亮的公園，所以我了解維持原貌的必要性。自從我小時候第一次造訪之後，就深深為它的美所著迷，並認為它是慶祝特別日子的最佳場地。無論是否能在公園裡舉行婚禮，煩請通知我一聲。

謝謝您撥空讀這封信。

婚禮企畫者
羅倫 · 泰
敬上

題目中譯

1. 這封信的目的是什麼？

   (A) 報告違規
   (B) 要求延期
   (C) 解釋看法
   (D) **請求許可**

2. 泰女士初次造訪該公園是什麼時候？

   (A) 7 月的第一個週末
   (B) **她還小的時候**
   (C) 2008 年 7 月 7 日
   (D) 10 月底

3. 泰女士提供什麼樣的保證？

   (A) **他們自己會打掃乾淨**
   (B) 他們會填滿所有的座位
   (C) 她的團體人數夠多
   (D) 她會找新的客戶

解題技巧

答案 (D)

這篇文章的主題從第二段開始發展，因此，第二段第一句的 I am inquiring as to... 就是正確答案的關鍵。只要發現這一句的 hosted 和第一段最後的 accommodate 是相關字，就能輕鬆找到正確答案。

答案 (B)

題目中的 first 是搜尋文章的關鍵字，就出現在文章第三段的 since I first visited it as a child 中。關鍵字在大多數時候都是像 first 這種表示順序的單字，或是比較級的單字。若用 visit 來搜尋文章，就可在第一段第一行找到，但是這一段並不是正確答案所在。

答案 (A)

題目中的 guarantee 是搜尋關鍵字。先搜尋到第二段第四行裡的同義字 assure，就能從 We ... can assure you that we will leave the area cleaner than how we found it. 中找到正確答案。

註解

tip-top (adj.) 第一流的，最佳的
accommodate (v.) 容納；使適合；供應
inquire (v.) 詢問
be charmed by... 被…迷住的

From: Bender Books

To: Mark Fernandez

Subject: Your order confirmation

Thank you for shopping with us. Your order has been packaged and is ready to leave our warehouse. The details of your order appear below. Within 24 hours of receiving this e-mail, you may track the delivery status of your order by visiting http://www.ups.com/tracking/tracking.html.

When a tracking number is included, please note that it has been assigned before the package was delivered to the carrier. If your tracking number does not appear immediately, the carrier may still be processing this information. You may need to check the carrier's website periodically for updated information.

Your order qualifies for FREE DELIVERY. For further details, please visit http://www.benderbooks.com/. For further assistance, please e-mail us at service@benderbooks.com, or call us toll-free at 1-800-555-1234.

We appreciate your business and look forward to your visiting us again soon.

benderbooks.com

The following has been packaged and is ready to leave our warehouse:

Bill To: Mark Fernandez

Ship To: Mark Fernandez, NW 2nd Ave, Miami, FL 33142

The Great Juggling Kit: All You Need to Know to Develop Amazing Juggling Skills

ISBN: 0760722714 Feb 5, 2009

The World's Foremost Military Historians
ISBN: 0425176428 Feb 5, 2009

A Rogue Economist Explores the Hidden Side of Everything
ISBN: 006073132X Feb 5, 2009

Carrier: UPS. To speed up delivery, we may send separate items in your order from different warehouses, in which case more than one package will be shipped to you. Sales tax varies by state.

1. What does this e-mail confirm?
   (A) A book order cannot be processed
   (B) A book has been successfully returned
   (C) A change in delivery policy
   (D) A book order being shipped

2. How should customers keep track of their orders' status?
   (A) Check a webpage
   (B) Make a phone call
   (C) Send an e-mail
   (D) Write a letter

3. Mr. Fernandez's order includes books on all of the following EXCEPT
   (A) juggling.
   (B) history.
   (C) international peacekeeping forces.
   (D) economics.

confirmation 確認
warehouse 倉庫
track 追蹤
delivery status 運送 狀況
assign 指定
carrier 貨運業者
periodically 定期地
appreciate 感謝

1 Ⓐ Ⓑ Ⓒ Ⓓ
2 Ⓐ Ⓑ Ⓒ Ⓓ
3 Ⓐ Ⓑ Ⓒ Ⓓ

寄件者：班德圖書
收件者：馬克．佛南德茲
主旨：訂購確認單

謝謝您在本網站購物。您訂購的商品已包裝完成，準備從倉庫寄出。您的訂單明細如下所示。收到這封電子郵件的 24 小時之內，您可以上 http://www.ups.com/tracking/tracking.html 追蹤訂單的運送狀態。

如果附上了追蹤編號，請注意那是本網站將包裹交給貨運業者前就已經指定的編號。如果您的追蹤編號沒有即時出現，那可能是貨運業者還在處理這項資訊。您可能要定期上貨運業者的網站查詢最新資訊。

您的訂單符合免費運送的資格。如需進一步的資訊，請上 http://www.benderbooks.com/。如需進一步的協助，請寫信到 service@benderbooks.com 或撥打免付費電話 1-800-555-1234。

感謝您的購買並希望您再度光臨。

benderbooks.com

以下物品已包裝完成，準備從倉庫寄出：
付款者：馬克．佛南德茲
收貨者：33142 佛羅里達州邁阿密市西北第二大道　馬克．佛南德茲

《偉大的雜耍箱：發展驚人雜耍技巧的所有知識》
ISBN: 0760722714 2009 年 2 月 5 日

《世界最重要的軍事歷史學家》
ISBN: 0425176428 2009 年 2 月 5 日

《無賴經濟學家的明察秋毫》
ISBN: 006073132X 2009 年 2 月 5 日

貨運業者：UPS。為了加快運送速度，您所訂購的商品可能會由不同的倉庫出貨，如此一來，您可能會收到一個以上的包裹。銷售稅視各州規定而異。

題目中譯

1. 這封電子郵件要確認什麼？

(A) 有一筆書的訂單無法受理
(B) 有一本書已經成功退貨
(C) 貨運政策改變
(D) 有一筆訂書的運送

2. 顧客要如何追蹤訂單狀態？

(A) 檢查網頁
(B) 打電話
(C) 寄電子郵件
(D) 寫信

3. 佛南德茲先生的訂單不包含以下哪一本書？

(A) 雜耍
(B) 歷史學
(C) 國際維和部隊
(D) 經濟學

解題技巧

答案 (D)

從信件一開頭的 From: 和 Subject: 就可以知道這是一封來自網路書店的「訂購」確認信。從這一點可以推測出正確答案，另外也可以從 delivery 或 tracking number 等字眼判斷出信件內容與確認「運送」事宜相關。

答案 (A)

若要在文章中迅速找出題目中的 customers keep track...，只要找到第一段最後一句 you may track the delivery status of you order by... 就行了。

答案 (C)

這一題問的是所訂購的商品，所以要先看清楚訂購明細。由於 juggling, historians, economist 等單字都出現在各個書名當中，因此可以排除選項 (A)、(B)、(D)。

註解

periodically (adv.) 定期地，週期地
updated (adj.) 最新的，更新的
juggling (adj.) 雜耍的
foremost (adj.) 最重要的，最先的
rogue (adj.) 無賴的
explore (v.) 探索

December 26, 2008

1593 Marathon Court, APT. 49
Lexington, KY 40505

Credcapital Card Company
P.O. Box 1230
Rapid City, SD 57709

Re: Objection to unauthorized charges
Account number: 2903 2114 1012 6603

Dear Sir or Madam:

Per my two conversations with Jason from your Credit Department on Wednesday, December 17, 2008, this is to confirm that an unauthorized charge was made to this account on November 2, 2007 in the amount of four thousand nine hundred ($4,900.00) dollars. This was done in the form of a cash advance issued as a check payable to Kathy Schwartz. This charge was not authorized by me; therefore, I object to this charge and refuse to be responsible for it. The check in question was made out by and cashed by her and her alone. She is responsible for the amount of the cash advance. I will continue to make timely payments on the boat loan, as I have done since opening this account.

This account has been dormant and no charges have been made against it for over a year. I never intended nor authorized charges to be made against this account. In fact, this charge card is one of three that were issued without my consent in conjunction with the aforementioned boat loan.

Please be advised that any charges by Kathy Schwartz on this account are improper and unauthorized. I will not be liable for any such charges.

Very truly yours,

Barry Schmell

1. What is the purpose of this letter?
   (A) To notify a creditor that Mr. Schmell refuses to pay
   (B) To contact a customer regarding an overdue loan
   (C) To request an extension on a bill soon-to-be due
   (D) To authorize Kathy Schwartz to use the account

2. What did Kathy Schwartz do?
   (A) She recently purchased a boat from Mr. Schmell.
   (B) She spoke with Jason by phone about the bill that was past due.
   (C) She used Mr. Schmell's credit card without permission.
   (D) She disputed the credit card bill with Mr. Schmell.

3. How many times has the credit card been used in the past year?
   (A) 0
   (B) 1
   (C) 2
   (D) 3

objection 反對.異議.
unauthorized 未經許可的.
charge 簽帳.
conversation 談話.
responsible 負責.
dormant 未使用的.
conjunction with 連同.
aforemention 上述的.

原文中譯

2008 年 12 月 26 日

40505 肯塔基州列克星敦市
1593 馬拉松廣場 49 號公寓

57709 南達科他州湍急市
郵政信箱第 1230 號
信用資金卡公司

回覆：對未經授權的簽帳提出異議
帳號：2903 2114 1012 6603

敬啓者：

依據我與貴信用卡部門員工傑森在 2008 年 12 月 17 日星期三兩次談話的內容，這封信是要確認在 2007 年 11 月 2 日有一筆未經授權的簽帳，四千九百元（4900 元），以預借現金支票的方式由這個戶頭開出，抬頭為凱西．史華茲。這筆簽帳沒有經過我的授權，因此我反對承認這筆簽帳，也拒絕為此負責。這張有問題的支票由她自己開出，也由她自己兌現，所以她必須為此預借現金的金額負責。我會繼續按時繳交從開戶以來就開始繳的船貸分期付款。

這個戶頭停止不用已經超過一年的時間，不曾有人使用這個戶頭簽帳。我也從來沒有打算或授權使用這個戶頭簽帳。事實上，這張簽帳卡是沒有經過我的同意，連同船貸一併發給我的三張簽帳卡之一。

請注意，凱西．史華茲用這個戶頭所進行的任何簽帳行為，既不恰當也未經過授權，因此我將不為任何此類的簽帳負責。

貝瑞．史梅爾
敬上

1. 這封信的目的是什麼？

(A) **通知債權人，史梅爾先生拒絕付款**
(B) 聯絡客戶有筆貸款逾期
(C) 要求延長即將到期的帳單
(D) 授權凱西・史華茲使用某個戶頭

答案 (A)

從收信者為信用卡公司，加上信件主旨為 Objection to unauthorized charges 可知，這封信的目的在針對未經授權的簽帳提出申訴。

2. 凱西・史華茲做了什麼？

(A) 她最近向史梅爾先生買了一艘船。
(B) 她與傑森通電話討論了過期帳單。
(C) **她未經許可就使用了史梅爾先生的信用卡**。
(D) 她為了信用卡帳單與史梅爾先生發生爭執。

答案 (C)

第一段的 The check in question was made out by and cashed by her and her alone. 是重點句，由此可知，開出並兌現支票的人都是凱西・史華茲本人。

3. 這張信用卡在過去一年使用過幾次？

(A) **0 次**
(B) 1 次
(C) 2 次
(D) 3 次

答案 (A)

題目中的 How many times... 和 used 是搜尋關鍵字。由於第一段的內容與支票有關，而與信用卡的使用無關，因此正確答案不會在這裡。第二段的 ...no charges have been made against it for over a year 這部分才是題目所指的內容。

註解

objection to... 反對…，對…有異議
unauthorized charge 未經授權的簽帳
account (n.) 戶頭
refuse (v.) 拒絕
be responsible for... 對…負責
dormant (adj.) 靜止的，暫停作用的
consent (n.) 同意，承認

Pat Alido
Haines Public Policy Non-Profit
Hopkins Lane, P.O. Box 48
Haddonfield, NJ 08012-0048

Dear Mr. Alido:

Hello, I was referred to you by Ryan Miller after we just recently had a conversation about some of my qualifications and how they might be better suited in another area of the Haines NPO.

I graduated from the Hussian School of Art in Philadelphia with an associate's degree in Specialized Technology. Although I am currently employed by Haines as a security guard, I am interested in the graphics art related positions that Ryan has talked about with me. He mentioned that with my background, I might be able to transfer to a position that would take full advantage of my education and skills through past employment. He had also indicated that you may be able to assist me in regards to these positions.

If a transfer is possible, I would be more than happy to discuss with you my qualifications in further detail. Attached is my résumé, job references, and a sample of the graphics design work I have done. Please feel free to contact me at my home phone number, (856) 439-0185.

Sincerely,

Tom Sakamoto

1. What is the purpose of this letter?
   (A) To request a job transfer
   (B) To announce a retirement
   (C) To authorize a new design project
   (D) To introduce a new staff member

2. What job does Mr. Sakamoto currently have?
   (A) Non-profit fund raiser
   (B) Graphics designer
   (C) Security guard
   (D) Performing artist

3. What is NOT included with this letter?
   (A) A résumé
   (B) A list of past supervisors
   (C) A copy of diploma
   (D) A sample of work

1 Ⓐ Ⓑ Ⓒ Ⓓ
2 Ⓐ Ⓑ Ⓒ Ⓓ
3 Ⓐ Ⓑ Ⓒ Ⓓ

派特．艾立度
海恩斯公共政策非營利組織
08012-0048 新澤西州哈登菲爾德鎮
霍普金斯路郵政信箱第 48 號

艾立度先生：

您好。不久之前我與雷恩．米勒談過，認為我的資歷或許比較適合海恩斯非營利組織的其他部門，因此他提到您。

我畢業於費城的胡賽因藝術學院，輔修專業技術。雖然我目前是海恩斯的警衛，但卻對我和雷恩洽談的平面設計藝術相關職位感到興趣。他提到我的背景或許能幫助我轉到一個可充分發揮在校所學及過去工作技能的職位。他同時也表示，您或許可以幫助我爭取到這一類的職位。

如果能調職，我會非常樂意與您詳細討論我的資格。隨信附上我的履歷、工作推薦人，以及我做過的平面設計稿。請隨時撥打我家裡的電話與我聯絡：(856) 439-0185。

阪本湯姆
敬上

1. 這封信的目的是什麼？

(A) **要求調職**
(B) 宣布退休
(C) 授權一件新的設計案
(D) 介紹一位新進員工

答案 (A)

這一題問的是寫這封信的目的。可從第一段推測出來，但第二段的 I am interested in the graphics art related positions ... I might be able to transfer... 直接表達出寫信人的心情，讀到這裡就能確定正確答案了。

2. 阪本先生目前的工作是什麼？

(A) 非營利組織募款員
(B) 平面設計師
(C) **警衛**
(D) 表演藝術家

答案 (C)

以 job 和 currently 當作搜尋關鍵字，就可以找到第二段的 I am currently employed by Haines as a security guard。如果能在寫第一題時就掌握了這個資訊，就能節省作答時間。

3. 這封信沒有附上什麼？

(A) 履歷
(B) 過去的主管名單
(C) **學歷副本**
(D) 作品樣本

答案 (C)

首先，重點在於是否發現題目的關鍵字就是 included，接下來則在於是否理解第三段的 attached 是相關字。Attached is... 之後沒有列出來的東西就是正確答案。

註解

qualification (n.) 資格，條件
associate's degree 副學士學位
transfer (v.) 調動（職務等）
take full advantage of... 充分利用…
résumé (n.) 履歷
reference (n.) 介紹人，介紹信

From: Eze Popo

To: Ndidi Fredricks

Subject: Mentoring for Sandra O'Neill

Congratulations on being selected as a mentor in the GOR Ubani Mentoring Pilot Program. The aim of the program is to assist young, black scientists and researchers in more rapidly developing successful careers in a research environment. A key component in the success of this program is an effective mentoring relationship between yourself and the mentee.

The program provides the following for the grant holder: a year's funding for proposed research activities, mentoring opportunities, regular assessment, and assistance with goal setting and performance management. We help grant holders get a head start on their careers by providing training in conference presentations and helping them develop professional writing skills.

In addition, the program provides the following for the mentor: $4,000 towards the mentor's research activities for the duration of the pilot program (2009-10), subject to satisfactory fulfillment of the tasks.

As a mentor you are expected to participate in the evaluation of your own performance, your mentee's performance, and the program itself. You will also participate regularly in goal-setting and outcome evaluation with your mentee. For an accurate assessment of progress made, you must submit your progress reports by the end of June and the end of October 2010. You also must attend initial orientation sessions organized by the GOR Ubani Program in March 2009, and attend one meeting every six months. You will need to communicate with your institution's Mentoring Committee in order to receive full funding.

We look forward to your participation in the program, and are sending you all the application materials by mail. If you have any questions or concerns, please feel free to contact us at your convenience.

Sincerely,

Eze Popo

Director, GOR Ubani MPP

1. Who has been offered the opportunity to be a mentor?
   (A) Eze Popo
   (B) Ndidi Fredricks
   (C) Sandra O'Neill
   (D) Gor Ubani

2. What kind of person would be helped by this program?
   (A) A young entrepreneur
   (B) A female engineer
   (C) A minority scientist
   (D) An excellent student

3. Which of the following is NOT required of a mentor?
   (A) Evaluating his or her own performance
   (B) Planning an orientation meeting
   (C) Helping the mentee set goals
   (D) Attending meetings organized by the GOR Ubani Program

4. What kind of service does the GOR Ubani Mentor Program provide grant holders?
   (A) Conference presentation opportunities
   (B) Job search assistance
   (C) Professional writing training
   (D) Research operation assistance

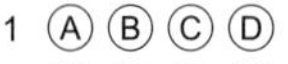

寄件者：伊茲．波波
收件者：恩底迪．佛德瑞克斯
主旨：擔任珊德拉．歐尼爾的指導顧問

恭喜您獲選為果耳烏班尼指導顧問試行計畫的顧問之一。這項計畫的目的之一，是要協助年輕的黑人科學家和研究員，在研究環境中能夠更快速發展成功的事業。有一個關鍵因素能讓這項計畫成功，就是您與被指導者之間能建立起一個有效的顧問指導關係。

這項計畫提供補助金得主如下所述：提出的研究活動能獲得一年的經費、顧問指導的機會、固定的評估、協助建立目標與成效管理。藉由提供會議發表的訓練及協助發展專業寫作技巧，我們能幫助補助金得主快速展開事業。

此外，這項計畫提供顧問如下所述：支付顧問 4000 元，作為試行計畫 (2009-10) 期間的研究活動費用，但是要視任務達成的滿意度而定。

身為指導顧問，您必須參與自我表現、被指導者表現，以及計畫本身成效的評估。您也要定期與被指導者針對目標的設立與成效進行評估。為了能正確評估進展，您在 2010 年 6 月底和 10 月底都必須交出進度報告。您同時也必須參與果耳烏班尼計畫於 2009 年 3 月所舉辦的首次介紹會，然後每六個月參與一次會議。您必須與貴機構的顧問指導委員會接洽，才能獲得全額的資金。

我們期待您加入這項計畫，並將全部的申請資料郵寄給您。如果您有任何疑問或擔憂，請隨時與我們聯絡。

果耳烏班尼指導顧問試行計畫主管
伊茲．波波
敬上

1. 是誰獲得機會擔任指導顧問？
   (A) 伊茲 · 波波
   (B) 恩底迪 · 佛德瑞克斯
   (C) 珊德拉 · 歐尼爾
   (D) 果耳 · 烏班尼

答案 (B)

從文章的第一行 Congratulations on being selected as a mentor 可以知道這封電子郵件的收件者佛德瑞克斯先生獲選擔任指導顧問。

2. 哪一種人將受惠於這項計畫？
   (A) 年輕的企業家
   (B) 女性工程師
   (C) 弱勢的科學家
   (D) 優秀的學生

答案 (C)

從第一段的 The aim of the program is... 知道「本計畫的目的在鼓勵年輕黑人科學家和研究員盡早在其研究領域累積傲人的資歷」。minority 是「少數」的意思。

3. 以下哪一項不是指導顧問必須做的事？
   (A) 評估自身的表現
   (B) 規畫介紹會議
   (C) 幫助被指導者建立目標
   (D) 參與果耳烏班尼計畫所舉辦的會議

答案 (B)

重點在於確認第四段第一句一開頭 As a mentor you are expected... 所引出來的主題是「指導顧問的義務」。選項中沒在這一段出現的 (B) 是正確答案。

4. 果耳烏班尼指導顧問計畫提供補助金得主何種服務？
   (A) 會議發表機會
   (B) 協助找工作
   (C) 專業寫作訓練
   (D) 協助進行研究

答案 (C)

這一題問段落主旨。一看到 grant holders 就要注意第二段第一句的 The program provides the following for the grant holder:。從這一段最後的 professional writing skills 可知要選 (C)。

註解

mentoring (n.) 指導教育；良師制度
component (n.) 構成要素，成分，元件
mentee (n.) 被指導者
duration (n.) 持續期間
subject to... 受限於…，服從於…
at your convenience 在您方便時

Golden Dragon Travel
Online travel services since 1998
Recognized for good performance by the Singapore Tourist Bureau

Dear Mr. Tomi Wong:

We would like to thank you for once again choosing Golden Dragon Travel. We strive to meet all of our business customers' needs. Included with this itinerary are your tickets. Please check that you have tickets for each leg of your trip and contact us if anything is missing.

Date	Flight Time	Flight No.	City	Notes
May 10	Dep 2200	SA 326	Singapore	
11	Arr 0450		London (LHR)	taxi to hotel
13	Dep 1800	BA 366	London (LHR)	
13	Arr 1930		Manchester	met by Mr. Jones
15	Dep 0900	BM 211	Manchester	met by Ms. Sands
15	Arr 1000		Glasgow	
15	Dep 1830	BM 244	Glasgow	go to terminal 3
15	Arr 1930		London (LHR)	
15	Dep 2130	SA 327	London (LHR)	
16	Arr 0500		Singapore	

Notes:

1. The London hotel for the 11th and 12th of May is Hotel Metropole. A single room suite has been booked in your name. The address is: Regent Street, London WCI 48Q. Telephone 020-9104-3448.
2. Hotel accommodation in Manchester is being arranged by Mr. Jones.

If there is anything else we can do for you, please do not hesitate to contact us. We at Golden Dragon are proud of the high level of service that we provide to all of our clients. I am enclosing a brochure describing some of our new Asia-Europe travel services. Please take a moment to look them over. We may be able to help you more than you know.

Thank you once again for your reservation. Have a great trip!

Nancy Chi

1. Why will Mr. Wong travel to England?
   (A) For leisure
   (B) For study
   (C) For business
   (D) For surgery

2. Where will Mr. Wong meet Mr. Jones?
   (A) Singapore
   (B) London
   (C) Glasgow
   (D) Manchester

3. What does Ms. Chi ask Mr. Wong to do?
   (A) Study a brochure
   (B) Send her his itinerary
   (C) Arrange a hotel reservation with Mr. Jones
   (D) Contact her upon arrival

4. Which of the following is Mr. Wong's flight to Glasgow?
   (A) SA 326
   (B) BA 366
   (C) BM 211
   (D) BM 244

1 Ⓐ Ⓑ Ⓒ Ⓓ
2 Ⓐ Ⓑ Ⓒ Ⓓ
3 Ⓐ Ⓑ Ⓒ Ⓓ
4 Ⓐ Ⓑ Ⓒ Ⓓ

金龍旅遊網
成立於 1998 年的線上旅遊服務網
經新加坡觀光局認可為服務品質優良

王湯米先生您好：

感謝您再次選擇金龍旅遊網。我們竭力滿足所有商務客戶的需求。您的機票連同旅程表一併附上。請確認每一段旅程的機票，如果有任何遺漏，請與我們聯絡。

日期	班機時刻	班機編號	城市	附註
5 月 10 日	22:00 起飛	SA 326	新加坡	
11 日	04:50 抵達		倫敦（希斯洛機場）	計程車接送到旅館
13 日	18:00 起飛	BA 366	倫敦（希斯洛機場）	
13 日	19:30 抵達		曼徹斯特	瓊斯先生接待
15 日	09:00 起飛	BM 211	曼徹斯特	山德斯女士接待
15 日	10:00 抵達		格拉斯哥	
15 日	18:30 起飛	BM 244	格拉斯哥	前往第三航廈
15 日	19:30 抵達		倫敦（希斯洛機場）	
15 日	21:30 起飛	SA 327	倫敦（希斯洛機場）	
16 日	05:00 抵達		新加坡	

附註：
1. 5 月 11、12 日在倫敦的下榻旅館為大都會飯店。已以您的名義預訂一間單人套房。地址：WCI 48Q 倫敦攝政街；電話：020-9104-3448。
2. 曼徹斯特的住宿由瓊斯先生安排。

有任何需要我們服務的地方，請隨時與我們聯絡。金龍旅遊網以提供客戶高規格的服務為傲。隨信附上我們的旅遊手冊，內容介紹我們所推出的全新歐亞旅遊服務，敬請撥空閱覽，我們所能提供的服務或許超出您的想像。

再次感謝您的預約並祝您旅途愉快。

齊南西

題目中譯	解題技巧
1. 王先生為什麼要去英國？ (A) 為了休閒娛樂 (B) 為了唸書 **(C) 為了生意** (D) 為了動手術	**答案 (C)** 首先可以先確認這封信是由旅行社寄給客戶的。從第一段的 We strive to meet all of our business customers' needs. 就能知道信件的內容是關於商務旅行。
2. 王先生將在哪裡和瓊斯先生會面？ (A) 新加坡 (B) 倫敦 (C) 格拉斯哥 **(D) 曼徹斯特**	**答案 (D)** 旅程計畫可由旅程表得知。從旅程表的 Notes（附註）中 met by Mr. Jones 就可以知道正確答案，這種題目不需要花費時間就能答對。
3. 齊女士請王先生做什麼？ **(A) 閱讀旅遊手冊** (B) 將他的旅程表寄給她 (C) 與瓊斯先生一起預約旅館 (D) 抵達時與她聯繫	**答案 (A)** 齊女士是這封信的寄件者，負責旅行社的聯絡業務。她對客戶的請求出現在最後一段 Please take a moment... 中，也就是非常客氣地請客戶閱讀旅遊手冊。
4. 以下哪一個是王先生飛往格拉斯哥的班機？ (A) SA 326 (B) BA 366 **(C) BM 211** (D) BM 244	**答案 (C)** 一看到表格裡的 Glasgow（格拉斯哥），就找出「抵達」格拉斯哥的班機，但是記得不要和從格拉斯哥「起飛」的班機搞混。

註解

itinerary (n.) 旅行日程

leg (n.) 旅程的一段

February 1, 2009

Transpacific Airways
1129 N. Pendergrass St.
Portland, OR 98765

Dear Sir:

I have been a long-term user of Transpacific. The convenient location of the Seattle-Tacoma Airport's hub makes it a natural choice for all of my flights to Asia. Currently, though, I am having a problem getting a refund on a recent trip. My travel agent suggested that I contact you in writing.

My originating flight from Portland to Seattle, on October 30, 2008, was held up because of inclement local weather. Not wanting to miss my flight out of Seattle, I asked the Transpacific staff at the counter to cancel and refund my originating flight to Seattle, then rented a car and drove myself to the location.

I made the flight in time, thanks to the help of your staff at Sea-Tac. But, I have yet to receive a refund for the canceled flight. I have made repeated calls to your 1-800 customer service staff, and I even visited the Transpacific counter at the Portland Airport. However, I have been told that my refund has been denied.

I am enclosing a copy of the receipt for the canceled Portland to Seattle flight. Notice that the staff at the Portland service counter apparently credited my credit card for $400, but I have yet to receive it. I am requesting that you immediately refund the $400.

I know that we are a small company. We take anywhere from 10 to 15 flights a year to Asia, most destined for our trading partners in Thailand and Singapore. So, we may not be a large priority to you. However, you should still honor the word of your customer representatives. I look forward to hearing from you.

Thank you,

David Saurus
Saurus Import-Export Ltd.

1. Why does David Saurus like to use Transpacific Airways?
   (A) It has a tie-in program with his company.
   (B) It offers the best frequent flyer program.
   (C) It's the cheapest airline for flying to Asia.
   (D) Its international flights leave from a nearby airport.

2. Why was Mr. Saurus's flight to Seattle postponed?
   (A) Bad weather in Portland
   (B) Congestion in Seattle
   (C) Extra security checks
   (D) Aircraft mechanical failure

3. Who has Mr. Saurus NOT spoken to about this problem?
   (A) His travel agent
   (B) Transpacific staff in Portland
   (C) A Portland Airport representative
   (D) A Transpacific customer service

4. What does Mr. Saurus ask Transpacific Airways to do?
   (A) Refund his ticket
   (B) Provide him a free ticket
   (C) Update his mileage report
   (D) Contact him to discuss the problem

long-term 長期以來.
refund 退費
originating 原本的.
inclement 天氣不佳.
in time 及時.
receipt 收据.

1 (A) (B) (C) (D)
2 (A) (B) (C) (D)
3 (A) (B) (C) (D)
4 (A) (B) (C) (D)

原文中譯

2009 年 2 月 1 日
泛太平洋航空公司
98765 奧勒岡州波特蘭市
北潘德葛拉斯街 1129 號

敬啓者：

長期以來我都是泛太平洋的忠實乘客。位於西雅圖塔科馬機場的服務中心，地點相當便利，自然成為我飛往亞洲的選擇。不過，我最近一次的旅程卻無法拿到退費。旅行社建議我以書面的方式與貴公司聯繫。

我原訂於 2008 年 10 月 30 日由波特蘭飛往西雅圖，卻因當地氣候不佳而使計畫中斷。因為不想錯過從西雅圖起飛的班機，所以我請泛太平洋的櫃台員工幫我取消原訂飛往西雅圖的班機，並且幫我申請退費，之後我就租車自行前往。

在西雅圖塔科馬機場經貴公司員工的協助，我及時搭上了班機，但是我到目前為止都還沒有收到取消班機的退費。我曾經數次撥打貴公司 1-800 客服電話，甚至親自造訪了波特蘭機場的泛太平洋櫃台，但是貴公司卻告訴我，我的退費被拒絕了。

隨信附上取消的波特蘭飛往西雅圖班機的收據影本。請注意，波特蘭服務櫃台的員工顯然退了 400 元到我的信用卡裡，但是我到現在為止都還沒有收到。我要請貴公司立刻退還我 400 元。

我知道我們是一家小公司，一年飛往亞洲的次數大概只有 10 到 15 次，多半都是去拜訪我們位在泰國和新加坡的貿易夥伴。因此，我們可能不是貴公司的重要優先客戶。但是，貴公司仍然應該實踐貴公司客戶代表所做的承諾。期待貴公司的回音。

謝謝您。

索羅斯進出口貿易公司
大衛・索羅斯

題目中譯

解題技巧

1. 大衛．索羅斯為什麼喜歡搭乘泛太平洋航空？
   (A) 該航空公司與他的公司有合作方案。
   (B) 這家航空公司提供最好的常客專案。
   (C) 這家航空公司飛往亞洲最便宜。
   (D) **這家航空公司的國際航班從鄰近的機場起飛**。

答案 (D)

在文章中尋找題目裡的關鍵字 like to use，而第一段裡的 a natural choice... 和 like 的意思剛好一致。只要在這個對應內容裡確認了 convenient location，就能知道正確答案了。

2. 索羅斯先生飛往西雅圖的班機為什麼會延誤？
   (A) **波特蘭的氣候不佳**
   (B) 西雅圖塞車
   (C) 額外的安全檢查
   (D) 飛機機械故障

答案 (A)

注意，題目裡 flight to Seattle postponed 的 to 和 postponed 剛好可以對應到第二段一開頭的 to Seattle 和 was held up because...。因應以 why 開頭的題目，文章中 because... 之後的內容就是正確答案。

3. 索羅斯先生沒有和誰談過這個問題？
   (A) 他的旅行社
   (B) 波特蘭的泛太平洋員工
   (C) **波特蘭機場的代表**
   (D) 泛太平洋的客服人員

答案 (C)

關鍵就在於能不能看出這四個選項和 spoken 的對應關係。(A) 和第一段的 My travel agent suggested...；(B) 和第三段 I even visited the Transpacific counter at the Portland Airport.；(D) 和第三段的 I have made repeated calls to your 1-800 customer service staff，各自對應。

4. 索羅斯先生請泛太平洋航空公司做什麼？
   (A) **為他的機票退費**
   (B) 提供他免費機票
   (C) 更新他的里程數紀錄
   (D) 和他聯繫來討論這個問題

答案 (A)

以 ask 作關鍵字在文章中搜尋。在第四段的 I am requesting... 中可以找到同義字 request，從這裡可以知道索羅斯先生在要求退費。

註解

hub (n.) 中心；中繼站
refund (n.) 退款；償還
inclement (adj.) 天氣險惡的
deny (v.) 拒絕
honor (v.) 實踐；尊敬

University of West Dakota
The Checkley School of Management

World MBA Tour 2009

Isn't it time to advance your career and enhance your life?
Attendance is free!

Date: March 16, 2009
Time: 6:00-8:00 P.M.
Place: Singapore Focal Point Convention Center, Room 301

Our program's international student advisor, Mr. Tom Little, will deliver a welcome speech at 6:00. There will also be a presentation by alumni and current students from Singapore, Malaysia, and Thailand at 7:00 to familiarize you with the first semester class' core curriculum. Admissions officers, current students from six countries, and alumni will be on hand to answer your questions about our prestigious one- and two-year MBA programs after the presentation. A university technical officer will also be on hand to tell you about our distance learning MBA program.

RSVP by March 7 to:
MBA-Singapore@checkley.wdakota.edu
Or register online at www.singreg.checkley.wdakota.edu

* Depending on the number of registrations we receive, we may have to move the event to a larger room, but we will definitely be at SFPC.

****

From: Peter Wu
To: Admissions Director, the Checkley School
Subject: MBA Tour 2009

Dear Sirs:

I heard about your MBA program's presentation at the Focal Point Convention Center and I would like to reserve a seat. Since graduating from Singapore National University, I have been working at the trading desk of a large Asian bond division of a local bank. However, in the near future, I would like to expand my career into international finance. I have been thinking of getting an MBA for several years, and I started studying for the GMAT test a couple of months ago. I am not sure if I will be able to apply this year or next year, but either way, I would greatly appreciate having your program's brochure and the RSVP sent to my office.

Thank you. I look forward to seeing you at Focal Point.

Peter Wu

1. All of the following will participate in the presentation EXCEPT
   (A) admissions officers.
   (B) professors.
   (C) current students.
   (D) alumni.

2. Who will discuss the university's Internet study program?
   (A) Current Checkley School students
   (B) Southeast Asian alumni
   (C) The MBA program director
   (D) A university employee

3. Where does Mr. Wu work?
   (A) He works at a regional company.
   (B) He works at a large multinational company.
   (C) He works at a university.
   (D) He is currently unemployed.

4. What can be inferred about Mr. Wu?
   (A) He is no longer interested in finance.
   (B) He knows at least one of the current Checkley students.
   (C) He might not apply this year.
   (D) He has a great amount of international business experience.

5. How does Mr. Wu want to be contacted?

   (A) By e-mail
   (B) By fax
   (C) By mail
   (D) By telephone

1 (A) (B) (C) (D)
2 (A) (B) (C) (D)
3 (A) (B) (C) (D)
4 (A) (B) (C) (D)
5 (A) (B) (C) (D)

西達科塔大學
伽克里管理學院

2009 世界企管碩士學程巡迴說明會

該是你提升事業、豐富生命的時候了吧？
免費參加！

日期：2009 年 3 月 16 日
時間：晚上 6 ～ 8 點
地點：新加坡焦點會議中心 301 室

本學程的國際學生顧問湯姆．利特先生，將在 6 點的時候發表歡迎演說。7 點時還有校友及來自新加坡、馬來西亞、泰國的在學學生，帶領大家熟悉第一學期的核心課程。如果對於我們知名的一年制、二年制企管碩士學程有任何問題，在說明會結束後，現場將有招生人員、來自六個國家的在學學生，以及校友來為各位解答。現場也會有學校技術人員，為各位解說我們的企管碩士遠距教學學程。

敬請於 3 月 7 日前回覆到：
MBA-Singapore@checkley.wdakota.edu
或到 www.singreg.checkley.wdakota.edu 進行線上註冊

＊我們將依報名人數多寡決定是否改到大間的會議室進行，但是地點一定是在新加坡焦點會議中心。

****

寄件者：吳彼得
收件者：伽克里管理學院招生主任
主旨：2009 企管碩士學程巡迴說明會

敬啓者：

聽說貴單位將在新加坡焦點會議中心舉行企管碩士學程說明會，所以我想要預約。我從國立新加坡大學畢業後，就一直在一家當地銀行的大型亞洲債券部門負責交易服務。但是在不久的將來，我想要將事業擴展到國際金融。我考慮取得企管碩士學位已經好幾年了，也在數個月前開始準備 GMAT 測驗。我不確定我今年或明年能不能提出申請，但是無論如何我都會十分感謝貴單位將學程簡章與回函寄到我的辦公室。

謝謝，並期待能在焦點會議中心見到您們。

吳彼得

題目中譯

1. 以下人物都會參與說明會，除了
   (A) 招生人員。 (C) 在學學生。
   (B) **教授**。 (D) 校友。

解題技巧

答案 (B)

迅速瀏覽文章，一下子就能找到題目中 presentation 這個字對應的部分，這題問的是出席者，因此閱讀文宣部分就能知道答案。

2. 誰會詳談學校的網路教學學程？
   (A) 伽克里學院的在學學生
   (B) 東南亞裔校友
   (C) 企管碩士學程主任
   (D) **學校員工**

答案 (D)

這一題問的是負責解說學程的人，只要確認文宣的內容即可，搜尋關鍵字是 Internet study。文宣部分使用的是同義字 distance learning，而解說該學程的人是 a university technical officer，由此可看出正確答案。

3. 吳先生在哪裡工作？
   (A) **他在當地公司工作**。
   (B) 他在大型跨國公司工作。
   (C) 他在大學裡工作。
   (D) 他目前失業中。

答案 (A)

題目問的是吳先生，所以不用讀上半部的文宣內容。關鍵字就是題目中的 work，而在吳先生的電子郵件中就可以找到 local bank，故可判斷 (B)、(C)、(D) 都不正確。

4. 可以推斷出吳先生的什麼事？
   (A) 他不再對金融有興趣。
   (B) 他至少認識一位伽克里的在學學生。
   (C) **他今年可能不會提出申請**。
   (D) 他在國際貿易方面有豐富的經驗。

答案 (C)

在 What can be inferred about... 這類的題目中欠缺搜尋關鍵字，因此重點在於是否能迅速看出選項中敘述有誤的地方。(A) 在 I would like to expand... 之後的內容有提到，所以不是正確答案。(B) 的 student、(D) 的 international business 在整封電子郵件裡都沒出現過。(C) 和 I am not sure... 之後的內容一致。

5. 吳先生希望對方怎麼和他聯絡？
   (A) 寫電子郵件
   (B) 傳真
   (C) **寄信**
   (D) 打電話

答案 (C)

注意吳先生的電子郵件，將 contacted 當作搜尋關鍵字，從 I would greatly appreciate ... to my office. 可以知道正確答案。通常聯絡方式多出現在文宣、書信或文章的結尾。

註解

alumni (n.) 校友（alumnus 的複數形）
semester (n.) 一學期，半學年
core curriculum 基礎課程，核心課程
on hand 在場
prestigious (adj.) 聲望很高的
RSVP 敬請回覆
brochure (n.) 小冊子

From: Dean Smith
To: All HQ
Cc: Marketing
Subject: A big welcome to Mary!

Mary will take over the day-to-day management of our marketing division starting next Monday, and I want all of us to give her a warm welcome. She has been running her own firm, Mary Blacksmith Marketing, for the past 14 years. I know that many of you are familiar with her work there, and I would encourage all of you to talk to her over the next few months and benefit from her experiences and insights.

Prior to starting her own firm, Mary Blacksmith spent 9 years in marketing and sales with IBM Canada. She had a variety of responsibilities—from managing marketing, to sales and communications with something like 1,500 small and medium-sized companies, to being an accounting executive for the largest food retailer in Québec.

At Mary Blacksmith Marketing, Mary conducted group interviews with consumers of all ages, executives, doctors, and other professionals. She has prepared and completed research projects in a wide variety of fields, and has moderated trade focus groups in both French and English—and not just here in Canada. She has also had the privilege of moderating in Europe.

In addition, Mary has published a number of articles on the attitudes and behavior of consumers in Québec towards private labels and has given workshops at two conferences (2005 and 2008). I believe that we will all benefit from having her presence in our office.

****

From: Mary Blacksmith
To: All HQ
Subject: Greetings and Salutations!

As Chairman Smith has so kindly introduced me, I would like to say HULLO to everyone. As you have heard, I will be leading the marketing research division starting next Monday. I am happy to be at Jones, Barnes & Petty, and I want to take this opportunity to affirm that we can improve our survey and product development groups by implementing more cross-functional teamwork. Everyone has something to learn from working in a cross-functional team, and I am no exception!

I want to make sure that everyone working under me feels fairly treated and evaluated. I will be on the road periodically, but when I am at HQ, I want to make sure everyone knows about my open door policy: if my door is open, you are welcome to come in and discuss your concerns with me. I welcome your ideas!

Mary Blacksmith
Marketing Research Director

1. What is the purpose of these e-mails?
   (A) To announce a retirement
   (B) To introduce a new manager
   (C) To encourage new management applications
   (D) To commend a manager for their performance

2. What can be inferred about Ms. Mary Blacksmith?
   (A) She has never held a position of authority.
   (B) Most of her experience is in accounting.
   (C) Her specialty is food retailing.
   (D) She speaks both French and English.

3. What has Ms. Mary Blacksmith NOT done?
   (A) Moderated in Europe
   (B) Managed her own company
   (C) Worked for the government of Québec
   (D) Published articles on marketing

4. Why did Ms. Mary close her business?
   (A) To establish a new private label
   (B) To work with more small and medium-sized companies
   (C) To join a branch of the Québec government
   (D) To accept a managerial position in a private firm

5. What can be inferred about the new manager?
   (A) She is eager to hear her subordinates' ideas.
   (B) She will be doing all her work at the office's headquarters.
   (C) She is enthusiastic about returning to Canada.
   (D) She plans to reorganize the division.

1	Ⓐ	Ⓑ	Ⓒ	Ⓓ
2	Ⓐ	Ⓑ	Ⓒ	Ⓓ
3	Ⓐ	Ⓑ	Ⓒ	Ⓓ
4	Ⓐ	Ⓑ	Ⓒ	Ⓓ
5	Ⓐ	Ⓑ	Ⓒ	Ⓓ

原文中譯

寄件者：狄恩．史密斯
收件者：總部全員
副本：行銷部
主旨：熱烈歡迎瑪莉的加入！

從下星期一開始，瑪莉將會接管行銷部所有的日常管理業務，我希望大家都能熱烈地歡迎她。過去 14 年來，她經營自己的公司，瑪莉布萊克史密斯行銷公司。我知道你們很多人都很清楚她在那裡的工作成就，所以我想鼓勵大家在接下來的幾個月內多和她聊一聊，從她的經驗與見解獲益。

在成立自己的公司之前，瑪莉．布萊克史密斯在加拿大 IBM 做了九年的行銷業務。她曾負責多項工作──從行銷管理，到與 1500 家中小型企業進行業務往來與溝通，到成為魁北克最大食品零售商的會計主管。

瑪莉在瑪莉布萊克史密斯行銷公司進行了各種年齡層、主管、醫生、其他專業人士等消費族群的群體訪談。她籌備並完成之研究計畫的領域廣泛，並能同時以法語和英語主持貿易焦點團體的集會，而且不僅在加拿大這裡而已，甚至還曾獲邀到歐洲去主持。

瑪莉也針對魁北克消費者對私人品牌的態度和行為發表過許多文章，也曾在兩場研討會 (2005, 2008) 中負責舉辦了專題討論會。我相信我們都會因為她的加入而受惠。

****

寄件者：瑪莉．布萊克史密斯
收件者：總部全員
主旨：向大家打招呼並致意！

史密斯主席如此熱情地介紹我，我也要一樣熱情地向大家打招呼。你們已經聽說了，下星期一開始就會換我來領導行銷研究部。我很高興能加入瓊斯、白恩斯與裴蒂公司，也想藉這個機會強調，只要多加強跨部門的團隊合作，就能改進我們的調查與產品發展小組。在跨部門的團隊裡，大家都有需要學習的課題，我也不例外！

我想確保每一位在我底下工作的人，都能覺得自己受到公平的待遇和評估。我定期會在外面出差，但是當我在總部的時候，我希望大家都了解我的開門政策：只要我的門是開的，我都歡迎你們進來和我討論你們的困擾，而我也很歡迎你們的任何構想！

行銷研究主任
瑪莉．布萊克史密斯

1. 這些電子郵件的用意是什麼？
   (A) 宣布退休事宜
   (B) **介紹新主管**
   (C) 鼓勵大家應徵新的管理職位
   (D) 稱讚某位主管的表現

答案 (B)

從郵件的主旨很容易就能判斷出正確答案。郵件的目的就是將瑪莉介紹給公司的所有員工認識。

2. 可以推斷出瑪莉．布萊克史密斯女士的什麼事？
   (A) 她未曾擔任過主管職位。
   (B) 她多數的經驗都與會計有關。
   (C) 她的專長是食品零售。
   (D) **她會說法語和英語**。

答案 (D)

解題的重點在於了解選項 (A) 的 never、(B) 的 most、(C) 的 specialty 都是比較極端的字眼，這些在 NEW TOEIC 的閱讀測驗裡大多都是不正確的選項。對應部分出現在文章中的第三段第二句。

3. 瑪莉．布萊克史密斯女士沒有做過什麼事？
   (A) 在歐洲擔任主席
   (B) 管理自己的公司
   (C) **替魁北克政府工作**
   (D) 發表行銷方面的文章

答案 (C)

從文章中的 her own firm, has moderated..., has published a number of articles 等字眼可知正確答案是 (C)。從第四段的 the attitudes and behavior of consumers in Québec towards... 可以知道是有關市場行銷的內容。

4. 瑪莉為什麼要結束自己的公司？
   (A) 為了成立新的私人品牌
   (B) 為了與更多的中小企業合作
   (C) 為了加入魁北克政府的某個部門
   (D) **為了接受某家私人公司的管理職位**

答案 (D)

文章中並未直接提到結束自己公司的原因，但瑪莉說了 I am happy to be at Jones, Barnes & Petty，表示她樂於成為該公司的員工，故選 (D)。

5. 可以推斷出新主管的什麼事？
   (A) **她積極地想要聽取下屬的構想**。
   (B) 她的所有工作都會在公司總部完成。
   (C) 她對於要回到加拿大感到很興奮。
   (D) 她打算重新整頓部門。

答案 (A)

最後一段的所有內容幾乎都是鼓勵下屬和自己對話，從 open door policy, welcome to come in and discuss, welcome your ideas 等字眼就能找出正確答案。只要了解整段文章的主旨，就能作答。

註解

insight (n.) 見解
moderate (v.) 主持（會議討論、節目等）
privilege (n.)（依法律、契約等而享有的）特權
salutation (n.) 正式的問候語
HULLO「哈囉」的意思
cross-functional teamwork 跨部門團隊合作
periodically (adv.) 定期地

From: Thelma Johnson
To: Fred Jenkins
Subject: Interview

Dear Mr. Jenkins,

Thank you for coming to my office last week for your interview. I must say that my supervisor, Mrs. Walker, and I were impressed with the breadth of your experience and the depth of your knowledge of sales, marketing, finance, and distribution.

As you are aware, we had a few interviewees come in at the end of last week and this morning. However, your experience in both sales/marketing and finance made you the obvious choice—you really stood head and shoulders above the rest—so I am pleased to offer you the regional sales director position. I would like you to come back to the office sometime this week to discuss salary and benefits, but since we have already spoken of this a bit, I assume there will be little to negotiate.

The best times for me are either Thursday afternoon or any time this Friday. And, if not then, early next week would also be fine. I would like you to inform me of your decision ahead of time, so that I can set up a teleconference introduction with your new subordinates, as I am sure they will be happy to meet you.

I eagerly await your response,

Thelma Johnson
HRM director
CRG Distributors

****

From: Fred Jenkins
To: Thelma Johnson
Subject: Interview

Mrs. Johnson,

Thanks for your kind comments and offering the position of regional director, but I must regretfully decline. As you know I have been interviewing with several distributors in the metro area, and yesterday I received and accepted an offer from one close to my residence, so I will not have to uproot my family. The location made it too tempting not to accept.

If at some time in the future you have a managerial or director position you are seeking to fill that is within the metro area, I would be more than happy to sit down and discuss it with you. I have a lot of respect for your company and those who run its operations. You are top-flight distributors. Unfortunately, this time things just will not work out. Thank you again for your time and consideration.

Sincerely,

Fred Jenkins

1. What is the purpose of Thelma Johnson's e-mail?
   (A) To provide a list of production options
   (B) To give notice that she's leaving the company
   (C) To accept a promotion
   (D) To offer a job to an applicant

2. Where does Mrs. Johnson work?
   (A) At a retailing company
   (B) At a distribution company
   (C) At a manufacturer
   (D) At an IT company

3. What is NOT mentioned as an area of Mr. Jenkin's expertise?
   (A) Sales experience
   (B) Marketing knowledge
   (C) Financial expertise
   (D) Accounting skills

4. When does Mrs. Johnson want to meet Mr. Jenkins again?
   (A) The beginning of this week
   (B) The end of this week
   (C) The middle of next week
   (D) The end of next week

5. Why does Mr. Jenkins NOT accept the position?
   (A) He has already accepted another position.
   (B) He has found a better-paying job.
   (C) He decided not to leave his present position.
   (D) He was dissatisfied with the salary and benefits.

1 Ⓐ Ⓑ Ⓒ Ⓓ
2 Ⓐ Ⓑ Ⓒ Ⓓ
3 Ⓐ Ⓑ Ⓒ Ⓓ
4 Ⓐ Ⓑ Ⓒ Ⓓ
5 Ⓐ Ⓑ Ⓒ Ⓓ

原文中譯

寄件者：黛瑪．強森
收件者：福瑞德．詹金斯
主旨：面試

詹金斯先生您好：

謝謝您上週到我的辦公室來面試。我必須說，我的主管沃克女士和我對於您的經驗之廣，以及對業務、行銷、金融與銷售知識之深都留下深刻的印象。

如您所知，上週末及今天上午，我們還有幾位面試者前來面試。不過，您在業務、行銷與金融方面的經驗，讓您明顯地成為不二人選——您確實比其他人選還要優秀——所以我很榮幸能邀請您擔任區域業務主管一職。我想請您本週再找個時間來我的辦公室討論您的薪資與福利，但是既然我們先前已經稍微談過這個話題，我想大概不需要花太多時間討論。

我本週有空的時間是星期四下午或是星期五全天。如果這兩天都不行，那麼下週的前幾天也可以。我希望您能事先回覆我您的決定，方便我安排電話會議，將您介紹給您未來的下屬。我相信他們將會很高興認識您。

熱切期待您的回音。

CRG 銷售公司
人力資源管理主管
黛瑪．強森

****

寄件者：福瑞德．詹金斯
收件者：黛瑪．強森
主旨：面試

強森女士：

感謝您給予我如此高的評價，並且邀請我擔任區域主管一職，但是我很遺憾必須回絕此一邀約。如您所知，我同時到市區這一帶的多家銷售公司面試，並於昨天獲得並接受了一份職位。這家公司離我家很近，讓我能夠不用舉家遷移。這份工作的地理位置優勢，讓我難以拒絕。

如果貴公司未來在市區這一帶有經理或主管的職缺，我會非常樂意與您坐下來好好談一談的。我非常尊敬貴公司與貴公司經營者，您們是頂尖的銷售公司。可惜的是，這一次事情並無法盡如人意。再次謝謝您花時間在我的事情上面。

福瑞德．詹金斯
敬上

題目中譯

1. 黛瑪．強森的電子郵件有什麼目的？
   (A) 提供生產的選擇清單
   (B) 通知大家她即將離職
   (C) 接受升職的機會
   (D) **提供應徵者工作機會**

解題技巧

答案 (D)

確認強森女士發送這封電子郵件的內容為何。從第一段寫著 your interview 立刻就能知道正確答案。也能由第二段的 so I am pleased to offer you the regional sales director position 來確認答案。

2. 強森女士在哪裡工作？
   (A) 零售公司
   (B) **銷售公司**
   (C) 製造公司
   (D) 科技公司

答案 (B)

題目問的是強森女士在哪裡工作，所以只需要看第一封由強森女士發送的電子郵件。電子郵件的最後都會標明她所屬的公司名稱，由此可看出正確答案。

3. 文中提及詹金斯先生的專長，不包含以下哪一項？
   (A) 業務經驗
   (B) 行銷知識
   (C) 金融專長
   (D) **會計能力**

答案 (D)

詹金斯先生的專長和經驗都在強森女士所發送的電子郵件中提到，搜尋關鍵字是 expertise。從第一段的 of your experience and the depth of your knowledge of sales, marketing, finance, and distribution 中就能找出正確答案。

4. 強森女士希望什麼時候再與詹金斯先生會面？
   (A) 這個星期一開始
   (B) **這個星期接近週末時**
   (C) 下個星期中間
   (D) 下個星期接近週末時

答案 (B)

從題目中的 When ... want to meet Mr. Jenkins again 找出文章中與時間相關的部分。從第三段的 The best times ... Thursday afternoon or any time this Friday 中選擇最接近的選項。

5. 詹金斯先生為什麼不接受這個職位？
   (A) **他已接受其他職位。**
   (B) 他找到薪水更高的工作。
   (C) 他決定不要離開他現在的工作。
   (D) 他對薪水及福利條件不滿意。

答案 (A)

在詹金斯先生回覆的電子郵件中，開頭提到要回絕這份工作的邀約，因為他已經答應去其他公司工作了。

註解

be impressed with... 對…印象深刻
stand head and shoulders above... 鶴立雞群，遠遠超出
subordinate (n.) 部下
uproot (v.) 連根拔起
tempting (adj.) 誘惑人的，迷人的
top-flight (adj.) 第一流的

February 1, 2009

Human Resources Representative
Animix Studios
One Time Warner Center
New York, NY 10019

Dear Human Resources Representative:

As a forthcoming graduate in audio engineering (June, 2009), I am interested in joining Animix. My interest in your company was sparked during a series of projects I completed as part of my audio engineering training. I know you need talented people, so please allow me to tell you why you should consider me for an interview.

I will graduate at the top of my audio engineering class at the Sound Audio Engineering Institute of Technology in Brooklyn. Through class assignments and part-time jobs, I have demonstrated the ability to be a productive member of technical project teams for both music and film. I even created a video synchronization for the movie *Paladin*, which is included on the attached DVD. Many of my projects dealt with the same production processes you provide clients.

For more detailed information on my experience and skills, please see my enclosed résumé. I also urge you to contact my references—both my instructors and part-time job supervisors. I would deeply appreciate the opportunity to work at Animix Studios, as I have admired your company for many years.

Sincerely,

Orville Valdez
ov_890707_doom@hotmail.com

To: Orville Valdez
From: Traci McKibbon
Sub: Résumé

Mr. Valdez,

First, I would like to say happy New Year and thank you for your interest in Animix! At this point in time we are not actively soliciting applications; however, I forwarded your qualifications to our Technical Team's hiring leader and he said he would keep your file on record. I do not want to speculate on whether or not we will be in contact with you, but your file will be kept in our permanent database. I am sure that with your level of technical expertise you will find many employment opportunities. So, you may want to periodically send us an update on what you have been doing in order to keep our database up-to-date. I wish you the best in your job search.

Traci McKibbon
HRM

P.S. I loved the *Paladin* piece!

1. Where does Ms. McKibbon most probably work?
   (A) A radio station
   (B) A university
   (C) A recording studio
   (D) A recruiting firm

2. What does Mr. Valdez NOT mention as part of his experience?
   (A) Training projects
   (B) University classes
   (C) Video synchronization work
   (D) Technical team leader

3. Why does Mr. Valdez send Ms. McKibbon a DVD?
   (A) To impress her with a gift
   (B) To provide a demonstration of his work
   (C) To give proof of his university school work
   (D) To show work he did with Animix

4. What is true about Mr. Valdez?
   (A) He has never worked before.
   (B) He enjoyed his internship.
   (C) He is not qualified for this position.
   (D) He performed well at his university.

5. What does Ms. McKibbon recommend Mr. Valdez do?
   (A) Contact the Technical Team's hiring leader
   (B) Send his résumé to the database manager
   (C) Provide information on his career progress in the future
   (D) Fill out and send in an application

1 Ⓐ Ⓑ Ⓒ Ⓓ
2 Ⓐ Ⓑ Ⓒ Ⓓ
3 Ⓐ Ⓑ Ⓒ Ⓓ
4 Ⓐ Ⓑ Ⓒ Ⓓ
5 Ⓐ Ⓑ Ⓒ Ⓓ

原文中譯

2009 年 2 月 1 日

人力資源代表
動畫迷工作室
10019 紐約州紐約市
時代華納中心 1 號

人力資源代表您好：

我即將畢業於錄音工程系（2009 年 6 月），有意加入動漫迷。我對貴公司產生興趣，源自於我完成一系列作品的期間，這是錄音工程訓練的一環。我知道貴公司需要有才華的人，所以請容許我告訴您為何貴公司應該考慮讓我有面試的機會。

我將以第一名的成績畢業於錄音工程系，我們的聲音錄音工程技術學院位在布魯克林。透過課堂作業與打工，我證明了自己有能力加入音樂與電影的技術製作小組，成為有所貢獻的組員。我甚至將電影《帕拉丁》進行影片同步化，就在附件的 DVD 當中。我有許多作業的製作過程與貴公司提供給客戶的製作過程相同。

如果要更詳細了解我的經驗與專長，請參考我隨信附上的履歷。同時也請您能與我的推薦人聯絡——不論是我的指導教授或是打工的主管。我將會好好珍惜在動漫迷工作室工作的機會，因為我仰慕貴公司已經很多年了。

奧維爾・維爾德茲
敬上
ov_890707_doom@hotmail.com

****

收件者：奧維爾・維爾德茲
寄件者：崔西・麥基本
主旨：履歷

維爾德茲先生您好：

首先向您說聲新年快樂並感謝您有興趣加入動漫迷。目前我們並沒有積極在尋找應徵者。不過，我已將您的資歷轉寄給我們的技術小組招募主管，他表示會將您的資料留下來建檔。我不想冒然猜測我們是否會和您聯絡，但是您的資料將會存放在我們的永久資料庫內。我相信憑著您如此優秀的技術專長，一定能找到許多工作機會。因此，或許您可以定期寄信告訴我們您最近在做什麼，讓我們的資料庫能存有最新資訊。祝福您找工作一切順利。

人力資源管理
崔西・麥基本

附註：我非常喜歡《帕拉丁》的影片！

1. 麥基本女士最有可能在哪裡工作？
(A) 廣播電台 (C) **錄音工作室**
(B) 大學 (D) 招募公司

答案 (C)

麥基本女士在動漫迷工作室負責人力資源管理的工作。看到專攻錄音工程學的學生詢問應徵事項，就能知道這家公司的業務性質。

2. 以下哪一項經驗維爾德茲先生沒有提到？
(A) 訓練計畫
(B) 大學課程
(C) 影片同步化作業
(D) **技術小組組長**

答案 (D)

題目問到維爾德茲先生的資歷，所以讀第一封信即可。這封信的第二段中敘述維爾德茲先生曾經有過的經驗，(A)、(B)、(C) 三者都是他的經歷。至於 (D) 則是麥基本女士要轉送維爾德茲先生履歷的對象。

3. 維爾德茲先生為什麼要寄 DVD 給麥基本女士？
(A) 用禮物討她歡心
(B) **展示他的作品**
(C) 作為他大學作業的證明
(D) 展示他與動漫迷一起做過的工作

答案 (B)

如果了解這封信的內容是關於一名即將畢業的學生，詢問有意應徵之公司的職缺狀況，就能立刻找出正確答案，即為了獲得面試機會，所以先送上試錄作品。

4. 以下關於維爾德茲先生的哪一點是正確的？
(A) 他以前從來沒有工作過。
(B) 他很喜歡他的實習工作。
(C) 他的資格不符合這份工作。
(D) **他在大學的表現非常好**。

答案 (D)

這類題目無法從問題中鎖定文章的對應部分。將選項 (A) 的 never worked、(B) 的 internship、(C) 的 not qualified for this position、(D) 的 performed well 當作關鍵字，在文章裡搜尋之後，可以在第二段第一行找到提及在校成績的內容。

5. 麥基本女士建議維爾德茲先生做什麼？
(A) 跟技術小組招募主管接洽
(B) 把他的履歷寄給資料庫經理
(C) **提供他未來工作發展的資訊**
(D) 填寫並寄出申請表

答案 (C)

麥基本女士在信件的結尾寫著 you may want to periodically send us an update on what you have been doing in order to keep our database up-to-date，可看出她建議維爾德茲先生往後可以寄來相關經歷的最新訊息。

註解

forthcoming (adj.) 即將來到的
admire (v.) 對…表示仰慕
solicit (v.) 懇求
speculate on... 推測…，思索…

14

作答時間 3 分鐘

Roadside Inns of America Customer Comment Card

* Both of the fields are optional.

1. Was your room clean and well-supplied?

2. Any other comments:

My husband and I stopped at the Irish Elk for dinner tonight while passing by on the interstate. We didn't stay at the hotel, and I must say that the meal was terrible. First, I ordered the grilled cod, but I received halibut, I think. It certainly was NOT cod. But in addition to that, my husband's sirloin was some kind of roast. It was tough and dry. He ordered it medium rare, but it was thoroughly cooked. We thought it was a little bit odd that we were asked to pay for dinner BEFORE we ate, but now I see why—if you serve such terrible food to your patrons, of course they would refuse to pay for it! We will not be coming back to any Roadside Inn franchise ever again.

Dear Mrs. Foley,

I am writing in reply to your customer comment card dated June 30. I was most disappointed to learn of your dissatisfaction with the meal you had at Roadside. I can assure you that such complaints are rare.

I have spoken to the proprietors of the restaurant, who lease both the kitchen and restaurant from us. They are responsible for all food served on the premises. They have asked me to send on their sincerest apologies to you and your husband. They have assured me that such an occurrence will never happen again.

Concerning the food you were served, they have apologized and wish to inform you that the cod you received was fresh and was indeed cod. The reason you were served round steak instead of sirloin was due to a supplier error. However, you should have been informed that there was no sirloin available.

The reason you were asked for payment in advance is that we do have a lot of "walk-outs," as the bar staff is not responsible for handling the money or food and the staff is not always present in the restaurant. Some people take advantage of this and leaving without paying.

Our comment cards are sent from the hotel to a private customer service firm which analyses them and informs me of any complaints. Prior to your complaint, I had not received a complaint for several months.

I hope the above has done something in the way of addressing the issues raised in your letter.

Yours truly,

Adrian Rockford
General Manager

1. What is the purpose of Mrs. Foley's comments?
   (A) To compliment the hotel on their room service
   (B) To complain about the food at a restaurant
   (C) To suggest several new menu items
   (D) To request information about a future banquet

2. What can be inferred about Mrs. Foley's Customer Comment Card?
   (A) She did not write down information about how to contact her.
   (B) It was her first visit to the Irish Elk.
   (C) She did not answer every question on the card.
   (D) She has refused to pay for her meal.

3. Who is Adrian Rockford?
   (A) A frequent customer at the Irish Elk
   (B) A chef at the Irish Elk restaurant
   (C) An employee of a customer service firm
   (D) A manager at the Roadside Inn

4. What is Mrs. Foley's complaint about cod?
   (A) It was a different kind of fish.
   (B) It was overcooked.
   (C) It was grilled.
   (D) It was priced incorrectly.

5. Why does the Irish Elk require payment in advance, according to Adrian?
   (A) Because many hotel customers leave in the middle of the night
   (B) Because customers have complained about the food and refused to pay
   (C) Because some of the restaurant staff have stolen money before
   (D) Because some customers try to leave the restaurant without paying

美國羅德賽旅館顧客意見卡

＊兩個欄位都可選填。

1. 您的房間是否乾淨且供應完善？

2. 其他意見：

我和我先生今晚跨越州際公路時，停在愛爾蘭麋餐廳用晚餐。我們沒有住在那間旅館。我必須說，晚餐真是糟透了。首先，我點的是烤鱈魚，上來的我想卻是比目魚之類的東西，總之絕對不是鱈魚。除此之外，我先生點的沙朗牛排也變成某種炭烤肉，又乾又硬。他點的是五分熟，上來的卻是全熟。我們覺得在用餐前就得先付錢有點奇怪，但是現在我懂了，如果您給顧客那麼可怕的食物，他們當然會拒絕付錢！我們永遠不會再踏進羅德賽旅館了。

****

佛利女士您好：

我寫這封信是為了回應您於 6 月 30 日所寫的顧客意見卡。對您在羅德賽的用餐經驗竟然那麼不愉快，我感到失望極了。我向您保證，像您這樣的投訴很少見。

我已經與向我們承租廚房和餐廳，並負責供應餐廳內所有食物的餐廳負責人談過了。他們請我代為向您與您的先生表達最誠摯的歉意，也向我保證這種情況永遠不會再發生。

對於您吃到的餐點，他們道了歉，也想告訴您，您吃到的鱈魚是新鮮的，而且確實是鱈魚。至於您為何吃到牛腿肉而不是沙朗牛排，則是因為缺貨。不過，應該要有人告訴您沙朗牛排缺貨才對。

您之所以必須先付款，是由於我們確實有非常多「不付錢就走人」的顧客。因為吧台人員不負責管錢或處理食物，而餐廳員工也不一定一直待在餐廳裡，有些人會利用這一點，不付錢就走人。

我們的顧客意見卡會由旅館送到私人顧客服務公司進行分析，再將顧客投訴的事件告訴我。在您投訴之前，我已經有好幾個月不曾接獲任何投訴了。

希望以上的說明多少能解釋您在信上所提到的問題。

總經理
艾德里安．洛克佛德
敬上

1. 佛利女士的意見有什麼目的？
   (A) 稱讚旅館的客房服務
   (B) 抱怨餐廳的食物
   (C) 建議菜單新加幾樣東西
   (D) 詢問未來宴會的資料

答案 (B)

從顧客意見卡上 2. Any other comments: 下面第二行寫到的 the meal was terrible 可以知道申訴的內容。這是一個與主旨相關的題目，看文章開頭就能知道答案了。

2. 從佛利女士的顧客意見卡可以推斷出什麼事？
   (A) 她沒有留下她的聯絡資料。
   (B) 這是她第一次去愛爾蘭麋餐廳。
   (C) 她沒有回答卡片上所有的問題。
   (D) 她不付晚餐錢。

答案 (C)

這題與顧客意見卡有關，所以要看第一篇文章。隨時留意文章中 first, second 等字眼或比較級的內容。文章完全沒提到「第一次在這家餐廳吃飯」，所以不能選 (B)。由於意見欄的第一項是空白，從這點就能知道正確答案。

3. 艾德里安・洛克佛德是誰？
   (A) 愛爾蘭麋餐廳的常客
   (B) 愛爾蘭麋餐廳的主廚
   (C) 顧客服務公司的員工
   (D) 羅德賽旅館的經理

答案 (D)

這題問的是收到顧客意見卡後回信者的職業，因此可直接由信件最後署名下方的職稱來確認。

4. 佛利女士對鱈魚有何不滿？
   (A) 是不同種類的魚。
   (B) 煮得過熟。
   (C) 是用烤的。
   (D) 價格標示不正確。

答案 (A)

在顧客意見卡中找出題目中的 cod，這個字出現在 2. Any other comments: 下面第二行 First, I ordered the grilled cod... 的部分，之後的內容就是正確答案。

5. 據艾德里安所說，愛爾蘭麋餐廳為什麼要求事先付錢？
   (A) 因為旅館許多房客都會在半夜的時候離開
   (B) 因為顧客都對食物有所抱怨而拒絕付錢
   (C) 因為以前有些餐廳員工曾經偷過錢
   (D) 因為有些顧客不付錢就想離開餐廳

答案 (D)

從題目的 according to Adrian 知道要讀信中 Dear Mrs. Foley, 之後的內容，搜尋關鍵字是 payment in advance。從第四段的 we do have a lot of "walk-outs," 可知是因為有許多吃霸王餐的人。

註解

on the premises 房屋內，店鋪內
sincere apology 誠心的道歉
payment in advance 預先付款
address (v.) 處理（問題等）

Chapter 3

Business Document

商用文件

NEW TOEIC® TEST

15

作答時間 1 分鐘

In-House Negotiation Training Seminar

Wednesday, October 18
Rooms 212 and 214

8:30 A.M. Coffee and doughnuts with our guest negotiation trainers, Milt Packhard and Margaret Eckhart

9:00-10:00 A.M. Warm-up exercises. Discussion on when and when not to negotiate.

10:00-11:30 A.M. Morning Workshop

A-Team: Developing an effective plan and strategy for negotiations (Milt):
- — on the phone
- — face-to-face
- — via e-mail and snail mail

B-Team: Developing trustworthy relationships (Margaret):
- — developing a common language
- — techniques to pull information from others
- — reading client and employee behavior

11:30 A.M.-1:00 P.M. Lunch in the cafeteria with Milt and Margaret

1:00-2:30 P.M. Afternoon Workshop
A-Team and B-Team switch rooms and classes

2:30-5:00 P.M. Negotiation simulations

* Roger Miller and Ken Van der Haden (and possibly others) from the Legal Department will participate in the afternoon simulations.

1. What are the company's in-house legal specialists scheduled to do?
   (A) Hold seminars to help company managers learn effective negotiation techniques
   (B) Lead a discussion of when and when not to negotiate
   (C) Discuss negotiation strategy with Milt and Margaret
   (D) Participate in negotiation practice exercises

2. When will the A-Team have a workshop on negotiation language and behavior?
   (A) From 9:00 to 10:00 A.M.
   (B) From 10:00 to 11:30 A.M.
   (C) From 1:00 to 2:30 P.M.
   (D) From 2:30 to 5:00 P.M.

1 Ⓐ Ⓑ Ⓒ Ⓓ
2 Ⓐ Ⓑ Ⓒ Ⓓ

內部協商訓練講座

10 月 18 日星期三
212、214 室

8:30 A.M.	與我們的客座協商講師米爾特・派克哈德和瑪格麗特・艾克哈特共享咖啡與甜甜圈
9:00 ～ 10:00 A.M.	暖身練習。討論何時該協商，何時不該協商。
10:00 ～ 11:30 A.M.	上午專題討論會 A 組　擬定有效的協商計畫與策略（米爾特）： 電話上 面對面 透過電子郵件與傳統郵件 B 組　建立可靠的關係（瑪格麗特）： 建立共同的語言 從別人身上獲得資訊的技巧 解讀客戶與員工的行為
11:30 A.M. ～ 1:00 P.M.	與米爾特和瑪格麗特在餐廳共進午餐
1:00 ～ 2:30 P.M.	下午專題討論會 A 組與 B 組交換教室與課程
2:30 ～ 5:00 P.M.	協商模擬練習

* 法律部門的羅傑・米勒和肯・凡德海頓（可能還有其他人）將參與下午的模擬練習。

題目中譯

1. 公司內部的法律專家預定要做什麼？

(A) 舉辦講座幫助公司主管學習有效的協商技巧

(B) 主導什麼時候該協商，什麼時候不該協商的討論會

(C) 與米爾特和瑪格麗特一起討論協商策略

(D) 參與協商練習活動

解題技巧

答案 (D)

文章中沒有出現 in-house legal specialists 這個詞，所以要找出類似的用法。文章最下面的注意事項 Roger Miller and Ken Van der Haden ... from the Legal Department... 就是對應內容，也就是說，他們要參加下午的模擬練習。

2. A 組何時將進行協商語言與行為的專題討論會？

(A) 從上午 9 點到 10 點

(B) 從上午 10 點到 11 點半

(C) 從下午 1 點到 2 點半

(D) 從下午 2 點半到 5 點

答案 (C)

在知道以 A、B 兩組分工，下午交換教室和課程之後，先找到文章中出現 language 和 behavior 這兩個字的地方，再判斷題目中的 negotiation language and behavior 指的是哪一個 workshop（專題討論會）。

註解

negotiation (n.) 協商，談判

simulation (n.) 模擬

Oct. 6, 2008

Mr. Alfred H. Cheung
PP&G Incorporated
Cebu City

Sir:

This is to authorize LJ Trucking to receive delivery of PP&G's container instead of Ultra Model Incorporated.

As agreed, an LJ trucker will return the container to the PP&G container yard within 48 hours (2 days) from the date it was originally pulled from the PP&G container yard. Failure to return the van within 48 hours will result in a fee of two hundred dollars per day. Any damages to the van or container shall be chargeable to LJ, and in case of total loss, we will charge the full amount at the present rate to LJ Trucking.

We are hoping for your immediate approval on this matter.

Respectfully yours,

Ana Marie C. Villanueva
Plant Manager

1. What is the purpose of this letter?
   (A) To notify of the approval of a change in trucking company
   (B) To notify a client of a change in shipping policy
   (C) To announce a new business shipping line
   (D) To remind Mr. Cheung of the shipping company

A

2. Which of the following will NOT result in charges to the trucking company?
   (A) Late delivery of the container
   (B) Damages to the van
   (C) Use of an additional trucker
   (D) Total loss of the container

incorporated 有限公司.
authorize 授权.
trucking 貨運公司.
container 貨櫃.
return 歸还.
immediate 立即

1 
2 

原文中譯

2008 年 10 月 6 日

鍾艾佛瑞先生
PP&G 有限公司
宿霧市

敬啓者：

這封信的目的是要授權 LJ 貨車運輸公司領取 PP&G 的貨櫃，而不是特級模範有限公司。

如先前所同意的，從貨櫃離開 PP&G 貨櫃場當天算起，LJ 貨車司機會在 48 小時（即兩天）內將貨櫃歸還至 PP&G 貨櫃場。如果未能在 48 小時內將貨車歸還，一天將罰款 200 美元。貨車或貨櫃如果有任何損壞，必須由 LJ 支付費用；如果完全遺失，我們將會要求 LJ 貨車運輸公司依現值全額賠償。

我們希望您能立即批准這件事。

工廠經理
安娜．瑪莉．薇蘭奴娃
敬上

題目中譯

1. 這封信的目的是什麼？

   (A) **通知批准更換貨車運輸公司**
   (B) 通知客戶運輸政策有所變更
   (C) 公告新的商業運輸線
   (D) 提醒鍾先生有這間運輸公司

2. 以下哪一項不會導致貨車運輸公司的罰款？

   (A) 延遲運送貨櫃
   (B) 貨車損壞
   (C) **多加一位貨車司機**
   (D) 貨櫃完全遺失

解題技巧

答案 (A)

第一段裡提到從以前委託的貨車運輸公司 Ultra Model Incorporated 換到另一家貨車運輸公司 LJ Trucking。只有 (A) 的 a change in trucking company 符合。(B) 的 client 以及 (D) 的 remind 都不恰當。

答案 (C)

討論遭到罰款的內容。在第二段第四行可以找到 charge 的相關字 fee，也就是對應的內容。雖然也可用消去法，但如果知道信中完全沒有關於貨車司機的敘述，就能更快作答。

註解

authorize (v.) 授權（資格等）
chargeable (adj.) 應支付的
approval (n.) 批准，認可

From: Patrick Hargrave

To: Melanie McQuerie

Subject: Business Development Manager (Immediate Release)

The Musky Pelican is accepting applications for a business development manager to expand our banquet business. The successful candidate will:

- Promote, organize, and significantly increase conferences and business banquets; achieve budget requirements and control overall costs.
- Ensure that accounting and internal control systems are in place.
- Prepare P&L statements for special events.
- Compile detailed reports on results and activities.
- Ensure relevant details are communicated to Reservations.
- Develop and implement a conference marketing strategy.
- Maintain the client file system (past functions, guest history, etc.).
- Ensure client requirements are passed on to all relevant departments.
- Establish and maintain good relation with local tourism offices and convention bureaus.
- Attend trade shows.
- Perform other duties as requested by management according to business demands.

1. The Musky Pelican is most likely which of the following businesses?
   (A) A ski resort
   (B) A hotel resort
   (C) A yacht club
   (D) A car yard

2. What kind of report is the new business development manager NOT expected to file?
   (A) Profit & loss report
   (B) Activities report
   (C) Trade show report
   (D) Results report

development 發展.
release 發布.
application 应徵者.
candidate 候选人.
banquet 宴会.
promote 推廣.
significantly 大幅地.
conferences 会議.
budget 預算.
requirement 要求.
overall cost 總成本.
P&L statement 損益表.
compile 編輯

relevant 相关的.
reservation 訂位.
implement 執行.
function 活动.
convention 会議.
trade 贸易.
duty 義務、本分.
request 要求.
perform 履行.
demand 需求.

原文中譯

寄件者：派翠克．哈葛瑞夫

收件者：梅蘭妮．麥奎瑞

主旨：市場開發經理（立即發布）

麝香鵜鶘開始接受求職者應徵市場開發經理，一起擴展我們的宴會市場。資格符合的求職者必須要：

- 推廣、組織並大幅增加會議與商業宴會；達成預算要求並控制總成本。
- 確保會計與內部控制系統正常進行。
- 為特殊場合準備損益表。
- 彙整成果與活動的詳細報告。
- 務必與訂位組溝通所有相關細節。
- 開發並執行會議行銷策略。
- 維護客戶檔案系統（過去活動、客人紀錄等）。
- 確保客戶需求都能傳達給所有相關部門。
- 與當地的旅行社、會議籌辦單位建立並維持良好關係。
- 參加貿易展。
- 根據市場需求履行主管要求的其他職責。

題目中譯

1. 麝香鵜鶘最有可能是以下哪一種行業？
   (A) 滑雪度假村
   (B) 旅館度假村
   (C) 遊艇俱樂部
   (D) 汽車銷售廠

2. 以下哪一種報告不需要新任市場開發經理建檔？
   (A) 損益報告
   (B) 活動報告
   (C) 貿易展報告
   (D) 成果報告

解題技巧

答案 (B)

這是典型不用讀完全文就能作答的題目。先確認這一題問的是該公司的業務內容後，再讀文章。本文的第二行有 banquet（宴會）一字，接下來只要選擇和「宴會」有關的業務內容即可。

答案 (C)

先確認在這 11 個條列式項目中與「製作文件或資料」相關的動詞只有 prepare 和 compile，接著再根據第三和第四項目的內容來看，就能刪去 (A)、(B) 和 (D)。

註解

release (n.) 發布
banquet (n.) 宴會
P&L statement 損益表 (= profit and loss statement)
compile (v.) 編纂
implement (v.) 實施

Date: February 10, 2009

From: B. Robin

To: Mr. James Sampson

Re: Contractor-Home Owner's Agreement on the Acceptance of Work

Due to certain concerns I have with respect to my previous employer, I would ask that you kindly confirm that the following is accurate and factual:

1. You do not have any current contractual relations with the Baughman Service Group in regards to the abovementioned site address.

2. At no time did I solicit work from you for this project. Rather, you approached me independently in order to ask me to submit a quote for the project.

3. I have never made any negative comments toward you or anyone in your company about the work done by the Baughman Service Group or about any of the principals or employees of the Baughman Service Group.

I confirm the above as being true and correct,

Name: ______________________________

Date: ______________________________

1. Who should sign this contract?
   (A) A representative of the B. Robin Construction Ltd. Company
   (B) A representative of the Baughman Service Group
   (C) Mr. Sampson
   (D) A local building inspector

2. It can be inferred from the contract that Mr. B. Robin is
   (A) a real estate agent.
   (B) a manager at a large construction company.
   (C) a representative of the Ocean Park City Council.
   (D) a former employee of Baughman Service Group.

agreement 協議.
contractor 承包商.
certain 某些.
previous 先前的.
confirm 確認.
accurate 確定的.
factual 真实的.
independently 独立地.
quote 報価.
principal 主管.
solicit 懇求.

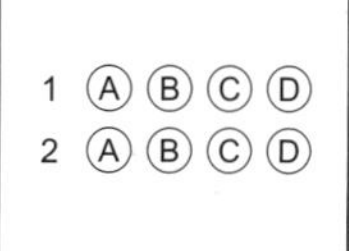

日期：2009 年 2 月 10 日
寄件者：羅賓
收件者：詹姆士 · 山普森先生
回覆：承包商與屋主接受業務協議

由於我與先前雇主有過某些問題，我希望您能確認以下敘述真實無誤：

1. 以上所列之建築基地地址，與鮑曼服務集團沒有任何現行合約關係。

2. 我從不曾主動要求您將這份工作承包給我。相反的，是您獨自找我，請我為這份工作提出報價。

3. 我從不曾對您或是對您公司的任何人，針對鮑曼服務集團所做的工作或鮑曼服務集團的任何一位主管或員工，說過任何壞話。

我確認以上真實無誤。

姓名：______________________________
日期：______________________________

題目中譯

1. 誰該簽這份合約？

(A) 羅賓建設有限公司的代表
(B) 鮑曼服務集團的代表
(C) 山普森先生
(D) 當地建築檢查員

2. 可以從合約中推斷出羅賓先生是

(A) 房地產經紀人。
(B) 大型建設公司的經理。
(C) 海洋公園市議會的代表。
(D) 鮑曼服務集團的前員工。

解題技巧

答案 (C)

這封信是單飛開業的羅賓先生為了證明自己並未從先前任職的公司那裡搶奪客戶，請客戶山普森先生當證人，以維護自身的清白。因此，應該在這份合約上簽名的人是收件者山普森先生。

答案 (D)

只要知道這整件事是為了什麼目的，以及向誰確認，就能輕鬆答對。亦或是注意到文章中並未出現 real estate agent, large construction company, City Council 等字，就會選 (D)。

註解

contractor (n.) 承包商
confirm (v.) 確認，證實
contractual relation 合約關係
at no time 絕不
solicit (v.) 懇求
quote (n.) 報價

To: All Customer Service Representatives
From: Darell Lari
Date: August 15
Subject: COMPLAINT RESOLUTION PROCEDURES

I want to post the procedures related to complaints once again, because we have been having some problems in this area. Please circulate this memo around the office and make sure everyone signs it this time.

1. All shoes are to be delivered to a client with specific instructions on the use of the shoes and a toll-free number on which they can contact Red Fox Inc. to resolve any problems.

2. As you know, the toll-free number is answered by the call center Monday through Friday, 10:00 A.M. through 4:00 P.M. (PST), and is equipped with a message service. Make sure to give clients accurate information on the hours of our call center if you speak to them. Also, tell them that if the call is received after business hours, we will return it the next business day. You can also direct clients to visit one of our office locations.

3. If a client calls with an issue, attempt to resolve the issue over the phone. If the shoes are slightly too big or too small, the representative who delivered the shoes will take them back and order the correct size.

4. If the client has a problem after their shoes have been delivered, contact the office, which will make an appointment for the representative who fitted the shoes or the owner to go out and meet the client. If the problem cannot be resolved, the representative will take the shoes back at no cost to the client.

5. All problems are resolved at no cost to the client.

1. What is the purpose of this memo?
   (A) To remind call center employees of a company policy
   (B) To introduce a new set of call center rules
   (C) To explain the reasons that customer complaints have arisen
   (D) To encourage call center employees to take a more active stance

2. What is NOT mentioned as a way to communicate with clients?
   (A) Calls to the call center
   (B) Owner visits
   (C) Messages sent through the website
   (D) Sales representative visits

3. If the client's problem CANNOT be solved over the phone, what should call center employees do?
   (A) Have a manager speak with the client
   (B) Contact an office manager
   (C) Send a note to the sales representative
   (D) Give clients directions to the nearest office location

收件者：所有客服代表
寄件者：戴瑞爾．賴瑞
日期：8 月 15 日
主旨：投訴解決步驟

我想要再次發布和投訴相關的步驟，因為我們在這方面一直有些問題。請在辦公室內傳閱這份備忘錄，並確認這一次每個人都確實簽名。

1. 所有鞋子送到顧客手上時，都要附上正確穿鞋的明確指示以及免付費電話，方便顧客有任何問題時能與紅狐有限公司聯繫。

2. 如各位所知，免付費電話由客服中心接聽，時間是週一到週五上午 10 點到下午 4 點（太平洋時間），也提供留言服務。在客服中心開放的時間內，如果接到顧客來電，務必提供他們正確的資訊。也要告知他們，如果是在下班時間內來電，我們將在下一個上班日回電。也可以指引顧客造訪我們的辦公室。

3. 如果顧客有問題打電話來，試著在電話中解決。如果鞋子稍微過大或過小，由負責運送鞋子的人員取回鞋子，並且重新訂購正確的尺寸。

4. 如果顧客在鞋子送達後才有問題，請聯絡辦公室，將會安排負責試穿工作的人員或是老闆和顧客會面。如果無法解決問題，負責人員會去取回鞋子，而且顧客不用負擔任何費用。

5. 顧客無須負擔任何解決問題的費用。

題目中譯

1. 這份備忘錄有什麼目的？

(A) **向客服中心員工提醒公司的政策**
(B) 介紹客服中心的新規定
(C) 解釋顧客投訴增加的原因
(D) 鼓勵客服中心的員工採取更積極的立場

2. 下面哪一項不是文章所述用來和顧客溝通的方式？

(A) 打電話到客服中心
(B) 老闆登門拜訪
(C) **透過網站發送訊息**
(D) 業務代表登門拜訪

3. 如果顧客的問題無法透過電話解決，客服中心的員工該怎麼做？

(A) 請經理和顧客談
(B) **聯絡辦公室經理**
(C) 傳送訊息給業務代表
(D) 指引顧客到最近的辦公室

解題技巧

答案 (A)

首先先確認備忘錄的收件者是客服代表。從步驟二的 Make sure to give clients accurate information... 之後提出和顧客對話時必須注意的事項，可以知道這項指示是針對客服中心的工作人員所說的。

答案 (C)

(A) 在步驟二裡提到，(B) 和 (D) 則在步驟四裡提到。速解的重點就在於步驟二第一行的 toll-free 和步驟三第一行的 over the phone，先判斷出步驟二和三是藉由電話來回應顧客，接著就直接跳到步驟四閱讀。

答案 (B)

題目中的 over the phone 在步驟三裡提到，接下來找尋 cannot be solved 對應的內容，發現就是步驟四一開頭的 If the client has a problem after their shoes have been delivered, contact the office...。把題目中的 problem 當作文章的搜尋關鍵字。

註解

circulate (v.) 使流通

be equipped with... 配備有…

20

作答時間 **1** 分鐘 

January 22, 2009

Mr. Jason J. Bellino
e-Daptive Media
2005 Nosferato Court
Chicago, IL 12345

RE: Hartford Website

Dear Jason:

Several complaints have been brought to my attention with regard to our website. These are items that were promised as part of our server package agreement with you, and as of this date, are still not functioning. Given the time frame, this is unacceptable.

Key items which do not work include:

1. Our mass e-mail. This was an important function for us, as it would allow us to communicate with our members. When we go to send a “broadcast” e-mail, we get a message that the server will not allow us to do so.

2. The Real Estate Agent and Affiliate Online Application. For over a year now, it has displayed the message “under construction, but coming soon.”

These are just two of the more major issues. There are some minor ones that can be corrected via e-mail or with a phone call to Maria, but the point I am making is that we are disappointed in your service after the sale. There are several ideas we would like to incorporate into the website, along with pushing the banner advertising idea; however, if we cannot even get the meat and potatoes of the site functioning as promised after all this time, we are reluctant to press the banner issue to our affiliates.

If need be, I can be available to meet or discuss and address these problems, any solutions, and/or ideas we have for the future. My cell number is (620) 555-1010 or you can contact Maria at the office. I am looking forward to hearing from you and resolving this situation.

Sincerely,

Joseph P. Hartford
Hartford President

1. What can be inferred about Mr. Hartford?
   (A) He has attended a presentation by Mr. Bellino.
   (B) He is seeking employment related to website construction.
   (C) He has already concluded a contract with Mr. Bellino.
   (D) He wants to purchase a new system.

2. What business is Mr. Hartford's company in?
   (A) Real estate
   (B) Website design
   (C) Food preparation
   (D) Graphic arts

3. Which is NOT discussed by Mr. Hartford as an issue?
   (A) Improving the mass mailing system
   (B) Introducing a new advertising method
   (C) Coming to an agreement soon
   (D) Fixing the online application

complaint 投訴、抱怨
agreement 合約
Real Estate Agent 房地產
Affiliate 加盟業
under construction 建構中
meat and potatoes 最基本的部份
If need be 假如有需要

1 Ⓐ Ⓑ Ⓒ Ⓓ
2 Ⓐ Ⓑ Ⓒ Ⓓ
3 Ⓐ Ⓑ Ⓒ Ⓓ

2009 年 1 月 22 日

傑森・貝林諾先生
電子適應媒體
12345 伊利諾州芝加哥市
諾斯菲拉托廣場 2005 號

回覆：哈特福特網站

傑森您好：

最近幾個對本公司網站的投訴引起我的注意，這些都涵蓋在本公司與貴公司的伺服器套裝軟體合約項目當中。但是直到今日，這些項目仍然還沒開始運作。想到這個案子進行的時間已久，這樣的結果實在讓人難以接受。

無法運作的主要項目包括：

1. 本公司的群組寄信功能。這個功能對我們非常重要，方便我們和會員溝通。每當我們要傳送「廣播」的電子郵件時，就會收到伺服器不讓我們這樣做的訊息。

2. 房地產業與加盟業的線上申請功能。這一年多來始終顯示「網頁建構中，近期推出」。

這還只是其中兩個主要問題而已。有些比較不嚴重的問題，可以透過寄電子郵件或是打電話給瑪莉亞而獲得解決，但是，我要強調的重點是，本公司對貴公司的售後服務感到很失望。除了推動橫幅廣告的構想外，本公司還有幾個構想想加入網站中。然而，這段時間以來，如果連網站約定要運作的核心部分都做不到時，那麼本公司當然不願意向加盟店推動橫幅廣告的構想。

有需要的話，我可以抽出時間見面來商討這些問題、解決方案、本公司對未來的想法等。我的手機號碼是 (620) 555-1010，不然您也可以打電話到辦公室找瑪莉亞。期待收到您的回信並解決這些問題。

哈特福特總裁
約瑟夫・哈特福特
敬上

題目中譯

1. 可以推斷出哈特福特先生的什麼事？

(A) 他出席了貝林諾先生的演講。
(B) 他在找架設網站的相關工作。
(C) **他已經和貝林諾先生簽了合約**。
(D) 他想要購買新的系統。

2. 哈特福特先生的公司從事哪一種行業？

(A) **房地產**
(B) 網站設計
(C) 食物調理
(D) 平面藝術

3. 哪一項並非哈特福特先生所討論的主題？

(A) 改善群組寄信的系統
(B) 引進新的廣告方式
(C) **盡快達成協議**
(D) 修正線上申請系統

解題技巧

答案 (C)

先確認寄信者是哈特福特先生，知道信件的內容是在向傑森．貝林諾先生抱怨後，就能馬上判斷出 (B) 和 (D) 不是正確答案。此外，從 as part of our server package agreement with you 可以知道已經簽約了。

答案 (A)

第二點針對公司伺服器無法運作的地方，提出「房地產業與加盟業的線上申請」，從這裡可以知道正確答案。本題從第一點無法找到答案。

答案 (C)

與其在文章中逐一確認 (A) ～ (D) 選項，更重要的是要知道這四個選項中除了 (C) 以外，其他三個都和網頁的功能有關，察覺到這個差異才是速解重點所在。此外，在第一題時就已經知道簽約了，也就能確定正確答案是 (C)。

註解

agreement (n.) 合約，協議
unacceptable (adj.) 無法接受的
under construction 建構中，施工中
along with... 與…一起，連同…
meat and potatoes 最基本的部分，最重要的部分
if need be 假如必要的話

March 2, 2009

Mr. Amando del Bosque
469 West Jersey
Suite 9910
Washington, D.C. 20051

Dear Mr. del Bosque,

Last Tuesday, I was extremely pleased to meet with you. I was quite impressed with your surveying skills and deep knowledge of the stone construction industry. Your experience and qualifications are precisely what our firm is looking for, and after speaking to your former supervisor, Mr. Lex Lewis, I am even more eager to add your skills and knowledge to our team. So, I am delighted to offer you the position of sales manager at Bedrock Limestone Co. I am certain you will be pleased with the benefits and the position our company is willing to provide.

Allow me to outline the terms of our offer. The salary is based at $50,000 per year, with attractive yearly bonuses tied to your net sales. In addition, we offer a signing bonus of $5,000, and will pay all your moving costs up to $3,000. You will have three weeks of vacation time per year and ten sick days.

We would like you to start soon. Indeed, tomorrow would not be too soon! Winter season is fast approaching and it is one of our busiest sales periods, particularly, as we have already discussed, with all the Washington metro construction being planned right now. So, you should get yourself oriented as soon as possible.

We would like you to start on March 10, but we understand the difficulties of moving from Washington, D.C. so quickly. We can place some calls to local apartment complexes, if you would like. Since we are confident you will be happy at Bedrock Limestone, we are willing to hold this position available to you until the end of March. Please contact me before then so that we can confirm your acceptance of this offer. I look forward to welcoming you to the wonderful state of Indiana: the limestone capital of the world!

Sincerely,

Betty Walton

Hiring Manager

1. What is the purpose of this letter?
   (A) To correct an earlier survey
   (B) To make a job offer
   (C) To settle an old score
   (D) To announce a new contract

2. What has Ms. Walton already done?
   (A) Spoken to Mr. del Bosque's former boss
   (B) Given Mr. del Bosque his bonus
   (C) Found a new sales manager
   (D) Exhausted her vacation days

3. What is the latest that Mr. del Bosque can start his new job?
   (A) March 4
   (B) March 10
   (C) March 17
   (D) March 31

4. What is NOT true about Mr. del Bosque's new job?
   (A) The salary starts at $50,000 per year.
   (B) There are three weeks of paid vacation time.
   (C) His moving expenses will be covered.
   (D) He is expected to report to work immediately.

1 Ⓐ Ⓑ Ⓒ Ⓓ
2 Ⓐ Ⓑ Ⓒ Ⓓ
3 Ⓐ Ⓑ Ⓒ Ⓓ
4 Ⓐ Ⓑ Ⓒ Ⓓ

2009 年 3 月 2 日

艾曼多．戴波斯克先生
20051 華盛頓特區
西澤西 469 號
9910 套房

戴波斯克先生您好：

很高興上星期二能與您會面，我對您的調查技巧與深厚的石造業知識感到印象深刻。本公司正需要借助您的經驗與資歷，加上與您的前任主管雷克斯．路易斯先生談過之後，我更希望將您的技術與知識納入我們的團隊。因此，我很高興能邀請您擔任基岩石灰岩公司的業務經理。我敢肯定，您一定會對本公司所提供的福利與職位感到滿意的。

請容我稍加描述此工作邀約的條件。基本薪資為年薪 5 萬元，連同與您的淨銷售息息相關的誘人獎金。除此之外，我們提供 5 千元的簽約獎金，另外還支付高達 3 千元的搬家費用。您一年享有三週的假期，外加 10 天病假。

我們希望您能盡快開始工作，就算從明天開始也不嫌快！冬季就快到了，這是我們最忙碌的銷售旺季，就像先前已經談論到的，尤其是華盛頓地鐵工程目前正在進行規畫。所以，您應該愈快熟悉一切愈好。

我們希望您能從 3 月 10 日開始上班，但是我們也了解，要迅速搬離華盛頓特區有些困難。如果您有意願的話，我們可以打電話給當地的集合公寓。由於我們確信您一定會喜歡在基岩石灰岩公司工作，我們願意為您保留這份工作直到三月底。請在那之前與我聯絡，向我們確認您是否要接受這份工作。我期待能歡迎您加入這個美好的印第安納州：世界石灰岩之都！

人資經理
貝蒂．瓦爾頓
敬上

題目中譯

1. 這封信的目的是什麼？

(A) 更正先前的調查
(B) **提出工作邀約**
(C) 清算舊帳
(D) 宣布一份新合約

解題技巧

答案 (B)

從第一段的 So, I am delighted to offer you the position 可以得知正確答案，但是解題技巧在於注意寄信者的頭銜。由於信上寫的職稱是人資經理，因此可以清楚知道信件內容與徵才有關。

2. 瓦爾頓女士已經做了什麼事？

(A) **與戴波斯克先生的前任主管談過**
(B) 給戴波斯克先生他的獎金
(C) 找到新的銷售經理
(D) 休完了她的年假

答案 (A)

在文章中迅速找出與 already 相關的部分，就在第一段第四行表示時間的連接詞 after 那裡，從 speaking to your former supervisor 可以得知正確答案。

3. 戴波斯克先生最晚何時可以開始他的新工作？

(A) 3 月 4 日
(B) 3 月 10 日
(C) 3 月 17 日
(D) **3 月 31 日**

答案 (D)

從最後一段中的 this position available to you until the end of March 就能知道正確答案是 (D)。此外，最後一段的一開頭就寫了希望開始工作的日期，如果可以立刻找到這一段，對於作答有相當的幫助。

4. 關於戴波斯克先生的新工作，哪一項不是真的？

(A) 年薪起薪為 5 萬元。
(B) 有三週的給薪假期。
(C) 公司會負擔他的搬家費用。
(D) **他必須立刻到新公司報到**。

答案 (D)

(A)、(B)、(C) 三者都是第二段中提到的工作條件。從書信日期（3 月 2 日）和第四段的 this position available to you until the end of March，就能確定寄信者並沒有催促戴波斯克先生立刻答覆的意思。

註解

signing bonus 簽約獎金

get oneself oriented 適應新環境；弄清楚方位

January 15, 2009

P.O.P. Distributing, Inc.
P.O. Box 61186
N. Miami, FL 33261-9093

Subject: Account Number 123456789

To Whom It May Concern:

This letter is in response to phone calls received this morning at approximately 9:10 A.M. The individual who called regarding our account was very rude and she even refused to give her name! A payment on the account was made online the previous day. I find it very hard to believe that you have no record of it after 24 hours. This is something that most definitely should be addressed.

I also asked to speak to someone about some complaints and the individual I spoke with during the second phone call only gave me her own, personal voicemail. This makes your company look a little shady.

I will not be ordering anything else from your company. I am very disappointed that you shipped each item I ordered separately and on different days. This made for more expense on my part for shipping, and definitely will stop me from ordering large orders during Christmas sales this winter. I just cannot count on getting your products in a timely manner, or at all in the case of one of my orders, which I was told was on back order, and so it wound up being canceled all together.

While I do appreciate the products themselves and their low cost, that does not outweigh the abovementioned issues.

Sincerely,

Mrs. Rosetta Jones
Owner, Harper Households, Ltd.

1. What is the purpose of this letter?
   (A) To register a complaint
   (B) To remind a customer of a shipped item
   (C) To encourage a response
   (D) To report a defect

2. Which of the following does Mrs. Jones NOT mention in her complaint?
   (A) Phone manners
   (B) Poor account management
   (C) High product costs
   (D) Late shipping of products

3. What can be inferred about Harper Households, Ltd.?
   (A) They will change accountants.
   (B) They will be in contact by voicemail.
   (C) They will find a new supplier.
   (D) They will offer more low-cost items.

4. Why did Harper Households NOT receive one of its orders?
   (A) It was discontinued.
   (B) It was not in stock.
   (C) It was too expensive.
   (D) It was damaged in transit.

1 Ⓐ Ⓑ Ⓒ Ⓓ
2 Ⓐ Ⓑ Ⓒ Ⓓ
3 Ⓐ Ⓑ Ⓒ Ⓓ
4 Ⓐ Ⓑ Ⓒ Ⓓ

原文中譯

2009 年 1 月 15 日
P.O.P. 銷售有限公司
33261-9093 佛羅里達州北邁阿密市
郵政信箱第 61186 號

主旨：帳號 123456789

敬啓者：

這封信是為了回應今天上午大約 9 點 10 分所接到的電話。有個人為了我們的帳戶打電話過來，但是卻非常無禮。她不願意留下她的名字。我們前一天就已經在線上將應付款項匯入該帳戶，我實在很難相信 24 小時後，貴公司還沒有任何紀錄。這件事我非提不可。

我也要求知道我可以找誰投訴，但是第二通電話上和我對話的人，只給了我她個人的語音信箱，這讓貴公司顯得不太可靠。

我再也不會向貴公司訂購任何其他東西了。我感到非常失望，因為貴公司將我訂購的每項貨品都分開運送，而且都不在同一天。這使我的運輸成本增加，讓我絕對不想為今年冬天的耶誕特賣下大筆訂單。我實在無法信任貴公司的產品會準時送達，我甚至曾有一項訂貨根本沒有送到，貴公司通知我要等調貨，結果最後根本就把訂單取消了。

雖然我喜歡產品本身和它們的低價位，但是這些優點卻抵不過以上所提及的問題。

哈波家用產品有限公司老闆
蘿賽塔．瓊斯女士
敬上

1. 這封信的目的是什麼？
   (A) **要投訴**
   (B) 提醒客戶有一件運送貨品
   (C) 鼓勵回應
   (D) 報告缺陷

答案 (A)

文章的目的就如同段落閱讀理論所提的出現在一開頭。第一句就指出了這封信是針對一通打給自己的電話，從下一句的 The individual who called regarding our account was very rude and she even refused to give her name! 就知道正確答案。

2. 瓊斯女士的投訴中並未提到下面哪一項？
   (A) 電話禮儀
   (B) 不良帳戶管理
   (C) **產品成本過高**
   (D) 產品運送延遲

答案 (C)

從第一題明確知道了主題是 (A)。(B) 可從第一段的 I find it very hard to believe that you have no record of it after 24 hours. 中知道，而 (D) 可從第三段的 I just cannot count on getting your products in a timely manner 中得知，所以兩者都可以刪去。

3. 可以推斷出哈波家用產品有限公司的什麼事？
   (A) 將更換會計師。
   (B) 將用語音信箱聯絡。
   (C) **將找尋新的供應商**。
   (D) 將提供更多低成本的物品。

答案 (C)

只要能注意到信末寄信者的署名就是題目中的 Harper Households, Ltd.（哈波家用產品有限公司），就能馬上知道正確答案。如果想在文章中確認答案，可從第三段開頭的 I will not be ordering anything else from your company. 得知。

4. 哈波家用產品為什麼沒有收到其中一筆訂單？
   (A) 停產了。
   (B) **沒有存貨**。
   (C) 價格太高。
   (D) 運送過程中受損。

答案 (B)

在文章中搜尋 not receive，可以在第三段的最後一句找到 being canceled。由此可知貨品並沒有送到，原因就在於 on back order（調貨），即表示「本公司無庫存」。

註解

shady (adj.) 不可靠的，成問題的
count on... 期待…，依賴…
be on back order 調貨
wind up... 結束…
outweigh (v.) 勝過，比…重要

Leadership Qualities

Of all the links between psychology and business, one of the most fruitful has been the focus on leadership by those in the psychological sciences. Psychological testing has uncovered some of the characteristics associated with successful leaders. We hope this list will help managers better understand their own strengths and weaknesses, and develop their skills.

As the pace of change in the business world has accelerated, leadership has never been more important. The managers of thirty years ago may have been able to succeed by following the status quo, but today they have to have a broader vision. Not only are leaders expected to teach, but they also need to be able to learn from their mistakes and learn from others with expertise. They need to be able to see how their society is changing, and they have to meet those changes.

The Leadership Potential Equation was developed in the 1950s to assess the leadership competence of military leaders. It is still used today to assess leaders in business, and make them aware of what and how they need to improve. Here's the short version of the list:

* Leaders must be emotionally stable people. They have to tolerate frustration and stress, and have the psychological maturity to deal with the problems they face.

* Leaders need to be competitive and decisive. It helps if they like a good challenge and have an assertive manner in dealing with others.

* Leaders must feel a sense of duty and diligence toward their work. After all, they are setting an example for others to follow. They must feel a strong desire to do their best and have the discipline to accomplish what they begin.

* Good leaders appreciate and encourage practical thinking. They understand that criticism is a valuable management tool.

* Leaders have self-confidence. They do not rely upon others for approval.

1. What is the purpose of studying leadership qualities?
   (A) To improve managers' emotional stability
   (B) To help managers understand and develop leadership skills
   (C) To ensure that we have visionary leaders in the future
   (D) To raise the corporate standard of excellence

2. What can be inferred about managers of the past?
   (A) Managers were not expected to be creative.
   (B) They were far more likely to study psychology than management.
   (C) They were more disciplined but less competitive than modern managers.
   (D) They often were recruited from the military.

3. The Leadership Potential Equation is based on what kind of leaders?
   (A) Business leaders
   (B) Innovative managers
   (C) Military leaders
   (D) Political leaders

4. What is NOT listed in the article as a quality of successful managers?
   (A) They can stand high levels of stress.
   (B) They always want to be the best.
   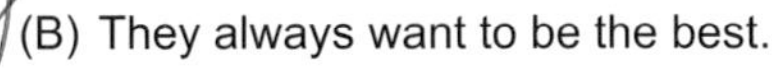
   (C) They accept criticism.
   (D) They understand the need for a consensus.

fruitful 成效.
weakness 弱點.
status quo. 維持現狀.
tolerate. 承受.
frustration. 挫敗.
maturity 成熟.
decisive 果決的.

assertive. 过於自信.

1	Ⓐ	Ⓑ	Ⓒ	Ⓓ
2	Ⓐ	Ⓑ	Ⓒ	Ⓓ
3	Ⓐ	Ⓑ	Ⓒ	Ⓓ
4	Ⓐ	Ⓑ	Ⓒ	Ⓓ

領導特質

在心理學與商業之間的眾多連結中，最有成效的就屬心理學對領導能力的重視。心理測驗揭露了某些成功領導者所具有的特質。我們希望這份清單能幫助主管了解自身的優點與弱點，進而發展自己的能力。

隨著商業世界的改變速度逐漸加快，領導能力也變得格外重要。30 年前的主管可能靠著維持現狀就能成功，但是，時至今日，他們的視野必須要更開闊。領導者不只必須教導他人，還必須從他們自己所犯的錯誤當中學習，並從其他有專長的人身上學習。他們必須要能看見社會是如何在改變，也要能順應這些改變。

領導潛能公式發展於 1950 年代，用於評量軍事領袖的領導能力。這個公式今天仍然用來評量商業領袖，讓他們了解到自己需要做什麼改變，以及如何達成。以下是清單的簡短版：

* 領導者必須是情緒穩定的人。他們得承受挫敗與壓力，心理上也要夠成熟才能處理他們面對的難題。

* 領導者必須有競爭力和果斷力。如果他們喜歡良性挑戰，而且待人處事上的態度是有自信的，那會更好。

* 領導者必須有責任感且勤於工作。畢竟，他們得要為其他人樹立典範。他們必須強烈地想要做到最好，也必須有紀律地將工作完成。

* 好的領導者喜歡也鼓勵實際的想法。他們了解，批評是有用的管理工具。

* 領導者都有自信。他們不會仰賴別人來肯定自己。

題目中譯

1. 研究領導特質的目的是什麼？
   (A) 改善主管的情緒穩定度
   (B) **幫助主管了解並發展領導能力**
   (C) 確保我們未來的領導者有遠見
   (D) 提高企業的優良標準

解題技巧

答案 (B)

這是個問主旨的題目，直覺就是閱讀第一段的內容，在這一段裡沒有提到的就不是正確答案。選項中的 emotional, visionary, corporate standard 都沒有出現在第一段。對應的部分就是在第三行 We hope... 之後的內容。

2. 可以推論出過去主管的什麼事？
   (A) **主管不需要有創意**。
   (B) 他們比較有可能學習的是心理學而非管理。
   (C) 他們比現代主管有紀律，但競爭力不足。
   (D) 他們通常都自軍中招募而來。

答案 (A)

在文章中搜尋題目裡的 managers 和 of the past，可以確實對應的部分出現在第二段的 managers 和 thirty years ago。選項的敘述與 succeed by following the status quo 最接近的就是正確答案。

3. 領導潛能公式發展自哪一種領導者？
   (A) 商業領袖
   (B) 創新的主管
   (C) **軍事領袖**
   (D) 政治領袖

答案 (C)

以 Leadership Potential Equation 作為關鍵字進行搜尋，可以在第三段的 The Leadership Potential Equation was developed in the 1950s... 中找到，這部分即為對應內容。

4. 成功的主管需要具備的特質，哪一項沒有列在文章中？
   (A) 他們能夠承受高度的壓力。
   (B) 他們永遠要當最優秀的人。
   (C) 他們接受批評。
   (D) **他們了解一致同意的重要性**。

答案 (D)

搜尋題目中的 quality，第三段中出現同義字 competence，故可判斷出這部分就是對應內容。接下來，找到列出的需求條件加以確認，從最後一項的 They do not rely upon others for approval. 得知應該選 (D)。

註解

status quo 現狀
equation (n.) 方程式，公式
maturity (n.) 成熟（度）
decisive (adj.) 果斷的；決定性的
assertive (adj.) 過於自信的；斷定的

To: Dean Martin
Re: nano tech 2009

Dean,

I just received confirmation that we've been invited to nano tech 2009 (International Nanotechnology Exhibition & Conference). Here's the promotional information:

Show Dates: February 18-20, 2009
Location: Tokyo, Japan
Facility: Tokyo Big Sight (Tokyo International Exhibition Center)
East Exhibition Halls 3, 4, 5, 6 & the Conference Tower
Booth Number: Yet to be determined

Nano tech 2009 will be the largest nanotechnology exhibition and conference in the world. There will be unparalleled opportunities to meet 400 exhibiting enterprises and research labs from around the world that are responsible for the rapid R&D progress in nanotechnology both at home and abroad. This event is one of the most comprehensive nanotechnology shows, and includes exhibitions of research and development in a great variety of industries. More than 250 Japanese and international companies will showcase their cutting-edge technology and products.

So my question is: Do you have a flyer we can use for this?

Justin Pere
Brobis R&D Division Manager

****

To: Justin Pere
Re: Re: nano tech 2009

JP,

Here's the basic product information:

The Brobis Group Research Lab will have its new ultra-low current measurement system with Cyrvex manipulator on display, as well as the Brobis 560K low current/high resistance measurement unit and the next generation nanovolt meter, which can eliminate thermoelectric power interference.

Our experts will be available to discuss all your testing and measurement challenges. We will have daily scheduled demonstrations of the following products:

* The New Model Cyrvex (accuracy/reliability demonstration)
* The enhanced Brobis 560K (measurement accuracy demonstration)

I think we can use it, but we'll need to get a translation. What I'm more worried

翻譯

about is our literature on the new nanovolt meter. I don't think we can use any of the literature translations we used last year with all the changes to the new model, and I can't remember who we got to produce it, either. The receipts are all in Japanese. Can you help me out on this one? Either find out who made the brochures last year or find me a new translator/printer. We need product brochures for the Cyrvex, Brobis 560K, and nanovolt meter.

Dean Martin
Business Promotion

1. What is being discussed in these e-mails?
   (A) A press conference to announce a new product line
   (B) The date and location of next year's conference
   (C) An international nanotechnology conference presentation
   (D) The best way of getting new product information translated into English

2. What did Mr. Pere just receive?
   (A) An invitation to a conference
   (B) A notice that a conference he planned to attend had to be rescheduled
   (C) A warning that one of his company's patents is being contested
   (D) A letter stating that several of his company's products will not be available for display

3. About how many research labs will participate in the conference?
   (A) 150 (C) 400
   (B) 250 (D) 560

4. What is Mr. Martin worried about?
   (A) Designing the presentation
   (B) Eliminating thermoelectric power interference
   (C) Explaining test and measurement challenges
   (D) Getting documents translated

5. What can be inferred about Mr. Martin?
   (A) He did not participate in last year's conference.
   (B) He has research and development experience.
   (C) He cannot find last year's product information.
   (D) He is Mr. Pere's colleague in a different division.

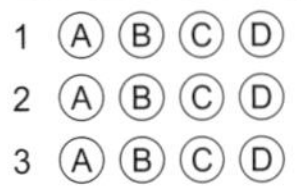

原文中譯

收件者：狄恩．馬丁
回覆：2009 奈米科技展

狄恩：

我剛獲得確認，我們受邀參加 2009 奈米科技展（國際奈米科技展覽與會議）。以下是宣傳資訊：

展出日期：2009 年 2 月 18 ～ 20 日
地點：日本東京
場地：東京國際展覽場東展覽館 3, 4, 5, 6 與會議塔
攤位編號：尚待決定

2009 奈米科技展將會是世界最大的奈米科技展覽與會議。屆時將有無可比擬的機會，一次見到 400 個來自世界各地，負責國內外奈米科技快速研發進展的參展企業與研究實驗室。這場活動是最完整的奈米科技展覽之一，包含各種工業領域的研究與開發展覽。超過 250 家來自日本與全世界的公司，將會展出他們最尖端的科技與產品。

所以我的問題是：你有沒有讓我們到時候可以派上用場的文宣？

波比斯研發組經理
賈斯汀．佩爾

****

收件者：賈斯汀．佩爾
回覆：回覆：2009 奈米科技展

賈斯汀：

以下是基本的產品資訊：

波比斯集團研究實驗室將展出全新超低電流測量系統，配有瑟非斯操作器，還有波比斯 560K 低電流／高電阻測量單位，及能排除熱電力干擾的新一代奈米伏特表。

我們的專家將在現場討論所有測試與測量的問題。我們每天會定期示範以下產品：

＊新型瑟非斯（示範其正確度與可靠度）
＊波比斯 560K 強化版（示範其測量準確度）

我想我們可以用這個，但是需要有人翻譯。我比較擔心的是我們新奈米伏特表的文案。我覺得我們不能用任何去年用過的文案翻譯，因為新型產品已經全然改變，而且我也想不起來文案當初是請誰寫的。（翻譯的）收據全用日文書寫。這一點能不能請你幫我的忙？不是去找出去年的手冊是誰做的，不然就是幫我找個新翻譯和新的印刷廠。我們需要為瑟非斯、波比斯 560K 及奈米伏特表做產品手冊。

市場推廣
狄恩．馬丁

題目中譯

1. 這幾封電子郵件在討論什麼？

(A) 發表新產品線的記者會
(B) 明年會議的日期與地點
(C) **國際奈米科技會議的發表**
(D) 將新產品資訊譯成英文最好的方法

2. 佩爾先生剛剛收到什麼？

(A) **參加會議的邀請函**
(B) 通知他原本計畫要參加的會議改期
(C) 警告他有人對公司的其中一項專利提出質疑
(D) 一封說明他的公司有幾樣產品將無法展出的信

3. 大約有多少間研究實驗室會參與這場會議？

(A) **150** (C) 400
(B) 250 (D) 560

4. 馬丁先生擔心的是什麼事？

(A) 設計這場發表會
(B) 排除熱電力干擾
(C) 解釋測試與測量的問題
(D) **翻譯文件**

5. 可以推論出馬丁先生的什麼事？

(A) 他沒有參加去年的會議。
(B) 他有研究與開發的經驗。
(C) 他無法找到去年的產品資訊。
(D) **他是佩爾先生在不同部門的同事。**

解題技巧

答案 (C)

佩爾先生在郵件中問到「是否有產品說明的文宣」，和文宣有關的只有 (C) 的 presentation。(A) 的記者會和 (B) 的會議日期與地點都和產品說明文宣的主旨不同，(D) 則和佩爾先生的郵件內容不符。

答案 (A)

以題目中的 Mr. Pere 和 receive 作為搜尋關鍵字，只要讀文章的開頭部分就能立刻作答。

答案 (A)

從佩爾先生所寫的郵件中可以得知，公司和研究機構共計 400 所，國內外公司約 250 家，兩個數字相減就能得出正確答案。

答案 (D)

重點在於能否立刻找出馬丁先生陳述主旨的部分。以 worried 這個字去搜尋，對應部分就在最後一段 but we'll need to get a translation，but 之後的內容就是主旨。

答案 (D)

馬丁先生這封郵件的主題是「翻譯」。(A) 是關於是否出席去年的會議；(B) 是佩爾先生的研發經驗，兩個選項都離題了。(C) 的「無法找到」和內容剛好相反，在最後一段第二行的 I don't ... last year 提到。

註解

unparalleled (adj.) 空前的；獨一無二的
showcase (v.) 展示，讓…亮相
thermoelectric (adj.) 電熱氣的
literature (n.) 文獻資料
be contested 爭論中

To: IBH Atlantic
From: Elena Ltd. On-site Team

Mr. Ray Savrin:

I enjoyed coming down to Charlotte last week. Thanks for the hospitality! Here are the specs we agreed on. I would like you to check them out and make sure we are on the same page. Our contract is on the standard package, so everything should be in order, but should you have any questions, please get back to me. I just sent the contract by snail mail, so you should get it in a few days. But, just in case, can you verify acceptance by e-mail until the contract is finalized? We are excited about this opportunity to serve you, especially because we think this project has such great potential.

I look forward to hearing from you,

Dave Spence

****

Statement of Work

Elena Ltd. will provide an on-site consultant at IBH Atlantic in Charlotte, NC, as requested, to continue the rollout of Elena Ltd.'s Enterprise Auditor product to the 1,000 servers identified by the IBH technical team. In addition, the on-site consultant will provide direct hands-on technical support to IBH's technical team as they manage and operate within their Elena Ltd. Enterprise Auditor product environment. This consultant will be knowledgeable in Elena's product set, focusing on IT infrastructure and end user client functionality as it is implemented in IBH's environment. This includes, but is not limited to, the Enterprise Auditor product and Elena custom reports for IBH.

Timeframe:
Approximately 4 months (83 working days) of on-site consulting over the course of 17 consecutive weeks commencing on May 7 and ending on September 1 of 2009. Coverage is for normal working hours, Monday through Friday, excluding holidays unless otherwise agreed upon.

Price and Payment:
The total cost of the project is $119,520, plus travel and lodging expenses. The travel and lodging expenses will be billed at actual rates.

Notes:
* Weekends and holidays are non-working days and are excluded.
* Additional consulting hours over 8 hours per day will be billed at a rate of $180 per hour.
* Additional days may be purchased at $1,440 per day based on a rate of $180 per hour.

1. What is the purpose of this e-mail?
   (A) To confirm an agreement
   (B) To notify a customer of a billing change
   (C) To authorize a new project
   (D) To report a special expense

2. Why did Mr. Spence travel to Charlotte last week?
   (A) To provide on-site assistance
   (B) To manage the installation of a new system
   (C) To negotiate a contract
   (D) To service the 1,000 server system

3. What kind of support will Elena provide?
   (A) Software
   (B) Server
   (C) Legal services
   (D) Client functions

4. Who will pay for travel expenses?
   (A) Dave Spence
   (B) Enterprise Auditor
   (C) Elena Ltd.
   (D) IBH Atlantic

5. What does Mr. Spence ask Mr. Savrin to do with this e-mail?
   (A) Forward it to the IBH legal department
   (B) Reply with a confirmation of project contract
   (C) Forward it to the technical team
   (D) Call Dave Spence to discuss the contract

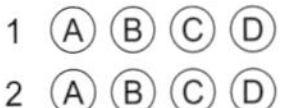

原文中譯

收件者：IBH 亞特蘭大
寄件者：艾蓮娜有限公司現場小組

雷・薩福林先生：

上星期去夏洛特市時很開心，謝謝您的熱情招待！以下是我們同意的詳細說明書，希望您看一下內容，確認我們的想法一致。我們的合約是標準配備，所以一切應該都沒問題，不過，如果您有任何疑問，請務必和我聯絡。我剛剛將合約郵寄出去，所以您應該這幾天內就會收到了。但是為了預防萬一，在合約完全簽訂前，能否請您先用電子郵件確認接受？我們很高興有這個機會能為您服務，特別是因為我們覺得這個方案有無比的潛力。

期待您的回信。

大衛・史班斯

****

工作說明書

艾蓮娜有限公司將會依要求，在北卡羅來納州夏洛特市擔任 IBH 亞特蘭大的現場顧問，以繼續將艾蓮娜有限公司的企業審計產品，首次展示在 IBH 技術小組所驗明的 1000 台伺服器上。除此之外，現場顧問也會在 IBH 技術小組管理、操作艾蓮娜有限公司的企業審計產品環境時，直接提供他們實際操作的技術支援。這位顧問會非常了解艾蓮娜的產品組合，將專注在資訊科技基礎建設，以及在 IBH 環境下執行時的終端使用者客戶功能。這個涵蓋，但並不侷限於企業審計產品與艾蓮娜給 IBH 的報表。

時間範圍：
在連續 17 週裡擔任大約四個月（83 個工作天）的現場顧問，從 2009 年 5 月 7 日開始到 2009 年 9 月 1 日結束。費用涵蓋正常工作時間，週一至週五，不包含假日，除非事先經過同意。

價格與付款：
整個方案的費用是 119,520 元，外加交通與住宿支出。交通與住宿支出採取實報實銷。

附註：
＊週末與假日屬非工作日，不算在內。
＊一天超過八小時的顧問時數，以一小時 180 元計算。
＊購買額外天數是一天 1440 元，以一小時 180 元計算。

題目中譯

解題技巧

1. 這封電子郵件的目的是什麼？

(A) **確認一份協議書**
(B) 通知客戶計費方式改變
(C) 授權新的專案
(D) 通報特別支出

答案 (A)

只要看到開頭招呼語之後的內容，就能知道郵件的主旨。I would like you... 之後的部分就是寄件者敘述的重點。

2. 史班斯先生上週為什麼去夏洛特市？

(A) 提供現場協助
(B) 為新系統安裝做管理
(C) **進行合約協商**
(D) 服務 1000 台伺服器系統

答案 (C)

第一行就指出郵件內容與旅行有關，而從之後接的 Here are the specs we agreed on. 可知郵件內容是在確認合約的說明書事宜。選項 (C) 的 negotiate 常在「形成共識」時使用。

3. 艾蓮娜會提供什麼樣的支援？

(A) **軟體**
(B) 伺服器
(C) 法律服務
(D) 客戶功能

答案 (A)

(C)、(D) 都可立刻刪去，但要判斷 (B) server（伺服器）是錯的則要花點時間。從 Elena Ltd. will provide ... to continue the rollout of ... to the 1,000 servers 可以知道，艾蓮娜公司提供伺服器的各項服務內容，因此 (B) 也可刪去。

4. 誰會負擔交通支出？

(A) 大衛．史班斯
(B) 企業審計
(C) 艾蓮娜有限公司
(D) **IBH 亞特蘭大**

答案 (D)

以 travel expenses 作為搜尋關鍵字。在標題為 Statement of Work 的下面有 Price and Payment:，可知寄件者就是索取費用的人。

5. 史班斯先生請薩福林先生怎麼處理這封電子郵件？

(A) 轉寄給 IBH 法務部門
(B) **針對合約的確認進行回覆**
(C) 轉寄給技術小組
(D) 打電話給大衛．史班斯討論合約

答案 (B)

尋找與題目中 ask 同義的字。郵件後段的 ...can you verify acceptance by e-mail until the contract is finalized? 就是向對方請求的說法，和 ask 有相同的意思，由此可知這個部分就是正確答案。

註解

spec (n.) 詳細說明書
on the same page 意見一致，有共識
snail mail 透過郵局寄送的信
verify (v.) 確認，驗證
hands-on 實際操作的
knowledgeable (adj.) 有豐富知識的
functionality (n.) 機能性
commence (v.) 開始，著手

Memo

To: All Regional Managers
From: Accounting Department, HQ
Date: May 10
Subject: New Cell Phone Expense Policy

I have discussed our new cell phone policy with most of the regional managers by now, but we want to make sure that news of the new policy has trickled down to all users. The new policy takes effect on July 1, so let us make sure to distribute it to everyone who is using a company cell phone. The procedures are as follows:

1. Regional managers must submit an approval form (attached) to all employees who are approved for a company cell phone. Managers will register your cell phone approval with HQ by June 1. You will receive an expense-claims number for each of the approved employees. This number must be entered in the new expense-claims form each month for our records.

2. Every month, approved employees need to file an itemized bill in addition to the new expense-claim form which you will receive by June 15. Do not claim calls not made for business purposes. Turning in the final bill without an itemized list will result in an unpaid claim.

We know and understand that cell phones are a vital link between our sales and technical staff in the field and our offices and customers. We also know that cell phone abuse is not uncommon. So, we will be tracking expenses carefully from now on. If you have questions or concerns about the new policy, contact me directly at the HQ Accounting Department.

Thank you,

Diane Summerton
Expense Manager
HQ Accounting Department

****

Cell Phone Expense Approval Form

Employee Name: Regional Office:
Job Title: Regional Manager:
Supervisor: Cell Phone Number:

To Supervisor: Please comment on the cell phone needs of this employee:

Supervisor's Signature　　　　Regional Manager's Signature

1. What is the purpose of this memo?
   (A) To remind employees not to use cell phones for personal use
   (B) To ask for new policy suggestions
   (C) To confirm that managers know about the new policy
   (D) To illustrate how the new expense-claims form works

2. Employees who claim cell phone expenses must do all of the following EXCEPT
   (A) get managerial approval.
   (B) enter the cell phone number on the claims-expense form.
   (C) provide a list of all cell phone calls.
   (D) provide an itemized list of all calls made over the last year.

3. What should a regional manager who has questions about this new policy do?
   (A) Contact Diane Summerton herself
   (B) Add any relevant documentation to the approval form
   (C) Review the procedures manual
   (D) Ask their local accounting staff for clarification

4. By what date do managers need to submit the approval forms?
   (A) May 10
   (B) June 1
   (C) June 15
   (D) July 1

5. Which information is NOT required by the Cell Phone Expense Approval Form?
   (A) Supervisor's name and signature
   (B) Frequently called numbers
   (C) Regional office
   (D) Cell phone number

備忘錄

收件者：全體區域經理
寄件者：總部會計部門
日期：5 月 10 日
主旨：新手機支出政策

到目前為止，我與多數區域經理都討論過我們新的手機政策，但是我們想要確認這項新政策的消息能夠傳達給所有使用者。新政策從 7 月 1 日起正式實施，所以我們要確保這項消息能夠傳給所有使用公司手機的人。程序如下：

1. 區域經理必須給每位被核准使用公司手機的員工一張核准單（已附上）。在 6 月 1 日前，經理會向總部註冊各位的手機使用許可，接著每位通過核准的員工會收到一組支出申報編號。這個編號必須填入每個月的新支出申報單，作為紀錄。

2. 除了 6 月 15 日前會收到的新支出申報單外，經核准的員工每個月需提出一份詳細的清單。非工作需要的通話費請勿申報。若要繳交最後的帳單但卻沒有詳細的清單，則申報支出將不予受理。

我們知道也了解，手機是業務人員和技術人員在辦公室內外工作時，與客戶聯繫的重要橋樑。我們同時也知道，濫用手機的情形很常見。因此，我們從現在開始將會嚴格追蹤這些支出。如果您對新政策有任何問題或疑慮，請直接打到總部會計部門與我聯絡。

謝謝您。

總部會計部門
支出經理
黛安・桑莫頓

****

手機支出核准單

員工姓名：　　　　區域辦公室：
職稱：　　　　區域經理：
主管：　　　　手機號碼：

致主管：請評論這名員工是否需要使用手機：

主管簽名　　　　區域經理簽名

題目中譯

解題技巧

1. 這份備忘錄的目的是什麼？
   (A) 提醒員工不要把手機用於私人用途
   (B) 詢問大家對新政策的建議
   (C) **確認經理知道這項新政策**
   (D) 說明新支出申報單的使用方式

答案 (C)

由於 I have discussed our new cell phone policy... 用的是現在完成式，可知針對手機支出政策已經討論過一陣子了。從 but 之後的 we want to make sure... 知道寄件者想要確認所有的經理都能知道新政策。

2. 申報手機支出的員工必須要做的事情不包含以下哪一項？
   (A) 取得經理的核准。
   (B) 將手機號碼填在支出申報單上。
   (C) 提供所有手機通話明細。
   (D) **提供過去一年所有手機通話明細**。

答案 (D)

在出現 EXCEPT 的題目中，逐一確認每個選項將非常浪費時間。由於是新政策，應該會與今後手機帳單的內容有關，因此 (D) 的 last year 絕對是錯的。

3. 對這項新政策有疑問的區域經理該怎麼做？
   (A) **聯絡黛安．桑莫頓本人**
   (B) 把所有相關文件都附在核准單上
   (C) 重看程序手冊
   (D) 請他們當地區域的會計人員說明

答案 (A)

若用題目中的 questions 來搜尋，就能在文章最後找到這個單字。這裡提到如果有任何問題或疑慮的話，可以和寄件者聯絡，因此只要確認文章最後的署名就能確定正確答案。

4. 經理要在幾月幾號前提出核准單？
   (A) 5 月 10 日　(C) 6 月 15 日
   (B) **6 月 1 日**　(D) 7 月 1 日

答案 (B)

用 submit 搜尋來找出相關字，只要知道第一項 Managers will register your cell phone... 中 register 的意思，就能迅速以消去法作答。

5. 手機支出核准單需要的資料不包含以下哪一項？
   (A) 主管姓名與簽名
   (B) **常撥打的電話號碼**
   (C) 區域辦公室
   (D) 手機號碼

答案 (B)

迅速作答的訣竅在於，細讀每個選項後就能發現到只有 (B)「常撥打的電話號碼」和其他為事務性質的選項不同。先預設 (B) 是正確答案，再確認它是否真的沒有出現在文章所列出的項目當中。

註解

trickle down 傳布；緩慢移動
take effect 實施
submit (v.) 提出
abuse (n.) 濫用
clarification (n.) 說明，解釋

Scarfe Consulting Expense Sheet

DATE	ITEM (NOTES)	TRAVEL	MEALS
8/3	CCO (Horowitz, Toronto)	200kms	$19.00
8/4	Finance Group Meeting	50kms	$45.00
8/8	Lunch Meeting (Chuck Kyd)		$36.26
8/10	Dinner (Oswald, strategic planning)		$45.00
8/11	Meeting (C. Kyd and K. Rich, planning)	50kms	
8/12	Meeting (O'Driscoll and Eggz, brochure)	50kms	
8/15	Meeting (Simcoe)	50kms	
8/16	Meeting (T. Kirk, strategic planning, and Eggz, brochure)	50kms	
8/17	Meeting (Janus, brochure & finance)	50kms	
8/18	Meeting (C. Kyd, K. Rich, planning)	50kms	$55.00
8/19	CCO Board Meeting (Toronto)	200kms	
	Hotel and Dinner		$107.50
8/24	Meeting (M. Profitt, B. Gallaher,	50kms	
	and dinner with Gallaher, finances)		$36.92
Total meals			$344.68
Total travel: 800kms @ $0.42/km			$336.00
Other			
* Cell Phone: 50% of Basic			$18.43
* 2 Flip Chart Pads @ $14.50/each (for CCO meetings)			$29.00
Total Expenses, August 2008			$728.11

Mike Cox

Mike Cox, Executive Director

****

To: Mike Cox

Subject: Expense Sheet

Mike,

I just got off the phone with our accountant, Mr. Harshberger, and he said we have to start separating mileage from other expenses when we file a claim. It's something related to documenting depreciation on the company car.

So, please fill out a separate mileage sheet when you turn your paperwork in from now on. I went ahead and had my secretary do it for you for this month. The meals, phone, and other expenses should still be filed on the current expense sheet.

Sorry for the hassle, thanks!

Roseanne Scarfe
Roseanne Scarfe, President

1. According to the expense sheet, how many times did Mike Cox travel to Toronto in August?
   (A) Zero
   (B) One
   (C) Two
   (D) Three

2. Who did Mr. Cox meet with three times in August?
   (A) Chuck Kyd
   (B) Oswald
   (C) K. Rich
   (D) Eggz

3. Who is Roseanne Scarfe?
   (A) Mike Cox's customer
   (B) Mike Cox's accountant
   (C) Mike Cox's boss
   (D) Mike Cox's travel agent

4. Why is a change in the expense filing system necessary?
   (A) Because they are changing accountants
   (B) Because they need to depreciate the car expenses
   (C) Because expenses have been far too high lately
   (D) Because Mike Cox will use public transportation to travel to Toronto from now on

5. When should Mr. Cox start using the new expense reports?
   (A) January 2008
   (B) August 2008
   (C) September 2008
   (D) January 2009

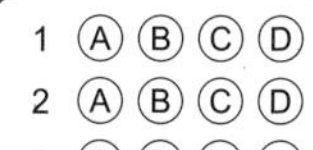

史卡佛顧問支出明細表

日期	項目（附註）	交通	用餐
8/3	CCO（霍羅威茲，多倫多）	200 公里	19.00 元
8/4	金融小組會議	50 公里	45.00 元
8/8	午餐會（恰克．凱德）		36.26 元
8/10	晚餐（奧斯華，策略規畫）		45.00 元
8/11	會議（凱德＆瑞奇，規畫）	50 公里	
8/12	會議（歐德斯可＆艾格斯，手冊）	50 公里	
8/15	會議（希姆科）	50 公里	
8/16	會議（科克，策略規畫；艾格斯，手冊）	50 公里	
8/17	會議（詹尼斯，手冊與金融）	50 公里	
8/18	會議（凱德＆瑞奇，規畫）	50 公里	55.00 元
8/19	CCO 董事會議（多倫多）	200 公里	
	旅館與晚餐		107.50 元
8/24	會議（波費特＆賈拉赫；與賈拉赫共進晚餐，金融）	50 公里	36.92 元

總餐費	344.68 元
總交通費：800 公里 @ 0.42 元 / 公里	336.00 元
其餘費用	
＊手機：基本的 50%	18.43 元
＊兩本活動掛圖紙 @ 14.50 元 / 一本（CCO 會議用）	29.00 元
2008 年 8 月總支出	728.11 元

常務董事　麥克．寇克斯

****

收件者：麥克．寇克斯

主旨：支出明細表

麥克：

我剛才和會計哈許柏格先生通過電話，他說我們在申報支出時，必須將里程數和其他支出分開，這與公務車的折舊攤提費用有關。因此從現在開始，請你每次繳交支出明細表時，再單獨填寫一張里程數明細表。我已經請我的祕書幫你把這個月的支出分開記錄了。餐費、電話費和其他支出，還是應該記錄在現行的支出明細表當中。

很抱歉給你添麻煩了，謝謝！

董事長　羅西安．史卡佛

題目中譯

1. 根據這張支出明細表，麥克・寇克斯 8 月時去了幾次多倫多？

(A) 零次 (C) **兩次**
(B) 一次 (D) 三次

2. 寇克斯先生在 8 月時和誰見了三次面？

(A) **恰克・凱德**
(B) 奧斯華
(C) 瑞奇
(D) 艾格斯

3. 羅西安・史卡佛是誰？

(A) 麥克・寇克斯的客戶
(B) 麥克・寇克斯的會計
(C) **麥克・寇克斯的老闆**
(D) 麥克・寇克斯的旅行社人員

4. 為什麼支出申報系統必須改變？

(A) 因為他們要更換會計師
(B) **因為他們要攤提車子的折舊費用**
(C) 因為最近的支出都太高了
(D) 因為從現在開始，麥克・寇克斯將會搭乘大眾運輸工具去多倫多

5. 寇克斯先生什麼時候開始必須使用新的支出報告？

(A) 2008 年 1 月
(B) 2008 年 8 月
(C) **2008 年 9 月**
(D) 2009 年 1 月

解題技巧

答案 (C)

在明細表的 ITEM (NOTES) 一欄中以 Toronto 搜尋就能馬上找到正確答案。麥克・寇克斯分別在 8 月 3 日和 8 月 19 日去了一次多倫多，所以總共去兩次。

答案 (A)

速解重點在於注意 NOTES，查看括號內的人名。和 Chuck Kyd（恰克・凱德）先生共見了三次，分別是在 8 月 8 日、11 日和 18 日。別因為 Chuck Kyd 簡寫成 C. Kyd 就搞混了。

答案 (C)

寄信者羅西安・史卡佛先生是老闆，可從 So, please fill out a separate mileage sheet when you turn your paperwork in from now on. 知道是老闆指示下屬整理支出明細表。

答案 (B)

從以 why 開頭的題目可以知道對應的內容不是指支出明細表部分，而是指信件的內容。第三行的 It's something related to documenting depreciation on the company car. 就是正確答案的對應部分。

答案 (C)

題目問的是何時開始使用新的支出明細表，那要看信件的最後部分。從 I went ahead and had my secretary do it for you for this month. 支出明細表的日期標明 8 月。8 月份的支出會在 9 月處理，因此 this month 指的就是 9 月。

註解

accountant (n.) 會計人員
depreciation (n.) 折舊攤提
hassle (n.) 麻煩；激烈且持久的爭論

TO: Bruce Campbell
FAX: (07) 3734-1234
FROM: Faux Fronts (Lin Chong)
SUB: Quotation for interior painting for Bruback Realty, 106 Market St., Sydney

Mr. Campbell,

I have not met you personally, but you come highly recommended from my colleague, Ted Simatran. We have a new subcontract client on Market Street, and I was hoping that you would be able to help us out with the interior painting. Ted said I should just send you a fax and ask you to go on over to the Bruback Realty building at 106 Market Street later this afternoon, if you are free.

If you can fax me back a quotation for the job, I would greatly appreciate it. I do not know what your crew's schedule looks like this week and next, but assuming the quotation is within reason, I would like to ask you to finish it by a week from Friday. I know this is short notice, and if you cannot get to it we will understand. This client is on a really tight schedule, and finishing the exterior is going to be taxing for us.

Looking forward to your reply,

Lin Chong

****

TO: Lin Chong—Faux Fronts
FAX: (07) 3216-0874
FROM: Bruce Campbell
SUB: RE: Estimate for 106 Market Street

Ms. Chong,

Here's the quotation. I don't think you'll find any problems with it. It's the usual service. We can get to it next Wednesday or Thursday at the very latest. Say hi to Ted for me. Thanks again,

Bruce Campbell

Areas to be painted:

1. Front entry door & surrounding area.
2. Front sash window.

Painting & Preparation:

1. All areas to be protected with drop sheets.
2. All loose & flaky paint to be scraped or sanded off.

3. Small holes & cracks will be filled and sanded back.
4. All stains will be washed off & sealed.
5. All areas to receive an oil-based undercoat and two coats of white semi-gloss enamel.
6. Only *Deluxe Paints* will be used.
7. All work will be carried out with tradesman-like professionalism.
8. All work is guaranteed and insured.

Materials & Labor	$480
Plus GST	$48
TOTAL	$528

1. What is the purpose of Ms. Chong's fax?
   (A) To introduce herself
   (B) To request an estimate
   (C) To claim some expenses
   (D) To correct a previous error

2. Why does Ms. Chong ask Mr. Campbell to go to Market Street today?
   (A) Because her client wants the work completed quickly
   (B) Because her company will start construction in the morning
   (C) Because Ted Simatran will return tomorrow
   (D) Because she wants to forge a good relationship

3. What company uses the building in question?
   (A) Faux Fronts
   (B) Bruback Realty
   (C) Market Street Construction
   (D) Deluxe Paints

4. What can be inferred about Mr. Campbell?
   (A) He is too busy to complete the job on time.
   (B) He is a respected artisan.
   (C) He works with Lin Chong often.
   (D) He has agreed to paint the building's exterior.

5. What is NOT mentioned as a service Mr. Campbell will provide?
   (A) Painting the entry door
   (B) Scraping and sanding off loose paint
   (C) Sealing and staining all floors
   (D) Filling and sanding holes

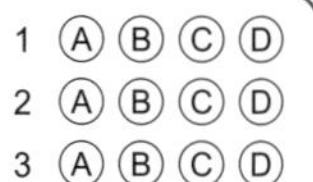

原文中譯

收件者：布魯斯．坎伯爾
傳真：(07) 3734-1234
寄件者：門面裝潢（鍾玲）
主旨：雪梨市市場街 106 號布魯貝克房地產室內粉刷的報價

坎伯爾先生：

我本人不曾見過您，但是我的同事泰德．西馬川非常推薦您。我們在市場街上有位新的轉包客戶，希望您能幫我們進行室內粉刷。泰德叫我直接傳真給您，請您有空的話，今天下午晚一點時到市場街 106 號的布魯貝克房地產大樓。

如果您能回傳給我一份報價單的話，我會非常感激的。不知道貴公司人員這週和下週的工作時程如何安排，但是如果報價合理的話，我希望您能在下週五之前完工。我知道這樣有點趕，如果您不能接下這份工作，我們也完全了解。這位客戶的時程真的非常趕，所以我們光是要完成外部粉刷，時間上就已經有點吃緊了。

靜待您的回音。

鍾玲

****

收件者：鍾玲（門面裝潢）
傳真：(07) 3216-0874
寄件者：布魯斯．坎伯爾
主旨：回覆：市場街 106 號的報價

鍾女士：
報價如下，我想應該不會有任何問題，這都是一般的服務。我們最慢大概下週三或四就可以開始動工。幫我向泰德打聲招呼。再次謝謝您。

布魯斯．坎伯爾

待粉刷的區域：
1. 前面入口大門及周遭區域。
2. 前面上下拉式窗戶。

粉刷與準備：
1. 所有粉刷區域全面用掛布保護。
2. 所有鬆散和片狀的油漆都會刮掉或磨掉。
3. 小洞與裂縫都會填平後再磨平。
4. 所有汙損都會洗淨後再封住。
5. 所有粉刷區域都會上一層油性底漆，兩層白色半亮光漆。
6. 只會使用豪華油漆。
7. 所有工作都會以工匠般的專業技術進行。
8. 所有工作都提供保證和保險。

材料與人工	480 元
商品及勞務稅（外加）	48 元
總額	528 元

題目中譯

1. 鍾女士的傳真有什麼目的？
   - (A) 自我介紹
   - (B) **要求對方報價**
   - (C) 申報某些支出
   - (D) 修正先前的錯誤

解題技巧

答案 (B)

這題問的是傳真的目的，從傳真信主旨的 quotation 就知道是「報價」。此外，從第一段的 you would be able to help us out with the interior painting 可以判斷傳真內容是一件委託工作，符合這些內容的就是正確答案。

2. 鍾女士為什麼請坎伯爾先生今天去市場街？
   - (A) **因為她的客戶希望工作快點完成**
   - (B) 因為她的公司一早就要開始動工
   - (C) 因為泰德・西馬川明天會回來
   - (D) 因為她想要營造良好的關係

答案 (A)

在傳真信中搜尋題目中的 Market Street 和 today。找到 go on ... 106 Market Street later this afternoon，接著看出布魯貝克房地產就是出現在主旨中的工地現場。此外，從第二段 This client ... really tight schedule 了解到時程上很緊湊，也就知道了正確答案。

3. 哪一家公司正在使用討論中的建築物？
   - (A) 門面裝潢
   - (B) **布魯貝克房地產**
   - (C) 市場街建設
   - (D) 豪華油漆

答案 (B)

「使用討論中之建築物的公司」指的就是工地現場的公司，因此工地客戶 Bruback Realty 就是正確答案。鍾女士的信中第一段結尾部分就是對應內容。

4. 可以推論出坎伯爾先生的什麼事？
   - (A) 他太忙所以沒有辦法準時完成工作。
   - (B) **他是個受人尊敬的工匠。**
   - (C) 他經常與鍾玲一起合作。
   - (D) 他同意要粉刷建築物外部。

答案 (B)

從第一段highly recommended ... Ted Simatran 能推論出正確答案，但由於這個不是直接的表達，因此必須先判斷出其他選項是錯的。從坎伯爾先生肯定的回答可知 (A) 不是正確答案，同時也能很快判斷出 (C) 和 (D) 與內容不符。

5. 坎伯爾先生將不提供哪一項服務？
   - (A) 粉刷入口大門
   - (B) 刮掉並磨掉鬆落的油漆
   - (C) **將所有的地板封住並上色**
   - (D) 填補並磨平缺口

答案 (C)

從坎伯爾先生報價單上的 Areas to be painted: 可確認報價部分是入口大門和周遭區域，以及上下拉式窗戶的粉刷。地板最初並未包含在報價範圍內。

註解

within reason 合乎情理的
short notice 臨時通知
taxing (adj.) 繁重的，勞苦的
insured (adj.) 保過險的
GST 商品及勞務稅 (= goods and services tax)

Chapter 4

Advertisement

廣告

NEW TOEIC® TEST

Harper Valley Campgrounds
New Zealand's best family camping experience

Amazing Activities!

- Sailing
- Snorkeling
- Wall and rock climbing
- Survivor courses
- Historical walks & treks
- Kayaking
- Ideal conditions for swimming
- Raft building
- Fishing and bird watching

Quality Facilities!

- Main camp dormitories can sleep up to 180
- Cook's quarters sleeps 4
- The lodge sleeps 34
- The cottage sleeps 4-10
- Tents to sleep up to 100, and several attractive remote sites
- Main camp mess hall has a large modern kitchen and can cater 200 people comfortably

Other facilities include: A gymnasium, an AV room, an art/resource room, a study room, a classroom for environmental studies (contact us about our staff lecturers), and large lavatory and showering blocks with separate facilities for adults.

All this comes at a very decent price as well!

If you would like to know more about this camp, go to
http://www.harpervalleycamp.co.nz
or call
(09) 493-1821

1. Who are Harper Valley Campgrounds' main customers?
   (A) Youth groups
   (B) Schools
   (C) Companies
   (D) Families

2. What is NOT offered by Harper Valley Campgrounds?
   (A) Rock climbing
   (B) Hiking
   (C) Educational lectures
   (D) White water rafting

1 (A) (B) (C) (D)
2 (A) (B) (C) (D)

哈波谷營地

紐西蘭最棒的全家露營經驗

精彩的活動！

- 航海
- 浮潛
- 攀牆、攀岩
- 野外求生課程
- 歷史步道和歷史之旅
- 划皮艇
- 理想的游泳環境
- 造筏
- 釣魚、賞鳥

優質的設備！

- 營區主要宿舍最多可睡 180 人
- 炊室可睡 4 人
- 森林小屋可睡 34 人
- 農舍可睡 4 ～ 10 人
- 帳篷可容納多達 100 人，有數個吸引人的偏遠地點
- 主要營地食堂有個大型現代廚房，能輕鬆供應 200 人用餐

其餘設備包含：一間健身房、一間視聽室、一間美術／資料室、一間自習室、一間環境研究教室（需要講師的資料，請與我們聯絡）、配備有成人專用設備的大間廁所與淋浴間。

這一切都不用花太多錢喔！

如果您想要更了解這個營地，請上我們的網站

http://www.harpervalleycamp.co.nz

或打電話到

(09) 493-1821

題目中譯

1. 哈波谷營地主要客戶是哪些人？
   (A) 年輕族群
   (B) 學校
   (C) 公司
   (D) **家庭**

解題技巧

答案 (D)

只要一看到標題第二行的 best family camping experience 就能馬上作答。

2. 哈波谷營地沒有提供哪一項設施？
   (A) 攀岩
   (B) 健行
   (C) 教育講座
   (D) **激流泛舟**

答案 (D)

查看活動項目可發現雖然有體驗「造筏」，卻沒有「泛舟」。

註解

raft (n.) 筏，救生艇
mess (n.) 食堂
cater (v.) 提供飲食與服務
decent (adj.) 有分寸的；大方的

Phuket Bilingual Job Board

January 2009

- **Reservation & Travel Sales** --Thai professional with English skills and hotel experience for a local resort.
- **Spa Manager** -------------------Young, experienced Thai spa manager for local resort. Must have good command of English and good managerial and people skills.
- **Translator** ----------------------Thai native to translate English/Thai for busy magazine publication.
- **Sports Manager** ---------------Must have managerial experience and sporting background. Some Thai and other languages are an advantage.
- **Thai Newspaper Reporter** ---Experienced Thai news reporter for local magazine. Must have good English skills and writing experience.
- **Shop Manager** -----------------Thai national with good English skills to manage furniture shop.
- **Thai Cooks** ---------------------Experienced Thai nationals to cook Thai and Western cuisine. Some spoken English is advantageous.
- **Kitchen Assistants** ------------Thai kitchen help urgently required in various busy restaurants and resorts.
- **Barmaids, Waitresses** ---------Urgent need for experienced Thai nationals to work in bars, restaurants, and resorts. Fairly good English is necessary.
- **Security Guards** ---------------Honest, responsible, and reliable Thai nationals needed to work night shifts.
- **Head Gardener** ----------------Experienced Thai to look after the landscaped gardens of a local resort.
- **Ship Mechanical Engineer** ---**URGENT!** A qualified Thai mechanic to live and work on-board a ship and maintain engines and equipment. Based in Samui.

To apply for any of these positions or to register for work opportunities please call (+66) 0 78239294 / Fax: 0 78239295
e-mail: admin@phuketjob.biz
or visit us at: 98-8 Moo 5, Chaweng Ring Road

1. English skills are required for all of the following jobs EXCEPT
   (A) a resort job.
   (B) a spa job.
   (C) a waitress job.
   (D) a security guard job.

2. What is the first step in applying for one of these jobs?
   (A) Visit the furniture shop
   (B) Contact a resort
   (C) Send an e-mail
   (D) Go to a school

1 Ⓐ Ⓑ Ⓒ Ⓓ
2 Ⓐ Ⓑ Ⓒ Ⓓ

普吉島雙語工作布告欄

2009 年 1 月

- 預約與旅遊業務------------當地度假村誠徵泰國專業人士，具備英文技能與旅館經驗。
- 溫泉美容經理---------------當地度假村誠徵年輕有經驗的泰國溫泉美容經理。必須精通英文，具備優秀的管理技能與社交手腕。
- 翻譯---------------------------泰國人，為繁忙的雜誌社進行英 / 泰文翻譯。
- 運動經理---------------------必須具備管理經驗與運動背景。懂泰文和其他語言者尤佳。
- 泰國報紙記者---------------當地雜誌社誠徵有經驗的報紙記者。必須精通英文，具備寫作經驗。
- 店經理------------------------家具店誠徵精通英文的泰國人。
- 泰國廚師---------------------有經驗的泰國人，烹煮泰式與西式料理。能說英語者尤佳。
- 廚房助手---------------------各家繁忙的餐廳與度假村急需泰國廚房助手。
- 酒吧女侍、女服務生-------急需有經驗的泰國人，在酒吧、餐廳及度假村工作。必須具備相當的英文能力。
- 保全警衛---------------------誠徵誠實、負責任、可靠的泰國人，需輪晚班。
- 總園丁------------------------誠徵有經驗的泰國人，照料當地度假村的造景花園。
- 船身機械工程師-------------急需！誠徵有資格的泰國技術人員，要能在船上生活、工作，維護引擎與器具。以蘇梅島為基地。

欲應徵以上任何職位或想登記找工作者

請電洽 (+66) 0-78239294 / 傳真到 0-78239295

寫信到 admin@phuketjob.biz

或親自到本公司：查威環道 5 目 98-8 號

題目中譯

1. 以下哪一項工作不需要具備英文能力？
   (A) 度假村的工作
   (B) 溫泉美容工作
   (C) 女服務生工作
   (D) **保全警衛工作**

2. 應徵這些工作的第一步要做什麼？
   (A) 造訪家具店
   (B) 聯絡度假村
   (C) **寄電子郵件**
   (D) 去唸書

解題技巧

答案 (D)

確認清單中是否有 English, languages 等單字。若得將選項中的工作一一對照清單，再確認是否符合需求內容，會浪費太多的時間。

答案 (C)

徵才廣告的應徵方式註明在最下方。沒有「用電話聯絡」的選項，因此另一個「寄電子郵件」的選項就是正確答案。

註解

cuisine (n.) 烹飪
urgently (adv.) 迫切地
landscape (v.) 美化…景觀
qualified (adj.) 有資格的，合格的

Crystal Valley University
Distinguished Lecture Series
Fall, 2009

The Distinguished Lecture Series is one way we help keep our faculty, students, and staff at the forefront of scholarly activity and human endeavor. This fall's lecture series' moderator will be Dr. Ronald Feldstein, Professor Emeritus of Religious Studies. All lectures will be held in the Wright Hall Auditorium. Although pre-registration is not required for faculty, staff, or students, it is recommended. Pre-registration is required of community attendees.

Monday, September 18

Frank Luntz

Frank Luntz may be the most widely recognized pollster in America. More media outlets have turned to Luntz for polling and consulting than to any other political pollster. Luntz has conducted focus group sessions for all four major networks and two cable news channels, the Wall Street Journal, and the BBC.

Thursday, October 19

Konrad Steffen

Climatologist Konrad Steffen, Director of the Cooperative Institute for Research in Environmental Studies at the University of Colorado, Boulder, has studied the impact of climate on the Earth's polar regions for three decades. His research has taken him to Canada, Switzerland, and China, in addition to his famous research on the Greenland ice sheet.

Wednesday, November 15

Peter Haug

Peter Haug, a professor of Manufacturing and Supply Chain Management, will discuss American offshore outsourcing of information technology, customer support services, and business processes to India.

1. What is the purpose of the Distinguished Lecture Series?
   (A) To provide exciting talks by faculty members who are experts in their fields
   (B) To bring leading international public opinion experts together for a debate
   (C) To reward large private donors for their contributions to the university
   (D) To keep people in the university community up-to-date on topics of modern interest

2. Who will discuss international business issues?
   (A) Ronald Feldstein
   (B) Frank Luntz
   (C) Konrad Steffen
   (D) Peter Haug

3. What topic will NOT be discussed by lecturers in this fall's series?
   (A) International outsourcing of services
   (B) Mass media management
   (C) Climate changes
   (D) Public opinion polling

1 Ⓐ Ⓑ Ⓒ Ⓓ
2 Ⓐ Ⓑ Ⓒ Ⓓ
3 Ⓐ Ⓑ Ⓒ Ⓓ

水晶谷大學
傑出講座系列
2009 年秋季

傑出講座系列是我們協助教師、學生及職員持續站在學術活動與人類成就之最前線的一種方式。今年秋季講座系列的主持人是羅納德 · 菲爾史坦博士，為宗教研究的榮譽博士。所有講座都會在萊特大禮堂內舉行。雖然教師、職員或學生不用事先報名，但是我們還是建議大家事先報名。想參加的社區民眾必須事先報名。

9 月 18 日星期一
法蘭克 · 浪茲

法蘭克 · 浪茲可說是美國最知名的民意調查專家。媒體找浪茲尋求民調與諮詢的比例，遠比找其他政治民調專家還高。浪茲曾經為四大電視網以及兩家有線新聞台，華爾街日報與英國廣播公司，舉辦過焦點團體課程。

10 月 19 日星期四
康拉德 · 史戴分

氣候學家康拉德 · 史戴分為科羅拉多大學博得校區環境研究合作研究中心主任，從事氣候變遷如何影響地球極區已經長達 30 年。他曾經在加拿大、瑞士和中國進行研究，他在格陵蘭冰層進行的研究也很出名。

11 月 15 日星期三
彼得 · 霍格

彼得 · 霍格是製造與供應鏈管理學的教授，他將會探討美國將資訊科技、客戶支援服務和企業流程境外委外到印度的議題。

題目中譯

解題技巧

1. 傑出講座系列的目的是什麼？
   (A) 由教職員按照其專長領域發表精彩的演說
   (B) 聚集重要的國際公共意見專家來進行辯論
   (C) 犒賞鉅額捐款給大學的私人捐贈者
   (D) **讓大學裡的社群能跟得上現代最流行的議題**

答案 (D)

這一題問的是講座系列的目的，因此必須和第一段的內容一致。相反地，如果出現了第二段開始之後的個別講座內容，就能判斷該選項不是正確答案。(A) 的 faculty、(B) 的 international、(C) 的 reward 等相關字都沒出現在第一段。

2. 誰將會探討國際商業議題？
   (A) 羅納德 · 菲爾史坦
   (B) 法蘭克 · 浪茲
   (C) 康拉德 · 史戴分
   (D) **彼得 · 霍格**

答案 (D)

浪茲先生是 pollster（民意調查專家）、史戴分先生是 climatologist（氣候學家），因此馬上就能判斷 (B) 和 (C) 不是正確答案。此外，(A) 菲爾史坦教授的專長是宗教學。

3. 今年的秋季講座系列中，講師不會探討哪一項主題？
   (A) 將服務全球委外
   (B) **大眾媒體管理**
   (C) 氣候變化
   (D) 公共意見調查

答案 (B)

在文章中搜尋選項的關鍵字 outsourcing, management, climate, opinion polling 等。management 出現在介紹霍格教授的文章中，但內容與製造與供應鏈管理有關，因此 (B) Mass media management 就是課程中沒有討論到的話題。

註解

distinguished (adj.) 著名的
forefront (n.) 最前線，最前部
endeavor (n.) 努力
moderator (n.) 會議主持人；仲裁者
pollster (n.) 民意調查專家 (= polltaker)
outlet (n.) 電台或電視台的分台
offshore (adj.) 離岸的；海面上的
polling (n.) 投票選舉；民意調查

January 20, 2009

Dear Neighbors,

I am pleased to announce that I am starting my own business as a Sumptuous Chef Kitchen Consultant. The Sumptuous Chef system provides items you can use to fix meals quickly and easily, freeing up more time to spend with friends and family, and allowing for less time to be spent in the kitchen. There are several hundred handy kitchen products we offer, most under $10.00. All products are professional quality tools which make being in the kitchen more enjoyable and rewarding.

I would like to invite you to my home for a demonstration of the Sumptuous Chef kitchen product lineup so that you can see the tools in action. Or, I can bring them to your home and give you an opportunity to observe the quality of Sumptuous Chef kitchen tools while I prepare a delicious recipe for you.

Sumptuous Chef is offering a variety of discounts for the remainder of the spring, so it would be a good idea to request your demonstration soon. Also, as one of my first clients, you will receive additional free gifts from the pantry line.

I look forward to speaking with you about a free demonstration. In the meantime, please take a moment to look at our online catalog at www.sumptuouschef.com. Thank you for your time!

Sincerely,

Margie Oberlin
Kitchen Consultant

1. What is the purpose of this letter?
   (A) To notify employees of a new lineup of kitchen goods
   (B) To announce a new local business
   (C) To generate interest in the new chef
   (D) To explain a series of new cooking terms

2. Where is the reader invited to go?
   (A) To the Sumptuous Chef Restaurant
   (B) To the writer's home
   (C) To the new kitchen store
   (D) To the pantry store

3. Which of the following is NOT mentioned as an advantage of holding a demonstration?
   (A) Discounts on products
   (B) A catalog
   (C) Free gifts
   (D) Free food

1 Ⓐ Ⓑ Ⓒ Ⓓ
2 Ⓐ Ⓑ Ⓒ Ⓓ
3 Ⓐ Ⓑ Ⓒ Ⓓ

2009 年 1 月 20 日

各位鄰居好：

很高興向大家宣布，我即將成立自己的公司：豪華主廚廚房顧問。豪華主廚系統提供您快速、簡便料理的產品，讓您有更多時間與朋友、家人相處，不用花那麼多時間在廚房裡做事。我們提供數百種各式各樣的廚房產品，多數單價都在 10 元以下。這些全都是專業且優質的產品，讓您在廚房裡更加享受、更加有收穫。

希望能邀請您來我家中，讓我為您示範使用豪華主廚廚房產品系列，讓您能親眼見識到如何使用這些器具。或是，我也可以將這些產品帶到您家中，讓您有機會在我為您準備美味的料理時，從旁觀察豪華主廚廚房用具的品質。

在春季結束前豪華主廚將提供各種不同折扣，所以請您把握機會盡早預約示範會。此外，身為我的首批客戶，您將會獲得額外的免費餐具贈品。

我很期待能與您詳談免費示範一事。同時，請您抽空看看我們的線上目錄 www.sumptuouschef.com。謝謝您花時間看這封信！

廚房顧問
瑪姬．歐伯林
敬上

題目中譯

1. 這封信的目的是什麼？

(A) 通知員工有新的廚房產品系列
(B) **宣布當地有新的公司**
(C) 引起大家對新主廚的興趣
(D) 解說一連串新的烹飪用語

解題技巧

答案 (B)

文章的主旨或目的必須寫在一開頭才符合段落閱讀理論。這篇文章的第一段第一行是 ...pleased to announce that I am starting my own business，從選項中直接找出 business 或同義字才是最快的方法。

2. 信中邀請讀者去哪裡？

(A) 去豪華主廚餐廳
(B) **去作者的家中**
(C) 去新的廚具店
(D) 去餐具用品店

答案 (B)

確認第一段主題是介紹新產品後，可以推測第二段以後的內容應該會與「招待」之類的訊息有關。從第二段的第一句 I would like to invite you to my home... 可以直接得知答案。這是一題能在短時間內作答的題目。

3. 以下哪一項不是舉辦示範會的好處？

(A) 產品有折扣
(B) **目錄**
(C) 免費贈品
(D) 免費食物

答案 (B)

示範會的內容出現在第二段和第三段，可在其中找到提到好處的地方。至於 (B) 的產品目錄，第四段提到可以在線上觀看，所以這一項並不是舉辦示範會的好處。

註解

rewarding (adj.) 有價值的，有益的
remainder (n.) 剩餘物，殘餘
pantry (n.) 餐具室，食品儲藏室
generate (v.) 引起

Upcoming Small Business Training Seminars in March

Allan County is proud to offer affordable seminars and workshops that provide a quick and easy way for small business owners to gain new skills and knowledge to improve their businesses. If you are contemplating starting your own business from scratch, you should attend our most popular workshop, "Starting Your Own Business," where in two three-hour segments, you will gain a clear understanding of the financial, managerial, and technical requirements of starting and operating a business. You will explore and evaluate the feasibility of your ideas, learn common pitfalls and how to avoid them, and discover ways to increase your chance of success.

Starting Your Own Business, Part 1
Thursday, March 5, 2009 (6 P.M.-9 P.M.)
  Self-Assessment & Feasibility Study
  Financial Projections & Pricing
  Bank Loans
  Licenses & Permits
($15/person, spouse or business partner free)

Business Record Keeping
Tuesday, March 10, 2009 (9 A.M.-12 P.M.)
  Legal Structure
  IRS Procedure
($15/person, spouse or business partner free)

Employment and Sales Tax Issues
Tuesday, March 10, 2009 (1 P.M.-3 P.M.)
  Tax Forms and Filing Requirements
  Exemption & Resale Certificates
($10/person, spouse or business partner free)

QuickBooks
Thursday, March 12, 2009 (8:30 A.M.-12:00 P.M.)
Friday, March 13, 2009 (8:30 A.M.-12:00 P.M.)
  Invoices and Records
  Bank Reconciliation
  Accounts Payable & Receivable
  Depositing & Checks
  Reporting Payroll, Sales Tax, and Transactions
($75/person, spouse or business partner free)

Starting Your Own Business, Part 2

Thursday, March 26, 2009 (6 P.M.-9 P.M.)

Insurance
Marketing
Legal Structure
Location / Commercial Real Estate

($15/person, spouse or business partner free)

($25 for 1 & 2, spouse or business partner free)

* Pre-registration is recommended. Unless otherwise noted, all courses are held at 15001 E. 29th St., Ste. 215 in LaGrange (Beaver Creek Shopping Center). QuickBooks will be held on the UIFW Campus, in Computer Lab CC5, in LaGrange.

1. Which seminar usually has the most participants?
   (A) Starting Your Own Business
   (B) Business Record Keeping
   (C) Employment and Sales Tax Issues
   (D) QuickBooks

2. When will a seminar on taxes be held?
   (A) Thursday, March 5, 2009 (6 P.M.-9 P.M.)
   (B) Tuesday, March 10, 2009 (9 A.M.-12 P.M.)
   (C) Tuesday, March 10, 2009 (1 P.M.-3 P.M.)
   (D) Thursday, March 26, 2009 (6 P.M.-9 P.M.)

3. The courses recommended for people who want to start their first business cover all of the following topics EXCEPT
   (A) bank loans.
   (B) record keeping.
   (C) insurance.
   (D) marketing.

4. Which lecture will be held at a university campus?
   (A) Starting Your Own Business
   (B) Business Record Keeping
   (C) Employment and Sales Tax Issues
   (D) QuickBooks

1 Ⓐ Ⓑ Ⓒ Ⓓ
2 Ⓐ Ⓑ Ⓒ Ⓓ
3 Ⓐ Ⓑ Ⓒ Ⓓ
4 Ⓐ Ⓑ Ⓒ Ⓓ

3 月即將來臨的小型企業訓練講習會

艾倫郡隆重推出一系列費用合理的講習會與工作坊，讓小型企業主能夠快速、輕鬆地學到新技能與新知識，讓各位的事業成長。如果您正在考慮從零開始自行創業，就該來參加我們最熱門的工作坊「自行創業」，讓您在兩次三小時的課程中，就能清楚了解創業與營運所需的金融、管理和技術條件。您將有機會探討與評估您的構想是否具有可行性，學會如何避開哪些常見的陷阱，進而找到方法增加您成功的機會。

自行創業（上）　2009 年 3 月 5 日星期四（晚上 6 點～ 9 點）
自我評估與可行性探討 / 財務預測與定價 / 銀行貸款 / 牌照與許可證
（每人 15 元，伴侶或生意夥伴免費）

商業紀錄管理　2009 年 3 月 10 日星期二（上午 9 點～中午 12 點）
法律架構 / 國稅局作業程序
（每人 15 元，伴侶或生意夥伴免費）

雇用與營業稅議題　2009 年 3 月 10 日星期二（下午 1 點～ 3 點）
稅務單據與申報條件 / 免稅與轉售證明
（每人 10 元，伴侶或生意夥伴免費）

商務財務管理教程　2009 年 3 月 12 日星期四（上午 8 點半～中午 12 點）
2009 年 3 月 13 日星期五（上午 8 點半～中午 12 點）
發票與紀錄 / 銀行存款調節表 / 應付帳款與應收帳款 / 存款與支票 / 提出薪資名單、營業稅與交易行為
（每人 75 元，伴侶或生意夥伴免費）

自行創業（下）　2009 年 3 月 26 日星期四（晚上 6 點～ 9 點）
保險 / 行銷 / 法律架構 / 地點 / 商用不動產
（每人 15 元，伴侶或生意夥伴免費）

（同時報名上、下者為 25 元，伴侶或生意夥伴免費）

* 建議事先報名。除非另有說明，否則所有課程都會在拉隆吉（海狸溪購物中心）15001 東 29 街 215 號房舉行。商務財務管理教程將會在拉隆吉 UIFW 校區電腦教室 CC5 上課。

題目中譯

解題技巧

1. 哪一場講習會通常最多人參加？
   (A) **自行創業**
   (B) 商業紀錄管理
   (C) 雇用與營業稅議題
   (D) 商務財務管理教程

答案 (A)

題目中出現最高級時，就要在文章中找出最高級對應的內容。只要發現到文章中第一段第四行的 most，就能找出正確答案。在課程項目及日期中並未說明哪一個是最受歡迎的。

2. 與稅務相關的講習會將在何時舉行？
   (A) 2009 年 3 月 5 日星期四（晚上 6 點到 9 點）
   (B) 2009 年 3 月 10 日星期二（上午 9 點到中午 12 點）
   (C) **2009 年 3 月 10 日星期二（下午 1 點到 3 點）**
   (D) 2009 年 3 月 26 日星期四（晚上 6 點到 9 點）

答案 (C)

搜尋第一段下方條列式項目中的 Employment and Sales Tax Issues，這題問的是課程時間表，因此不需要讀完文章就能作答，可節省時間。

3. 推薦給第一次自行創業者參加的課程，不包含以下哪一項主題？
   (A) 銀行貸款
   (B) **紀錄管理**
   (C) 保險
   (D) 行銷

答案 (B)

從題目的內容可以知道不在 Starting Your Own Business Part 1 和 Part 2 中的部分就是對應 EXCEPT 的內容。選項 (B) 的 record keeping 出現在文章中以粗體字表示的講習會項目中，由此可以判斷 (B) 不屬於 Part 1 和 Part 2 的內容。

4. 哪一場講習會將在大學裡舉行？
   (A) 自行創業
   (B) 商業紀錄管理
   (C) 雇用與營業稅議題
   (D) **商務財務管理教程**

答案 (D)

確定課程時間表中都沒提到地點後，那就必須盡快了解最後星號處的注意事項。告知地點時經常使用 hold（舉辦）這個動詞。

註解

affordable (adj.) 負擔得起的
contemplate (v.) 仔細考慮
from scratch 從無到有，從零開始
pitfall (n.) 陷阱，圈套
bank reconciliation 銀行存款調節表，銀行往來調節表
accounts payable 應付帳款
accounts receivable 應收帳款
payroll (n.) 薪水名單；雇用人數

Byron Bay Alternative Advertising

Standard media message delivery systems are more expensive and less effective than ever. So we help companies find strategies that are cheaper, more creative, and more effective for our clients. Consumers are constantly inundated with traditional methods of advertising, such as commercials, sales letters, Internet advertisements, billboards, etc. We seek to crack through the advertising noise by utilizing different media outlets to give the consumers fresh and different perspectives on your company or product. Alternative advertising may include the placement of ads on

* shopping bags
* coffee sleeves
* streetcars and buses
* pizza boxes
* restaurant menus
* murals and stickers

and a host of other inventive concepts that bypass the usual. Alternative outdoor advertising can include the use of "wild postings," including poster advertising on construction walls, telephone poles, vehicles, or any other blank outdoor space that has yet to be turned into a valuable advertising medium.

Placing ads in nightlife guides and dance culture magazines is one of the most popular forms of alternative advertising. It attracts a smaller, more targeted market (e.g. young people aged 18-30 who enjoy dance music). These guides are popular within major metro markets such as Sydney, Melbourne, Newcastle, Wollongong, and Byron Bay where the market is more densely populated by target readers. These guides are not sold in stores, but set up in take-away stands at local cafes, bars, hair dressers, restaurants, university campuses, and other locations that attract potential consumers. The magazines are free to the consumers, as around 70 percent of the magazines are full of advertisements about what is going on in the youth/dance music scene.

Contact us today for a free consultation and demonstration of our services.
Phone: (02) 6680-4192

1. What is the purpose of this flyer?
   (A) To show the effectiveness of advertising
   (B) To promote an advertising service
   (C) To announce a new business scheme
   (D) To advertise for a nightclub

2. According to this flyer, what is the problem with traditional advertising channels?
   (A) They are misleading.
   (B) They are too influential.
   (C) They are too common.
   (D) They don't meet the needs of the Internet economy.

3. For what kind of business is alternative advertising popular?
   (A) Internet companies
   (B) Pizza companies
   (C) Construction companies
   (D) Nightclubs

4. All of the following are mentioned as potential advertising media EXCEPT
   (A) buses.
   (B) radio advertisements.
   (C) dance culture magazines.
   (D) telephone poles.

1 Ⓐ Ⓑ Ⓒ Ⓓ
2 Ⓐ Ⓑ Ⓒ Ⓓ
3 Ⓐ Ⓑ Ⓒ Ⓓ
4 Ⓐ Ⓑ Ⓒ Ⓓ

拜倫灣另類廣告

現在的標準媒體訊息傳達系統遠比過去的都還要昂貴且缺乏效率，因此我們協助企業客戶找尋更便宜、更具創意及更有效的策略。消費者總是被傳統廣告方式給淹沒，例如電視廣告、推銷信、網路廣告、廣告看板等。我們想要打破這些廣告干擾，利用不同的媒體通路，讓消費者對貴公司或產品產生新鮮或不同的看法。另類廣告包含將廣告張貼於：

＊購物袋　　＊披薩盒
＊咖啡包裝袋　　＊餐廳菜單
＊有軌電車與公車　　＊壁畫和貼紙

還有許多超乎尋常的創意構想。另類戶外廣告還包含使用「海報游擊戰」，在工地牆壁上、電線杆上、車輛上，或是在任何可以發展成有價值廣告媒介的空白戶外空間內張貼海報。

在夜生活指南與舞蹈文化雜誌裡登廣告，是目前最流行的另類廣告手法之一。這能吸引一個較小但客群較集中的市場（例如 18 ~ 30 歲喜歡舞曲的年輕族群）。這些指南在雪梨、墨爾本、新堡、臥龍崗、拜倫灣等大都會市場中受到歡迎，因為這些市場有著密集的目標讀者人口。這些指南沒有在店裡販賣，而是放在當地咖啡廳、酒吧、理髮廳、餐廳、大學校園的抽取架上，或是其他能夠吸引潛在消費者的地點。雜誌供消費者免費索取，因為雜誌裡有 70% 的內容都是關於年輕族群、舞曲等最新消息的廣告。

馬上聯絡我們，就能享有免費諮詢與服務示範。
電話：(02) 6680-4192

題目中譯

1. 這張文宣的目的是什麼？
   (A) 展現廣告的效果
   (B) **推銷廣告服務**
   (C) 宣布新的商業計畫
   (D) 為一間夜店打廣告

2. 根據這張文宣，傳統廣告通路有什麼問題？
   (A) 會誤導民眾。
   (B) 太具有影響力。
   (C) **太過普通**。
   (D) 無法符合網路經濟的需求。

3. 另類廣告很受哪種行業歡迎？
   (A) 網路公司
   (B) 披薩公司
   (C) 建設公司
   (D) **夜店**

4. 以下哪一項不是文中所提具有潛力的廣告媒介？
   (A) 公車
   (B) **電台廣告**
   (C) 舞蹈文化雜誌
   (D) 電線杆

解題技巧

答案 (B)

如果從 (B) 的「推銷廣告服務」知道「廣告」本身就是被推銷的產品，就能馬上判斷出正確答案。(A) 的「展現廣告的效果」只是一種推銷廣告產品的手段，不可能成為這張文宣的目的。

答案 (C)

搜尋文章中可能是題目所指的 problem，在第一段的第四行會看到 inundated。這裡的意思是，廣告量太大會變成一個問題。選項中用了和 inundated 意思相近的 common，也就表示 (C) 是正確答案。

答案 (D)

搜尋關鍵字是題目中的 alternative advertising popular。只要看到第三段第一行的 Placing ads in nightlife guides and dance culture magazines is one of the most popular forms of alternative advertising. 之後，就能馬上知道正確答案。

答案 (B)

除了 (A) 的公車外，其他選項都沒列在清單中，因此這些選項必須在文章中確認。搜尋選項中的 radio, dance, telephone poles 等，沒出現的 (B) 就是正確答案。

註解

alternative (adj.) 可供選擇的
be inundated with... 被…淹沒
mural (n.) 壁畫，壁飾
inventive (adj.) 獨創的，發明的
bypass (v.) 繞過，迴避
densely (adv.) 密集地
take-away stand 抽取架

Business Risk Management Lecture Series

The importance of risk management can hardly be overstated. Awareness of risk has increased, as we currently live in a less stable economic and political environment. We hope these training lectures will provide managers with a solid understanding of business risk and how to manage it.

This risk management lecture focuses primarily on operational, project, and reputation risk management, looking at risk from different perspectives and analyzing the possibilities for its management in each situation.

Lecturer: ***Mr. Vincenzo C. Sirius***

Mr. Sirius is currently the Training Business Group manager at CCE Consulting, where he focuses on quality, productivity, engineering management, IE, and engineering electives, etc. He graduated with a bachelor of science in industrial engineering at Auburn University and earned his MBA at the University of Texas, Austin. He is a productivity specialist by profession. As project manager, he has organized international seminars and local study meetings. As well, he has done firm-level consulting, project management, and quality technology-oriented projects for both private and public organizations. He has over 12 years of experience in research, manufacturing, materials management, trading, industry-based needs assessment, trainings/seminars, firm-level consulting, and project management in his chosen fields, and has handled positions from professional technical staffer to consultant-retainer. His private work experience includes metal fabrication, casting, car manufacturing, food processing, construction management, logistics, and business consulting.

Venue and Date: Tutor Function Room, Inter Continental Plaza Hotel, Houston, Texas, March 31, 2009

We invite members of the greater Houston business community to the 5th lecture in our series of Business Risk Management Lectures. Please contact LaFontaine Montgomery to reserve your seat, (281) 986-1925, ext. 5518.

1. What is the purpose of this lecture series?
   (A) To help business managers learn to deal with risk
   (B) To generate interest in a local consulting service
   (C) To promote a university program
   (D) To explain Mr. Sirius' expertise

2. What kind of risk will Mr. Sirius NOT discuss?
   (A) Operational risk
   (B) Reputation risk
   (C) Project risk
   (D) Trading risk

3. Who is this lecture being arranged for?
   (A) Texas government economists and politicians
   (B) Consultants interested in improving productivity
   (C) Local business professionals
   (D) Professional technical staff supervisors

4. Mr. Sirius has worked as all of the following EXCEPT
   (A) a productivity specialist.
   (B) a project manager.
   (C) a business process reviewer.
   (D) a private sector consultant.

1 Ⓐ Ⓑ Ⓒ Ⓓ
2 Ⓐ Ⓑ Ⓒ Ⓓ
3 Ⓐ Ⓑ Ⓒ Ⓓ
4 Ⓐ Ⓑ Ⓒ Ⓓ

商業風險管理講座系列

風險管理的重要性再怎麼強調也不為過。我們目前處在一個經濟、政治都較為不穩定的環境中，所以我們的風險意識也就提高了。我們希望這些訓練講座能幫助主管徹底了解商業風險及管理之道。

風險管理講座主要聚焦在營運、專案及信譽風險管理，從不同角度檢視風險，分析在各種情況下管理的可能性。

講者：文森洛 · 賽勒斯先生

賽勒斯先生目前是 CCE 顧問公司的企業體訓練經理，他專注於品質、生產力、工程管理、工業工程、工程選修等。他是奧本大學工業工程學學士，也是德州大學奧斯汀分校企業管理碩士。他的職業是生產力專員。身為專案經理，他籌備過國際研討會與地區性讀書會。他也曾經為民間與公家機構進行公司級諮商、專案管理以及品質技術導向專案。他在研究、製造、材料管理、交易、各產業的需求評量、訓練 / 研討會、公司級諮商、專案管理等領域，有超過 12 年的經驗，而他所擔任過的職務包括專業技術人員到約聘顧問。他的私人工作經驗包含金屬製造、鑄造、汽車製造、食品加工、營建管理、物流與企業顧問。

地點與時間：德州休士頓洲際大飯店教育廳，2009 年 3 月 31 日

我們邀請大休士頓商業社群的成員前來參加我們的第五屆商業風險管理講座。預約座位請洽拉鳳寧 · 蒙哥馬利：(281) 986-1925 分機 5518。

題目中譯

1. 這個講座系列的目的是什麼？
   (A) **幫助企業主管學習處理風險**
   (B) 引起大家對當地顧問服務的興趣
   (C) 推廣大學課程
   (D) 說明賽勒斯先生的專長

2. 賽勒斯先生將不會探討哪一項風險？
   (A) 營運風險
   (B) 信譽風險
   (C) 專案風險
   (D) **交易風險**

3. 這場講座是為誰舉辦的？
   (A) 德州政府的經濟學者與政治人物
   (B) 對改善生產力有興趣的顧問
   (C) **當地企業專業人士**
   (D) 專業技術人員主管

4. 賽勒斯先生擔任過的職位不包含以下哪一項？
   (A) 生產力專員
   (B) 專案經理
   (C) **企業流程審查員**
   (D) 民間企業顧問

解題技巧

答案 (A)

這種文章理論上在一開始時就會寫明宣告的目的，就出現在第一段的第三行 ...these training lectures will provide managers...。由此可知這個講座系列的目的是「讓主管徹底了解商業風險管理之道」。

答案 (D)

文章第一段敘述講座的目的，第二段則說明講座的內容。...lecture focuses primarily on operational, project, and reputation risk management 就是對應的內容。

答案 (C)

將第一段第三行出現的 managers 和選項做對照。(A) 的 economists、(B) 的 consultants、(D) 的 staff supervisors 都和 managers 不符。

答案 (C)

賽勒斯先生的經歷在第三段有相關敘述。從 productivity specialist, firm-level consulting, project management 等內容，可知賽勒斯先生未曾有過的工作經歷就是 (C)。

註解

overstate (v.) 誇大，過分強調
awareness (n.) 認識，知道
IE (industrial engineering) 工業工程學
profession (n.) 職業，專業
oriented (adj.) 以…為導向的
retainer (n.) 雇員
fabrication (n.) 製作
casting (n.) 鑄造
logistics (n.) 物流，運籌
venue (n.) 會議地點，會場

AMC Racing 2010 Sponsorship Proposal

Racer: Freddy Wu

Freddy,

First, we would like to congratulate you and your team on an excellent season and championship win. Several of our racer customers have inquired about sponsorship from our company for 2010, so we have decided to put together sponsorship packages tailored to each racer. As you know, our builder/racer relationship has grown strong over the last few racing seasons. You have shown us that your drive and desire is second to none. We are proud to be part of your great team.

Just as your performance has helped move our company to a higher level, we feel that we have helped provide you with excellent service and quality craftsmanship that has helped keep you competitive in the highly aggressive sport of racing. Because of this relationship and our loyalty to you as a customer, we would like to offer you a generous personalized sponsorship program.

We would like to continue to provide you with VIP service between races during the entire 2010 season to ensure you make it to every race on time and in top shape. Specifically, we offer:

1. Provide you with a home for your car and trailer all season long.
2. Provide a free space and help with your cars' general upkeep between races. Your crew can use our facilities to pull motors, transmissions, etc.
3. Provide you with all parts and materials at our cost, plus shipping with no markup.
4. Provide fabrication and shop work at a rate of $45.00 per man hour, saving you $20.00 per hour.

In return we would like you to:

1. Provide us with a forward facing decal on the front bumper reading AMCRACING.COM, size 3"x40", and two side facing decals reading AMCRACING.COM, size 2"x18".
2. Provide us general rights to use your name and car images in our 2010 advertisements.

Please take your time to read this over and let us know what you think. We are really hoping to work with you again next year.

Morgan Keogh
AMC Racing

1. What is the purpose of this letter?
   (A) To generate interest in a new product line
   (B) To report last year's racing results
   (C) To respond to Mr. Wu's concerns
   (D) To propose a new sponsorship agreement

2. What can be inferred about Mr. Wu?
   (A) He will start racing in a more competitive league in 2010.
   (B) He has worked with AMC Racing before.
   (C) He wants to start creating his own promotional calendars for 2010.
   (D) He had disappointing racing results in 2009.

3. What kind of business is AMC Racing?
   (A) A car parts dealer
   (B) An advertising company
   (C) A race car builder
   (D) A race track operator

4. What is NOT part of AMC's offer to Freddy Wu?
   (A) Parking services
   (B) Use of their facilities
   (C) Discounted fees
   (D) Free auto parts

1 Ⓐ Ⓑ Ⓒ Ⓓ
2 Ⓐ Ⓑ Ⓒ Ⓓ
3 Ⓐ Ⓑ Ⓒ Ⓓ
4 Ⓐ Ⓑ Ⓒ Ⓓ

AMC 賽車 2010 年贊助提案

賽車手：吳佛瑞迪

佛瑞迪：

首先，我們要恭喜您與您的團隊在賽季的表現精彩極了，還拿了冠軍。我們有幾位賽車客戶，都已經向本公司詢問過 2010 年的贊助計畫，因此我們決定為每位賽車手量身規畫一套贊助計畫。如您所知，在過去幾個賽車季中，我方設計者與賽車手的關係日益茁壯。您已經向我們證明了您的賽車技能與企圖心無人可敵。我們很榮幸能成為您團隊的一分子。

您的表現幫助本公司更上一層樓，而本公司也認為我們提供給您的優良服務與優質工藝，幫助您在這競爭激烈的賽車運動上保持競爭力。由於這層關係，也由於本公司對您這位客戶的忠誠度，我們想要提供您優渥的個人贊助計畫。

我們想要繼續提供您 2010 年整個賽季期間的貴賓服務，確保您每次都能準時參賽並且都保持在最佳狀況。本公司特別提供：

1. 整個賽季期間賽車與拖車的停車場。
2. 免費空間，並在比賽期間協助賽車的一般性保養。您的隊員可以使用我們的設備來牽動馬達、變速器等。
3. 所有零件和材料全照成本價加上運費，不另外加價。
4. 製造和工廠工作以每人每小時 45 元計價，每小時幫您省下 20 元。

同時，本公司希望您提供：

1. 前保險桿正面空間，貼上寫著 AMCRACING.COM 的商標貼紙，尺寸是 3” x 40”；兩邊側面空間，貼上寫著 AMCRACING.COM 的商標貼紙，尺寸是 2” x 18”。
2. 授予我們普遍性的權利，讓我們能在 2010 年的廣告中使用您的名字與賽車圖片。

請慢慢閱讀此提案，再告訴我們您的想法。我們非常希望明年還能再與您合作。

AMC 賽車
摩根 · 吉奧

題目中譯

1. 這封信的目的是什麼？
   (A) 引起大家對新產品線的興趣
   (B) 報告去年的賽事結果
   (C) 回應吳先生的擔憂
   (D) **提出新的贊助合約**

2. 可以推斷出吳先生的什麼事？
   (A) 他將在 2010 年開始加入更具競爭力的車隊。
   (B) **他以前曾與 AMC 賽車合作過**。
   (C) 他想要開始製作自己的 2010 年宣傳月曆。
   (D) 他在 2009 年的賽事結果非常令人失望。

3. AMC 賽車屬於什麼樣的行業？
   (A) 汽車零件商
   (B) 廣告公司
   (C) **賽車設計商**
   (D) 賽車跑道操作者

4. 哪一項不是 AMC 賽車提供給吳佛瑞迪的服務？
   (A) 停車服務
   (B) 使用他們的設備
   (C) 費用打折
   (D) **免費汽車零件**

解題技巧

答案 (D)

這題問的是寫這封信的目的。可以從文章的標題推測出正確答案，也可以在第一段的 so we have decided to put together sponsorship packages tailored to each racer 中確定，so 有推論出結論的意思。

答案 (B)

從題目中不容易找出關鍵字，但由於這封信是寫給吳先生的，因此關於吳先生的資訊可以藉由搜尋文章中的 you 或 your 找到。只要了解第一段最後一句的 We are proud to be part of your great team.，就可以知道吳先生和 AMC 公司的關係。

答案 (C)

將 business 當作搜尋關鍵字，找出文章中與業務內容相關的字眼。在第一段找到 our builder/racer relationship 之後，就能確定正確答案。

答案 (D)

用題目中的 offer 來搜尋，可在第三段找到 we offer:，接下來的 1. ～ 4. 都是 AMC 提供的項目，沒出現在這個部分的就是正確答案。3. 的 at our cost, plus shipping with no markup 的意思是「以我們的成本價加上運費，不另外加價」。

註解

put together 整理（思路、意見等）
tailor (v.) 使適合
craftsmanship (n.) 技能，技藝
competitive (adj.) 競爭的
aggressive (adj.) 侵略的；積極進取的
personalized (adj.) 個別的
upkeep (n.) 保養，維持
markup (n.) 漲價；毛利

From: Carolina Henne
To: Bill Heard Used Autos
Subject: Volume Classifieds

In the past year, Latino Trader has become one of the best publicity mediums in the Latino market, which makes us very proud. This year, we plan to become the absolute best. We have prepared this proposal believing that we can likewise help your company become a leader in sales within the fastest growing market of the USA. This is a big opportunity to attract thousands of Latin consumers to your store.

Proposal	Regular Price	Your Price	Trial Price
2 full page ads in Latino Trader Auto Magazine	$900/week	$700/week	$600/week
Auto Classifieds in Latino Trader	$19/week	$15/week	$10/week
1-800 Tracking number	$100/week	$75/week	Free 30 day trial

The trial price will only be charged at the special rate for fewer than 30 days or four publications and needs to be paid in advance.

This proposal is just a sample of the variety of alternatives we offer, if you have anything else in mind, we can prepare a proposal based on the needs of your company. If you wish to discuss any of your advertising needs, please feel free to contact me.

Carolina Henne
Sales Representative

From: Bill Heard Used Autos
To: Carolina Henne
Subject: Re: Volume Classifieds

Carolina,

I've seen *Detodo Auto Magazine* and have been impressed with it, and we'd like to take advantage of the trial offer. I do have some questions though. I am wondering if the prices you quoted are for color photos, or just for b/w. I've seen both in your magazine. Also, what is the word limit for a classified ad? I've got about 10 to 12 cars that we are currently looking to move. If we were to place classified ads for them, would you be able to print them in a block, maybe outlining the block in a bold faced box? I think that would draw attention to them.

I need to know your payment information as well. Get back to me with that and I'll send the ads by e-mail, and send the check by post. Thanks a bunch!

Bill Heard

1. Where does Carolina Henne work?
   (A) At an automobile dealer
   (B) At a magazine
   (C) At an automotive garage
   (D) At a school

2. What must a business do to receive the trial price?
   (A) Meet with Ms. Henne
   (B) Respond within 30 days
   (C) Create an advertisement in Spanish
   (D) Pay up front

3. Why does Ms. Henne mention the growth of the Latino population in the USA?
   (A) To explain why her company is able to offer discounted advertising services
   (B) To promote the effectiveness of her company's billboard placement service
   (C) To emphasize that her company's classifieds reach new potential customers
   (D) To advise Mr. Heard on the content of his future advertisements

4. What is NOT mentioned as a concern of Mr. Heard?
   (A) The photos
   (B) The word limit
   (C) The size of the classifieds
   (D) The price

5. How would Mr. Heard like to pay for his classified advertisement?
   (A) By credit card
   (B) Sending a check by mail
   (C) By cash
   (D) Drop a check off at Ms. Henne's office

1 Ⓐ Ⓑ Ⓒ Ⓓ
2 Ⓐ Ⓑ Ⓒ Ⓓ
3 Ⓐ Ⓑ Ⓒ Ⓓ
4 Ⓐ Ⓑ Ⓒ Ⓓ
5 Ⓐ Ⓑ Ⓒ Ⓓ

原文中譯

寄件者：卡洛琳娜 ‧ 海恩
收件者：比爾賀德二手車
主旨：大量分類廣告

「拉丁商人」在過去一年裡變成了拉丁市場中最好的宣傳工具，這讓我們感到非常驕傲。今年我們打算成為最頂尖的宣傳工具。我們相信我們所準備的提案，也能幫助貴公司的銷售量在美國快速成長的市場中拔得頭籌。這是個非常好的機會，可以吸引數千名拉丁裔消費者光顧貴公司。

提案	普通價格	您的價格	試用價格
拉丁商人汽車雜誌兩面廣告	900 元／週	700 元／週	600 元／週
拉丁商人汽車分類廣告	19 元／週	15 元／週	10 元／週
I-800 追蹤號碼	100 元／週	75 元／週	30 天免費試用

試用價格只適用於 30 天內或四期刊物上，必須事先付款。

這份提案只是列舉某些我們提供的服務，如果您有任何其他的想法，我們也可根據貴公司需求擬訂其他提案。如果您有任何廣告需求想與本公司討論，請隨時與我聯絡。

業務代表
卡洛琳娜 ‧ 海恩

寄件者：比爾賀德二手車
收件者：卡洛琳娜 ‧ 海恩
主旨：回覆：大量分類廣告

卡洛琳娜：

我已經看過《德特朵汽車雜誌》，而且對它的印象很好，所以我們想要利用試用優惠看看。不過，我還有些疑問。我想知道您列舉的價格是彩色照片的價格，還是只是黑白照片的價格？我在您的雜誌中同時看過這兩種。除此之外，分類廣告的字數限制是多少？我目前有 10 到 12 輛車想推銷出去。如果我們將這些車放在分類廣告，您是否能將它們印成一整個區塊，甚至用粗體方塊將整個區塊標示出來？我想這樣可以讓大家注意到這些車子。

我也需要知道您的付款方式。請回覆我這些問題，我會將廣告以電子郵件的方式寄出，再到郵局將支票寄出。非常感謝！

比爾 ‧ 賀德

題目中譯

解題技巧

1. 卡洛琳娜 · 海恩在哪裡工作?
   (A) 汽車買賣商
   (B) **雜誌社**
   (C) 修車工廠
   (D) 學校

答案 (B)

從第一段開頭的 Latino Trader has become ... which makes us very proud. 中看到海恩女士以「我們 (us)」自稱，表示她是以公司代表的身分寫出這封郵件的。

2. 公司必須要做什麼才能享有試用價格?
   (A) 與海恩女士碰面
   (B) 在 30 天內回應
   (C) 用西班牙文寫廣告
   (D) **事先付款**

答案 (D)

在文章中搜尋題目裡出現的 trial price，可以在第二段鎖定住對應內容。而 The trial price will only be charged ... and needs to be paid in advance. 中的 needs to be paid 就是對應題目中 must ... do 的部分。

3. 海恩女士為什麼會提到拉丁族群在美國的成長?
   (A) 解釋她的公司為什麼能夠提供廣告費用折扣
   (B) 宣傳她的公司配置廣告看板服務的效率
   (C) **強調她公司的分類廣告能接觸潛在消費群**
   (D) 建議賀德先生未來廣告的內容

答案 (C)

第一封郵件的主要目的是向客戶推銷「多刊登廣告」。根據文章中提到美國拉丁裔人口的增加，使得市場擴大，推測出海恩女士想以此鼓勵客戶多刊登廣告。

4. 以下哪一項不是賀德先生的疑問?
   (A) 照片
   (B) 字數限制
   (C) **分類廣告的大小**
   (D) 價格

答案 (C)

賀德先生所擔心的事情出現在第二封郵件裡。重點在於看出 questions 就是 concern 的相關字。賀德先生的信完全沒提到廣告大小的事情。

5. 賀德先生希望怎麼付分類廣告的費用?
   (A) 刷信用卡
   (B) **郵寄支票**
   (C) 付現金
   (D) 把支票送去海恩女士的辦公室

答案 (B)

第二封郵件的最後一段就寫著付款方式。從 send the check by post 就能直接找到答案。

註解

be impressed with... 對…有印象
quote (v.) 舉出例子，引證
move (v.) 推銷（貨物）

March 1, 2009
Dr. Barry Whirlege
Suite 505, Pearl Street Mall
Brockton, MA 02301

Dear Dr. Whirlege,

We are pleased to submit a proposal for janitorial services in your facility located at the Pearl Street Mall in Brockton. Our services will include:

1. nightly vacuuming of carpets,
2. cleaning/disinfecting of bathrooms, and
3. emptying trash barrels and dusting where needed.

In addition, if you contract with us within the month of March, we will provide free carpet shampooing treatments as needed at no additional cost for the duration of your contract. All cleaning services are to be done five times per week (Monday through Friday), for a rate of $175 per week. We bill every two weeks. All janitorial cleaning supplies will be provided by Ace Cleaning Service.

All of our personnel are carefully screened and selected. Prior to and during field assignments, all personnel are thoroughly and continually versed in modern building maintenance, safety, and security, as well as in the proper care of equipment and supplies. Our employees are also aware of the rules and regulations governing their conduct in the field, including the use of common sense. Additional personnel will be trained in the procedures of your building in the event of absenteeism.

If you have any questions, please feel free to contact us at Ace Cleaning Service.

Sincerely,

Maria Croker
Office Manager, Ace Cleaning Service

Blue Ribbon Cleaners

Dear Dr. Whirlege,

Our cleaning crew saw that you have moved into Suite 505 at the Pearl Street Mall, and I would like to take this opportunity to say welcome! We provide cleaning services for 18 of the mall's clients, and would like to ask you for a few minutes of your time to explain our services to you. You may not recognize our name, as we are not one of the big chain cleaning companies, but it is our commitment to providing the finest of cleaning services that keeps our clients in the greater Boston area loyal. Just ask your new neighbors!

Most cleaning services focus on making an office presentable. That is, they wipe surfaces down to remove stains and dust. But, they do not take the time to use soapy water to actually disinfect office surfaces, and disinfection is exactly what a pediatrician needs! We do not just brush away the dust, we get down and on our hands and knees scrub floors. That is why so many doctors and dentists use our services.

Below you will find our office phone number. Why don't you or your office manager give us a call? I will personally come over to your office to review all of your offices' individual cleaning needs and give you an estimate on the spot.

Sincerely yours,

Wanda Fisher
Manager
(617) 555-1234

1. What services do both of these companies provide?
   (A) They provide temporary office workers.
   (B) They provide office utilities.
   (C) They clean offices.
   (D) They repair office equipment.

2. What feature is emphasized by Blue Ribbon Cleaners?
   (A) Cheap price
   (B) Quality service
   (C) Long years of experience
   (D) Free shampoo service

3. What is NOT part of Ace Cleaning Service's proposal?
   (A) Vacuuming carpet
   (B) Washing windows
   (C) Cleaning toilets
   (D) Dusting

4. What can be inferred about Wanda Fisher?
   (A) She has contacted Dr. Whirlege in the past.
   (B) She works in an office at Pearl Street Mall.
   (C) She owns a Blue Ribbon Cleaners franchise.
   (D) She hasn't met Dr. Whirlege.

5. What do both businesses ask Dr. Whirlege to do?
   (A) Call them for more information
   (B) Come in to their offices
   (C) Consult their homepages
   (D) Contact them by mail or e-mail

1 Ⓐ Ⓑ Ⓒ Ⓓ
2 Ⓐ Ⓑ Ⓒ Ⓓ
3 Ⓐ Ⓑ Ⓒ Ⓓ
4 Ⓐ Ⓑ Ⓒ Ⓓ
5 Ⓐ Ⓑ Ⓒ Ⓓ

2009 年 3 月 1 日
拜瑞 · 沃利巨醫生
02301 麻州布拉克頓市
珍珠街購物中心 505 套房

沃利巨醫師您好：

我們非常榮幸能向您提出本公司的清潔服務提案，為您在布拉克頓市珍珠街購物中心裡的診所服務。我們的服務包括：

1. 每晚使用吸塵器吸地毯，
2. 清潔並消毒洗手間，
3. 清空垃圾桶，有灰塵處即除塵。

除此之外，如果您在三月底之前與本公司簽訂合約，合約期間內本公司將視情況需要替您免費用清潔劑清洗地毯，絕不額外收費。所有清潔服務都是一週五次（週一到週五），一週 175 元。我們每兩週請款一次。所有清潔用品都會由王牌清潔服務公司提供。

本公司所有員工都經過審慎篩選。外派工作前及工作期間，所有人員都會通盤且持續了解如何進行現代大樓的維護、安全和保全，並會妥當看管設備與用品。本公司的員工也熟知各自領域的行為規範與法則，包含如何運用常識。在為您大樓服務的過程中，我們也會另外訓練人員以防有人中途請假。

如果您有任何問題，請隨時與王牌清潔服務公司聯絡。

王牌清潔服務公司辦公室主任
瑪麗亞 · 克洛克
敬上

藍帶清潔公司

沃利巨醫師您好：

本公司清潔人員發現您已經搬入珍珠街購物中心 505 套房，我想藉此機會歡迎您！我們為購物中心裡的 18 位客戶提供清潔服務，也希望能耽誤您幾分鐘的時間，向您解釋本公司的服務。您或許沒聽過本公司，因為我們不是大型連鎖清潔公司，但是我們致力於提供最好的清潔服務，讓大波士頓地區的客戶都成為我們的老主顧。只要問問您的新鄰居就知道了！

多數的清潔服務只重視把辦公室弄得很體面，也就是說，他們會把表面的灰塵和髒汙擦掉，但卻不會花時間使用肥皂水，將辦公室表面進行實際消毒，然而小兒科醫生需要的正是消毒！我們不僅除塵，還會跪在地上實際刷洗地板。這也是為什麼許多醫生和牙醫都選擇我們的服務。

下面附有我們辦公室的電話號碼。請您或您的辦公室管理人員撥個電話給我們吧？我將會親自到您的辦公室，檢視所有的清潔需求，現場就為您報價。

經理
汪達 · 費雪
敬上
(617) 555-1234

題目中譯

解題技巧

1. 這兩家公司提供什麼樣的服務？
   (A) 提供辦公室臨時員工。
   (B) 提供辦公室水電。
   (C) **清潔辦公室**。
   (D) 修理辦公室設備。

答案 (C)

從這兩封信的第一行各有 janitorial services（清潔服務）和 cleaning（清潔），可以知道是在推銷清潔服務。也可以從信件開頭及結尾的公司名稱一目了然。

2. 藍帶清潔公司強調什麼樣的特色？
   (A) 價格低廉
   (B) **優質服務**
   (C) 多年經驗
   (D) 免費用清潔劑清洗

答案 (B)

以題目中的 emphasized 當作線索，搜尋藍帶清潔公司的信件。從 ...our commitment to providing the finest of cleaning services... 及使用形容詞 fine 的最高級來強調，知道這裡就是對應的內容。

3. 哪一項不是王牌清潔服務公司的提案之一？
   (A) 用吸塵器吸地毯
   (B) **洗窗戶**
   (C) 清廁所
   (D) 除塵

答案 (B)

先確認王牌清潔服務公司信中第一段 Our services will include: 的內容，沒有包含在服務內容中的項目就是正確答案。信中以條列方式書寫，應該很容易看出正確答案。

4. 可以推論出汪達 · 費雪的什麼事？
   (A) 她過去曾經和沃利巨醫師聯絡過。
   (B) 她在珍珠街購物中心的辦公室工作。
   (C) 她擁有一間藍帶清潔公司的經銷權。
   (D) **她沒有見過沃利巨醫師**。

答案 (D)

從題目中的名字知道，必須搜尋藍帶清潔公司的信。從一開頭的 Our cleaning crew saw that you have moved into Suite 505... 可知寫信者從清潔人員那裡得知沃利巨醫師剛搬入，故可判斷出寫信者應該不認識沃利巨醫師。

5. 這兩家公司都請沃利巨醫師做什麼？
   (A) **打電話給他們以獲取更多資訊**
   (B) 去他們的辦公室
   (C) 參考他們的網頁
   (D) 用一般信件或電子郵件與他們聯絡

答案 (A)

所有的選項都和洽詢方式有關，這種資訊通常寫在信件末端。藍帶清潔公司的信中提到 phone number 和 call，而王牌清潔服務公司的信末也有 contact us at...，由此可知最接近的選項就是 (A)。

註解

janitorial service 清潔服務
disinfect (v.) 消毒
be versed in... 精通於…
absenteeism (n.) 經常無故缺席，怠工，曠課
commitment (n.) 承擔的義務
presentable (adj.) 漂亮的，像樣的
pediatrician (n.) 小兒科醫師
on the spot 當場，在現場

Sales Manager wanted by one of the largest German manufacturers and suppliers of doors, windows, and other joinery products

Successful candidates will be required to:

* Deal with new and previous clients.
* Manage customer accounts.
* Process orders and follow up on customer queries.
* Implement a high standard of customer service.
* Communicate precisely and quickly with team members.

Skills required for this position include:

* Excellent German and English communication skills.
* Strong team player skills.
* The ability to act on one's own initiative.
* 1-3 years office sales experience in a customer service environment.

This is an excellent opportunity for the right candidate. For more information, please contact Gertrude Lovelidge at (07) 635-1072.

From: McFadden, Drew
To: Lovelidge, Gertrude
Cc:
Subject: Sales Manager position in *The Daily Telegraph*

I am writing in response to your recently placed advertisement in *The Daily Telegraph* and wish to apply for the position. I have worked in commercial, customer-oriented positions for the last 15 years selling automation equipment to manufacturing industries both directly and through distributors.

Concerning your requirement for proficiency in German, I first studied German when working with the Swiss company Schaffer and Stroh in 1994. More recently, in 2006, I completed an intermediate German course at Luton University as part of the LCB (Language, Culture and Business) module which was introduced to improve the language competence of companies in Herefordshire. I also have direct experience generating and executing business plans as a result of managing the UK subsidiary of a USA-based inspection equipment manufacturer. I also attended the Business Growth Program run by the Herefordshire School of Management.

My current salary is £50,500 plus an 8% pension and car allowance, but I am prepared to be flexible on salary for a challenging and rewarding opportunity with good prospects.

I am very interested in the position advertized and feel that I satisfy the criteria listed. I have attached my résumé and I hope that you find my application of interest.

Sincerely,

Drew McFadden

1. Where does Gertrude Lovelidge work?
   (A) At a manufacturing company
   (B) At a newspaper
   (C) At a university
   (D) At a retailer

2. What is NOT mentioned as a requirement for this position?
   (A) Bilingual language ability
   (B) Educational background in business
   (C) Previous sales experience
   (D) Client management skills

3. Why does Mr. McFadden mention Luton University?
   (A) He taught some business courses there.
   (B) He is about to graduate from there.
   (C) He attended graduate school there.
   (D) He studied a foreign language there.

4. What has Mr. McFadden attached to his e-mail?
   (A) His résumé
   (B) His business plan
   (C) His references
   (D) His photograph

5. What can be inferred about Mr. McFadden?
   (A) He lacks the required experience, but is an enthusiastic learner.
   (B) He requires a higher salary than Ms. Lovelidge's company is offering.
   (C) His business planning experience is just what Ms. Lovelidge needs.
   (D) He appears to meet the job requirements and might accept a salary reduction.

1 Ⓐ Ⓑ Ⓒ Ⓓ
2 Ⓐ Ⓑ Ⓒ Ⓓ
3 Ⓐ Ⓑ Ⓒ Ⓓ
4 Ⓐ Ⓑ Ⓒ Ⓓ
5 Ⓐ Ⓑ Ⓒ Ⓓ

大型德國門窗及細木工製品製作公司徵求業務經理

合格的應徵者必須要：
* 負責新舊客戶
* 管理客戶
* 處理訂單並解決客戶疑問
* 執行高水準客戶服務
* 能與組員精確且快速地溝通

此職位需要具備的技能包含：
* 絕佳的德語和英語溝通技巧
* 良好的團隊精神
* 能夠主動積極行動
* 在客戶服務領域有 1 ～ 3 年的辦公室業務經驗

對合適的應徵者來說，這是絕佳的機會。如果需要更多資訊，請洽葛楚德 ‧ 拉佛利吉，電話是 (07) 635-1072。

寄件者：德魯 ‧ 麥法登
收件者：葛楚德 ‧ 拉佛利吉
副本：
主旨：《每日電訊報》上的業務經理一職

我寫這封信是為了回應您最近在《每日電訊報》上刊登的廣告，我希望應徵這個職位。過去 15 年來，我曾擔任商業、客戶服務導向的職位，直接或透過經銷商販賣自動化設備給製造業。

關於德語流利這項要求：1994 年我在瑞士公司夏佛與史拓工作時，第一次開始學德語。2006 年我在魯頓大學修完了中級德語，那是 LCB（語言、文化、商業）課程中的一部分，目的是為了要增進赫里福德郡內企業員工的語言能力而引進的課程。我也曾主導擬定與執行營運計畫書，管理美商檢驗設備製造商在英國的子公司。我同時也參加過赫里福德郡管理學院開設的企業成長課程。

我目前的薪資是 5 萬 5 百元英鎊，外加 8% 的退休與交通津貼，不過我並不堅持新工作的薪資，只希望能獲得有挑戰性、有收穫且前景看好的工作機會。

我對廣告裡的職缺十分有興趣，也覺得自己符合所列的所有條件。隨信附上我的履歷，希望能引起您的興趣。

德魯 ‧ 麥法登
敬上

題目中譯

1. 葛楚德 · 拉佛利吉在哪裡工作？
   (A) **製造公司**
   (B) 報社
   (C) 大學
   (D) 零售商

2. 哪一項不是這個職缺要求的條件？
   (A) 雙語能力
   (B) **商科教育背景**
   (C) 曾有業務經驗
   (D) 客戶管理技能

3. 麥法登先生為什麼提到魯頓大學？
   (A) 他在那裡教過商業課程。
   (B) 他即將從那裡畢業。
   (C) 他在那裡讀研究所。
   (D) **他在那裡學習外語**。

4. 麥法登先生的電子郵件附件是什麼？
   (A) **他的履歷**
   (B) 他的營運計畫書
   (C) 他的推薦人
   (D) 他的照片

5. 可以推論出麥法登先生的什麼事？
   (A) 他缺乏所需的經驗，但很樂意學習。
   (B) 他要求的薪水比拉佛利吉女士的公司所提供的還高。
   (C) 拉佛利吉女士就是需要他的營運規畫經驗。
   (D) **他似乎符合求職條件，而且可能也願意接受減薪**。

解題技巧

1. **答案 (A)**

搜尋 Gertrude Lovelidge 這個名字就能知道他所隸屬的公司。從廣告標題及提到自己的公司是 the largest German manufacturers and suppliers... 就能找出正確答案。

2. **答案 (B)**

題目問到應徵該職位的必備條件，所以搜尋 Successful candidates will be required to: 之後的內容。選項中將文章裡的說法稍微換了一下，雖然得花一點時間，但只要讀過內容就知道 (B) 不是必備條件。

3. **答案 (D)**

在郵件裡搜尋大學名稱。從第二段的 in 2006, I completed an intermediate German course at Luton University... 可以確認麥法登先生曾經學過德語。

4. **答案 (A)**

附件事項的說明大多出現在郵件的最後，故可直接搜尋郵件的後半段。從 I have attached my résumé 可以得到正確答案。

5. **答案 (D)**

由於題目問有關於麥法登先生的事情，所以就去搜尋郵件內容。從他具備 15 年的業務經驗知道 (A) 不正確。(B) 的 requires a higher salary，和第三段的 I am prepared to be flexible on salary 相反。(C) 的 business planning experience 並沒有列入應徵條件，所以要選 (D)。

註解

initiative (n.) 主動；率先
proficiency (n.) 精通，熟練
rewarding (adj.) 有益的，值得的
with good prospects 有良好前景的

Chapter 5

Report

報告

NEW TOEIC® TEST

September 30, 2008

Larry Barton
Vice President of Corporate Marketing
GGG Central Ontario Co.
450 West Lindon Court
Thornhill, ON L4T 9N4

Dear Larry,

Please find the attached roster of the hours worked, for your firm, by Colburn Communications Consultants during the third quarter of 2008.

I trust this is in order. If you have any questions, please do not hesitate to call or e-mail me. I hope this helps with your budgeting activities.

Regards,

Gary Colburn
Principal
Colburn Communications Consultants

Month	Project	Hours
July	Gap Analysis	9
	Meeting	2
	Strategic Document Development	2
	Database Analysis	2
	Rewards Program Research	2
August	Canadian Market Summary	13
	Preparing Board Presentation	3
	Database Analysis	4
September	Health/Dental Gap Analysis	4
	Auto Insurance Gap Analysis	4
	Pricing Research	34
GRAND TOTAL OF HOURS WORKED IN Q3, 2008		79

1. Where does Larry Barton work?
   (A) GGG Central Ontario Co.
   (B) The Canadian Market Track
   (C) Colburn Communications
   (D) The Canadian Federal Government

2. Which of the following analyses was NOT performed?
   (A) Gap analysis
   (B) Database analysis
   (C) Board presentation analysis
   (D) Auto Insurance analysis

1 Ⓐ Ⓑ Ⓒ Ⓓ
2 Ⓐ Ⓑ Ⓒ Ⓓ

2008 年 9 月 30 日

賴瑞．巴頓
企業行銷副總經理
GGG 中安大略公司
L4T 9N4 安大略省康山市
西林敦廣場 450 號

賴瑞您好：

附件為寇伯恩通訊顧問公司於 2008 年第三季為貴公司服務的時數表，請查收。

我確信正確無誤。若您有任何問題，請隨時撥電話或寄電子郵件給我。我希望這能有助於您編列預算。

寇伯恩通訊顧問公司
社長
蓋瑞．寇伯恩
敬上

月份	專案	時數
7 月	差異分析	9
	會議	2
	製作策略文件	2
	資料庫分析	2
	研究獎賞計畫	2
8 月	加拿大市場摘要	13
	準備董事會報告	3
	資料庫分析	4
9 月	健康與牙齒的差異分析	4
	汽車保險差異分析	4
	定價研究	34
2008 年第三季總工作時數		79

題目中譯

1. 賴瑞・巴頓在哪裡工作？

   (A) GGG **中安大略公司**
   (B) 加拿大市場追蹤
   (C) 寇伯恩通訊
   (D) 加拿大聯邦政府

2. 以下哪一項分析沒有做到？

   (A) 差異分析
   (B) 資料庫分析
   (C) **董事會報告分析**
   (D) 汽車保險分析

解題技巧

答案 (A)

信件的開頭部分通常都會有收信者姓名，還會有公司地址、公司名稱、職稱等。只要在 Larry Barton 這個名字的附近找一下，馬上就能找出正確答案。

答案 (C)

注意清單中的 Preparing Board Presentation 和 (C) 的 Board presentation analysis 是不同的。因此 (C) 是正確答案，其他選項全都經過分析。

註解

roster (n.) 勤務表，名簿

Polywall® Insulation Questionnaire

Polywall®—Insulated Homes Create a Better Indoor Environment. We spend as much as 90% of our time indoors, so why shouldn't we be concerned with improving the quality of our home environment? The benefits of better Indoor Environmental Quality (IEQ) include optimal energy efficiency, proper temperature and humidity levels, and reduced levels of noise, pollutants, and allergens. All of these benefits can be achieved by insulating your home with Polywall®. For a more detailed idea of how better buildings could help you and your family, please fill out and send us the following questionnaire and you will receive a customized tip sheet with simple ways to improve your home's IEQ.

1. Do you notice any of the following around your home: bad smells, cracks in the foundation or walls, or leaky roof?
   YES / NO

2. Does your home have uneven floor temperatures?
   YES / NO

3. Does your home generate high heating and cooling costs?
   YES / NO

4. Do you wish that sound from noisy areas of the home (e.g. children's play areas) didn't penetrate other rooms that should be quiet?
   YES / NO

5. Do you or a family member experience one or more of the following symptoms: headaches, eye/nose/throat irritation, or coughing?
   YES / NO

1. What is the recipient of this questionnaire requested to do?
   (A) Check the condition of their home's roof
   (B) Confirm their Polywall contract
   (C) Visit a Polywall branch
   (D) Return it to Polywall

2. Which of the following is NOT mentioned as part of the benefits brought from better Indoor Environmental Quality?
   (A) Energy efficiency
   (B) Extension in house life
   (C) Quiet atmosphere
   (D) Temperature control

3. The questionnaire asks about all of the following EXCEPT
   (A) humidity.
   (B) smell.
   (C) sound.
   (D) temperature.

1 Ⓐ Ⓑ Ⓒ Ⓓ
2 Ⓐ Ⓑ Ⓒ Ⓓ
3 Ⓐ Ⓑ Ⓒ Ⓓ

多層牆絕緣問卷

多層牆——做好絕緣的家能讓您有更好的室內環境。我們大概有 90% 的時間會待在室內，怎麼能夠不關心該如何改善居家室內環境呢？較佳的室內環境品質可以帶來的好處包括，最佳能源效率、適當溫度與濕度，以及降低噪音、汙染、過敏原的程度。只要用多層牆做好絕緣，就能獲得以上全部的好處。如果想進一步了解較佳的建築如何幫助您及您的家人，請填寫以下問卷寄回，就能收到為您量身打造的個人情報，教您用簡單的方法改善您居家的室內環境品質。

1. 您在家中是否注意到以下的狀況：臭味、地基或牆壁有裂痕，或是屋頂漏水？
   是／否

2. 您家中的地板是否溫度不均？
   是／否

3. 您家中的冷暖氣電費是否過高？
   是／否

4. 您是否希望家中吵雜區域的聲音（例如：兒童遊戲區）不會影響到應該要安靜的地方？
   是／否

5. 您或您的家人是否曾經不只一次有過以下的症狀：頭痛、眼睛／鼻子／喉嚨不適、咳嗽？
   是／否

題目中譯

1. 收到這份問卷的人應該要做什麼？
   (A) 檢查家中屋頂狀況
   (B) 確認他們的多層牆合約
   (C) 造訪多層牆的分店
   (D) 交回給多層牆

2. 以下哪一項不是室內環境品質可帶來的好處？
   (A) 能源效率
   (B) 延長房屋的壽命
   (C) 氣氛安靜
   (D) 溫度控制

3. 這份問卷不包含以下哪一項？
   (A) 濕度
   (B) 味道
   (C) 聲音
   (D) 溫度

解題技巧

答案 (D)

文章中關於「協助做問卷」的內容出現在第一段的倒數第三行 please fill out...，由此可知是「麻煩做完問卷送回」。

答案 (B)

在文章中尋找顯示 Indoor Environmental Quality 優點的地方，第三行的 The benefits of better Indoor Environmental Quality (IEQ) include... 部分就是對應內容。正確答案就是沒出現在這個部分的選項。

答案 (A)

humidity 在文章的第一段第四行中是以 proper ... humidity 的說法出現，但是在問卷中並沒有提到。temperature, bad smell, noisy 等字都出現在問卷中，所以都不是正確答案。

註解

insulation (n.) 絕緣，隔熱
optimal (adj.) 最適宜的，最佳的
pollutant (n.) 汙染物質
allergen (n.) 過敏原
crack (n.) 裂縫
leaky (adj.) 漏水的，有漏洞的
penetrate (v.) 穿透，刺穿

Are you a mother who wants to go back to work, but thinks she can't handle a full-time job?

It's just not possible for most of us to get off work at 4:00 P.M. every day to pick up our children at day care. It annoys co-workers and bosses, and ultimately you yourself will become frustrated trying to work full-time while trying to be a great mom.

It's stressful for single parents and working mothers to combine work and child-rearing. And, even if you find time to pick up your young ones, fix dinner, do the housework, and get the kids ready for bed, you won't have time to do anything else.

A flex-time work arrangement can help. Certainly, not every company allows for flexible time management, and it's not applicable to every kind of job. But, flexible working hours and alternative working arrangements are becoming more and more common, particularly among companies that struggle to keep talent. Therefore, you shouldn't hesitate to ask if your company also has a program which could give you more time with your family. But, it's likely that you'll have to bring it up, and you'll have to sacrifice benefits, such as vacation time, to keep your job security.

Job sharing is also becoming more prevalent, as are agreements to work from home once or twice a week, or even part-time. Check around to see whether there is someone like you who is looking for fewer hours who might be able to share your job with you. You may also want to seek out employment opportunities at companies that pride themselves on innovative work-life programs.

1. Who is most likely to benefit from the scheme described in the passage?
   (A) Small business owners
   (B) New college graduates
   (C) Unemployed fathers
   (D) Single mothers

2. Why are many companies willing to offer flex-time options?
   (A) They want to keep good workers.
   (B) They need to open day care centers.
   (C) They were not profitable before starting flexible time schemes.
   (D) They want to avoid additional vacation time expenses.

3. What is NOT stated in the article about companies?
   (A) More are offering flex-time arrangements.
   (B) More are providing job sharing opportunities.
   (C) Many require reduced benefits for flex-time workers.
   (D) Many will refuse to guarantee job security.

1 Ⓐ Ⓑ Ⓒ Ⓓ
2 Ⓐ Ⓑ Ⓒ Ⓓ
3 Ⓐ Ⓑ Ⓒ Ⓓ

你是想重回職場卻擔心自己無法勝任全職工作的媽媽嗎？

我們多數人真的沒有辦法每天下午四點鐘下班，去托兒所接小孩回家。這樣會讓同事和老闆不高興，最後也會讓你自己感到挫折不已，因為你得要在做全職工作的同時，還要當個偉大的媽媽。

同時兼顧工作和育兒，讓單親家長與職業婦女倍受壓力。就算你有時間接小孩、煮晚餐、做家事、把小孩哄上床，你也沒有時間再做別的事情。

彈性工時的安排很有幫助。當然，不是每家公司都容許彈性工時的安排，也不是每一種工作都適合這種制度。但是彈性工時與彈性工作安排變得愈來愈普遍，特別是對那些很難留住人才的公司，因此你應該毫不猶豫地問你的公司，有沒有能夠讓你與家人多一點時間相處的方案。但是你可能得自己主動提起，也必須犧牲像假期等的某些福利來保住你的工作。

工作分攤也是愈來愈普遍的做法，就像是協議一週在家工作一天或兩天，或甚至是兼職。找找看周遭有沒有和你一樣想把工作時數降低一些的人，就可以一起分攤工作。至於那些以實行工作和生活兼顧的創新計畫為傲的公司，你可能也會想要去找看看有沒有工作機會。

題目中譯

1. 誰最可能受惠於文章所提的方案？

(A) 小型企業主
(B) 大學應屆畢業生
(C) 失業父親
(D) **單親媽媽**

2. 為什麼有很多公司願意提供彈性工時的選擇？

(A) **想要留住好員工**。
(B) 需要開設托兒所。
(C) 實行彈性工時的計畫前並沒有獲利。
(D) 想要避免額外假期支出。

3. 文章並未提到關於公司的哪一項？

(A) 愈來愈多公司提供彈性工時的安排。
(B) 愈來愈多公司提供工作分攤的機會。
(C) 很多公司要求彈性工時的員工必須犧牲某些福利。
(D) **很多公司會拒絕保障員工的工作**。

解題技巧

答案 (D)

從第二段裡提到單親家長和職業婦女的辛勞，以及第三段第一句的 A flex-time work arrangement can help. 中可以立刻得知正確答案。

答案 (A)

從題目中的 flex-time 可以判斷出第三段是它的對應內容。公司引進彈性工時的理由可以從 becoming more and more common, particularly among companies that struggle to keep talent 可知這就是題目中 why 的對應內容。

答案 (D)

與公司相關的內容出現在第三和第四段，介紹一般的彈性工時和工作分攤制。(C) 在第三段最後的 you'll have to sacrifice benefits... 提到。(D) 從 will 就很容易判斷，因為論及一切關於公司的行為都會用現在式，不會用未來式。

註解

annoy (v.) 使生氣；使煩惱
stressful (adj.) 產生壓力的
prevalent (adj.) 普遍的，盛行的

Loans for Loved Ones

Many savers may have certificates of deposit coming to them soon, but are hesitant to roll them over with the measly 3-4% interest CDs are paying these days. Money market funds are no better in today's low interest environment. So, how can you improve your yield? Well, if your children are looking to buy a house and need a mortgage, a little creativity and a simple contract could help you both. Both parents needing returns and children looking to buy a first home can benefit from a family loan.

You see, by lending directly to your children, you eliminate the intermediary—the bank. On one hand, your children can avoid paying loan points and application fees. You, on the other hand, can get a higher return on your savings. With mortgage interest rates hovering around 7%, it is a substantial improvement over what banks are paying savers these days. You can even give your kids a half-point discount and receive a higher rate than the current 30-year Treasury bond is paying.

This kind of financial arrangement isn't for everyone. Some children are just not a good credit risk, so you need to be honest with yourself. Some parents who commit to this kind of loan find it difficult to collect later on. One solution can be to involve a lawyer who can, for a fee of $100 or so, draw up the necessary legal documentation and act as an independent third party between the parents and children. So, if you are interested in trying for this kind of finance, make sure to treat it as an arm's length business deal as much as possible—don't cut corners just because they are your children.

1. What is this article discussing?
   (A) A way to improve marketing techniques
   (B) A new community banking service
   (C) A do-it-yourself financial method
   (D) A new financial product

2. What is NOT mentioned as an advantage of this suggestion?
   (A) Higher savings returns
   (B) Lower mortgage rates
   (C) The simplicity of the contract
   (D) The rate of the 30-year bond

3. Why does the article recommend consulting a lawyer?
   (A) This financial arrangement may be illegal in some areas.
   (B) Some parents may have difficulty collecting payment from their children.
   (C) So that parents have the legal documentation necessary when filing taxes.
   (D) It's a bank mortgage requirement.

1 Ⓐ Ⓑ Ⓒ Ⓓ
2 Ⓐ Ⓑ Ⓒ Ⓓ
3 Ⓐ Ⓑ Ⓒ Ⓓ

借錢給你愛的人

許多存款戶都有即將到期的定存單，但是都不願意繼續再滾下去，因為現在定存單的利息僅僅不過 3 ～ 4%。在現今的低利率環境下，貨幣市場基金的表現也沒有好到哪裡去。那你要如何才能提高獲益呢？如果你的孩子想要買房子，需要貸款，那麼只要一點點創意，再加上一張簡單的合約，就能同時幫助你們雙方。想要獲得利潤的父母以及想要購買第一棟房子的孩子，雙方都受惠於家庭貸款。

你看，直接借錢給你的孩子，就能排除銀行這個中間人。一方面，你的孩子可以不用支付貸款百分點與申請費用。另一方面，你也能獲得更高的存款利息。現在的房貸利率大概是 7% 左右，遠比銀行支付存款戶的利息還要高。你甚至可以給孩子半個百分點的折扣，還是能獲得高於目前 30 年期財政部長期公債的利率。

這種財務安排並非適合所有人。有些孩子實在不能冒這種信用風險，所以你得要對自己誠實。某些提供這種貸款的父母，日後會難以回收。其中一個解決辦法就是聘請一位律師，只要 100 元左右的費用就能幫你草擬必要的法律文件，甚至擔任父母與孩子之間的獨立第三者。所以，如果你有興趣嘗試這種財務安排，記得盡量將這當作常規的商業交易——不要因為他們是你的孩子就圖方便走捷徑。

題目中譯

1. 這篇文章在討論什麼？
   (A) 改善行銷技巧的方式
   (B) 新的社區銀行服務
   (C) 自己來的理財方法
   (D) 新的金融產品

解題技巧

答案 (C)

由標題可以知道主旨是貸款，但是從第二段出現的 eliminate ... the bank（排除……銀行）就可以直接刪去選項 (B) 和 (D)。此外，(A) 從 marketing 這個單字就能判斷出與標題的主旨無關。

2. 以下哪一項不是此項提議的好處？
   (A) 更高的存款利潤
   (B) 更低的貸款利率
   (C) 合約很簡單
   (D) 30 年期債券的利率

答案 (D)

選項 (A) 和 (B) 都在第二段裡提到。(C) 出現在第一段的 a simple contract。也可以由文章的內容是「非透過金融機構的貸款」得知正確答案是 (D)，因為債券得透過金融機構才買得到。

3. 這篇文章為什麼建議諮詢律師？
   (A) 這項理財安排在某些地區可能違法。
   (B) 有些父母可能很難向孩子收回款項。
   (C) 如此一來父母要報稅時，才有必要的法律文件。
   (D) 這是銀行貸款的要求。

答案 (B)

在文章裡搜尋題目中的 lawyer，它就出現在第三段第四行。了解第三段前三行在說明親子間借貸的難處後，就知道這個部分是正確答案的對應內容。

註解

certificate of deposit (CD) 定存單
measly (adj.) 微不足道的；沒價值的
yield (n.) 投資收益；生產量
mortgage (n.) 抵押借款
arm's length 一臂之隔，保持距離
cut corners 抄近路，用最簡潔經濟的方式做事

Intellectual Property: Ideas and Inventions

There are some businesses for which ideas are a valuable asset. Lots of people have great ideas that they never act upon, only to find out later that someone else had the same idea, acted on it, and has brought a new product or service to market.

Of course, it's a long way from having an idea to actually making an invention. Inventions take a lot more market knowledge, effort, and time than ideas do. There is even an element of luck involved. Also, even if you create and manufacture an invention, there is no guarantee that it will ever go on to become a successful product. There are a lot of pitfalls, and avoiding them requires planning and support.

Nearly a quarter million inventors file patents, trademarks, and copyrights every year in the USA. The three, together, are known as "intellectual property." Sometimes, it's hard to figure out which is most appropriate, and some products need all three, since each protects a specific aspect of a creative work.

Of course, of all the inventions filed for protection each year, only a few are successful. So, it's not as if having a patent on a product will guarantee success in the market. It might not even be worth the thousands of dollars it can cost to get exclusive rights to a product which, possibly, no one wants.

1. According to the article, what is an important distinction between ideas and inventions?
   (A) Inventions are more easily accepted in the marketplace than are ideas.
   (B) Ideas take a lot more luck to find than inventions.
   (C) Ideas are more abstract than concrete inventions.
   (D) Inventions take more time and energy than ideas.

2. What does the author indicate about the amount of intellectual property?
   (A) It is unrealistic for most individuals, but more realistic for companies.
   (B) It is most common for vehicles.
   (C) Over 100,000 people file claims annually.
   (D) It is a requirement for success in the modern world.

3. Which of the following is NOT a form of intellectual property?
   (A) Patents
   (B) Copyrights
   (C) Inventions
   (D) Trademarks

1 Ⓐ Ⓑ Ⓒ Ⓓ
2 Ⓐ Ⓑ Ⓒ Ⓓ
3 Ⓐ Ⓑ Ⓒ Ⓓ

智慧財產權：概念與發明

對某些行業來說，概念是非常值錢的資產。許多人有很棒的概念卻從不付諸行動，最後才發現別人也有相同的概念且已付諸行動，因而為市場帶來新的產品或新的服務。

當然，從概念到發明是一條很漫長的路。發明需要對市場有更多的了解，付出更多的努力和時間，遠超過於概念所需。發明甚至還需要一點運氣成分。而且就算你成功發明、製作出來了，也不一定保證就會變成一項成功的產品。外面有許多陷阱，需要經過規畫、得到支持，才能避免。

美國每年有將近 25 萬名發明家申請專利、商標與著作權。這三者合在一起統稱為「智慧財產權」。有時候很難分辨到底哪一種比較適合，而有些產品則三種都需要，因為每一種僅能保護這些創意結晶的某一特定部分。

當然，每年申請專利保護的發明中只有少數會成功，因此不是有專利就保證一定會大受市場歡迎。有時候可能甚至不值得花上數千元去獨占一個或許根本沒有人要的產品。

題目中譯	解題技巧
1. 根據這篇文章，概念與發明之間有什麼重要的差別？ (A) 發明比概念容易為市場所接受。 (B) 要有概念比發明更需要運氣。 (C) 概念比實際發明更抽象。 (D) **發明比概念需要更多時間與精力**。	**答案 (D)** 注意題目中的 distinction，找到兩者進行比較的部分。留意第二段的比較級：Inventions take a lot more market knowledge, effort, and time than ideas do.，只要仔細閱讀比較級的內容就能知道正確答案。
2. 作者對智慧財產權的數量說了什麼？ (A) 對多數個人來說很不實際，但是對公司比較實際。 (B) 對車輛來說很正常。 (C) **每年有超過 10 萬人提出申請**。 (D) 這是現代社會中要成功的必要條件。	**答案 (C)** 以題目中的 amount 作為關鍵字，搜尋有關智慧財產權數量的內容。相關內容出現在第三段，這一段一開頭的 Nearly a quarter million inventors file patents... 就是有關於數量的描述，因此可得知正確答案。
3. 以下哪一項不屬於智慧財產權之一？ (A) 專利 (B) 著作權 (C) **發明** (D) 商標	**答案 (C)** 鎖定說明智慧財產權內容的第三段。只有 The three, together, are known as “intellectual property.” 這句話前面的內容與智慧財產權有關。發明並不包括在其中。

註解

pitfall (n.) 陷阱，圈套

file (v.) 申請；提起（訴訟等）

Timecard & Master Database Report

Submitted by: Souhal Tsouris

Master Database Upgrade Items:

1. Create a report that prints an alphabetical listing of all contracts in the database (1 hr.)

2. Modify existing reports to print alphabetically (2 hrs.)

3. Revise find feature (15 hrs.)
   a. Create "find contract" menu item.
   b. Selection of the above menu item will bring users to a screen similar to the "custom report" screen.
   c. Users will input search criteria and possible matches will be viewed on-screen with the ability to print to paper.

4. Modify the custom report to allow multiple code selections (15 hrs.)

5. Modify the "e-mail report" option to allow extraction of e-mail addresses (3 hrs.)

6. Modify all locations to include code descriptions (5 hrs.)

7. Update user and administrator manuals to reflect all changes made to the system (1 hr.)

Timecard Database Upgrade Items:

1. Time card by employee report (15 hrs.)
   a. Modify drop down menu for Employee IDs to also show employees' names.
   b. Allow for the selection of multiple employees.
   c. Create a drop down selection of payment periods with a multi-selection capability.

2. Update user and administrator manuals to reflect all changes made to the system (1 hr.)

1. What is the purpose of this document?
   (A) To list defects in a company database
   (B) To describe a newly installed computer system
   (C) To identify changes to be made to a database
   (D) To apply for a set of new services

2. What change is NOT listed in this document?
   (A) Changing the database print function
   (B) Allowing users to extract e-mail addresses
   (C) Modifying existing user manuals
   (D) Enlarging the master database storage limits

3. A multiple selection function will be added to all of the following tasks EXCEPT
   (A) custom reports.
   (B) e-mail selections.
   (C) employee payment periods.
   (D) employee selections.

1 Ⓐ Ⓑ Ⓒ Ⓓ
2 Ⓐ Ⓑ Ⓒ Ⓓ
3 Ⓐ Ⓑ Ⓒ Ⓓ

出勤卡資料庫與主要資料庫報告

提出者：蘇哈爾．梭利斯

主要資料庫升級項目：

1. 在資料庫裡建立一份報告，按字母順序印出所有合約（1 小時）

2. 修改現有報告為按字母順序印出（2 小時）

3. 修正搜尋特徵（15 小時）：
   a. 建立「搜尋合約」選單項目。
   b. 選擇以上選單項目，會將使用者帶到類似「自訂報表」的畫面。
   c. 使用者輸入搜尋條件，可能符合的項目會出現在螢幕上，還可以列印出來。

4. 修改自訂報表為可選擇多重編碼（15 小時）

5. 修改「電子郵件報告」選項為可選取電子郵件地址（3 小時）

6. 修改所有地點以包含編碼敘述（5 小時）

7. 更新使用者與管理人手冊，反映所有系統改變（1 小時）

出勤卡資料庫升級項目：

1. 根據員工報告的出勤卡（15 小時）：
   a. 修改顯示員工身分的下拉式選單，讓員工姓名同時顯示。
   b. 允許選擇多位員工。
   c. 建立具有多重選取功能的發薪期間下拉式選項。

2. 更新使用者與管理人手冊，反映所有系統改變（1 小時）

題目中譯

1. 這份文件的目的是什麼？
   (A) 列出公司資料庫的瑕疵
   (B) 描述新安裝的電腦系統
   (C) 點出資料庫所做的改變
   (D) 申請一套新的服務

2. 文件所列的改變不包含以下哪一項？
   (A) 改變資料庫列印功能
   (B) 允許使用者選取電子郵件地址
   (C) 修改現有使用者手冊
   (D) 擴大主要資料庫儲存限制

3. 以下哪一項作業不會加上多重選取功能？
   (A) 自訂報表
   (B) 電子郵件選項
   (C) 員工發薪期間
   (D) 員工選項

解題技巧

答案 (C)

兩個用粗體標示的標題都用了 Upgrade，因此要特別注意選項中的第一和第二個單字。(A) 的 To list... 和 (B) 的 To describe ... system 並不是 upgrade。(D) 的 To apply ... new services 是新申請事項，和改善目前的系統剛好相反。

答案 (D)

瀏覽一下選項就知道要看的不是出勤卡資料庫的項目，而是主要資料庫項目的變更。(A)、(B)、(C) 在 1. ～ 7. 的項目中都可以找到，(C) 的使用者手冊出現在 7. 中。

答案 (B)

搜尋關鍵字是題目中的 multiple。只要在 4. 中發現 multiple code selections，就能將 (A) 刪去。接下來的 5. 中並沒有出現 multiple。(C) 和 (D) 在文章中的對應部分各出現在 Timecard Database Upgrade Items 下面 1. 的 b. 和 c.。

註解

modify (v.) 變更，修改

revise (v.) 修改，校訂

March 11, 2009

Thompson Termite Inspectors
6161 West Plaza
Memphis, TN 43720

Michael Hurst
643 W. Lincoln
Memphis, TN 43689

Mr. Hurst:

I would like to take this opportunity to thank you for using a Thompson Termite Inspector. We take great pride in our inspectors and the fact that we are independent from any treatment that may be needed based upon inspection. This independence, combined with your home inspection, represents the ultimate independent inspection. We pride ourselves in working for you, the buyer.

During your inspection, unfortunately, was discovered a severe termite infestation, and your business site needs immediate professional attention. There are professionals that can treat and eliminate any problems, and although we do not recommend one pest control company over any other as a matter of policy (and law), your local inspector may know of some in your area.

There are a few steps to follow when looking for a pest control company. First of all, you want to make sure the company is licensed to do business in the state of Tennessee (pest control companies are regulated by the Department of Agriculture). You also want to make sure to get quotes in writing, stating the exact work to be performed. We recommend that you also get a guarantee in writing. There are a variety of treatments that are effective, so you will also want to consider the side effects of a treatment, such as potential allergic reactions.

Here at Thompson, we continually strive to improve ourselves and give the highest degree of satisfaction to our customers. If you have any questions or comments, please contact me, toll-free, at 1-800-239-0094.

Sincerely,

Jeff Thompson

Owner and President

1. Why is Thompson Termite Inspectors writing Mr. Hurst?
   (A) They found termites at his business.
   (B) They need his approval to start the new procedure.
   (C) They want to recommend a change of policy.
   (D) They need a written guarantee.

2. What does Mr. Hurst need to do next?
   (A) Sign a contract
   (B) Have an inspection
   (C) Hire a pest control company
   (D) Get a guarantee in writing

3. How can Mr. Hurst find a quality pest control company?
   (A) Call the Department of Agriculture
   (B) Ask his local inspector
   (C) Reply to Jeff Thompson's letter
   (D) Call the Thompson Termite Inspectors home office

4. Which of the following is NOT recommended in looking for a pest control company?
   (A) Check that it is licensed with the state government
   (B) Get a written guarantee and estimate
   (C) Ask for previous customer referrals
   (D) Evaluate any chemical treatments

1 Ⓐ Ⓑ Ⓒ Ⓓ
2 Ⓐ Ⓑ Ⓒ Ⓓ
3 Ⓐ Ⓑ Ⓒ Ⓓ
4 Ⓐ Ⓑ Ⓒ Ⓓ

2009 年 3 月 11 日

湯普森白蟻督察員
43720 田納西州孟菲斯市
西濱廣場 6161 號

麥克・赫斯特
43689 田納西州孟菲斯市
林肯西路 643 號

赫斯特先生您好：

我想要藉此機會感謝您使用湯普森白蟻督察員。我們對本公司的督察感到非常自豪，而且本公司的視察完全獨立，與視察結果所需的處理毫不相干。這項獨立性加上到貴府視察，正是終極的獨立視察。我們以能為買主您服務為榮。

很遺憾的是，視察期間發現您遭受白蟻嚴重肆虐，所以，您的商業據點需要立即進行專業處理。有些專業人士能夠為您處理、消除所有問題。雖然礙於本公司的政策（與法律）規定，我們無法特別推薦任何一家蟲害防治公司，但是您當地的督察員或許知道您附近地區有哪些選擇。

尋找蟲害防治公司時，有幾個步驟可遵循。首先，您要確認這家公司領有田納西州的營業執照（蟲害防治公司由農業部管理）。您也要確認收到書面的報價單並載明實際進行的工作。我們建議您還要要求一份書面保證書。有效的處理方式有很多種，所以您也要將處理方式的副作用納入考慮，例如引發過敏反應。

湯普森會持續努力自我改進，讓客戶獲得最大的滿足。如果您有任何問題或意見，請撥打免付費專線與我聯絡：1-800-239-0094。

老闆暨董事長
傑夫・湯普森
敬上

題目中譯

1. 湯普森白蟻督察員為什麼要寫信給赫斯特先生？

(A) **他們在他的公司裡發現白蟻**。
(B) 他們需要他的許可，才能進行新的程序。
(C) 他們想要建議改變政策。
(D) 他們需要書面保證。

2. 赫斯特先生下一步該怎麼做？

(A) 簽訂合約
(B) 進行視察
(C) **雇用蟲害防治公司**
(D) 取得書面保證

3. 赫斯特先生要怎麼尋找優質的蟲害防治公司？

(A) 打電話給農業部
(B) **問當地的督察員**
(C) 回覆傑夫．湯普森的信
(D) 打電話到湯普森白蟻督察員的總辦公室

4. 尋找蟲害防治公司的建議不包含以下哪一項？

(A) 確認領有州政府的營業執照
(B) 取得書面保證與報價
(C) **要求先前客戶的推薦名單**
(D) 評估化學處理方案

解題技巧

答案 (A)

題目問的是書信的主旨「為什麼要寫這封信？」。一般來說，主旨都會寫在一開頭，但是這封信的第一段只是單純表示感謝，所以主旨出現在第二段。

答案 (C)

在文章裡搜尋題目中的 need，發現第二段的第二行有 needs。your business site needs immediate professional attention 之後的內容就應該和尋找廠商有關。

答案 (B)

針對「如何才能找到蟲害防治公司？」的詢問，對應內容就在第二段的最後 your local inspector may know of some in your area 部分，從這裡可以知道當地督察員能夠協助尋找蟲害防治公司。

答案 (C)

重點在於能否發現題目中 recommended 的對應內容，出現在第三段第二行的 you want to...，這裡提出三點，不包含在內的就是正確答案。

註解

termite (n.) 白蟻
infestation (n.)（蟲、盜賊等）大批出現
strive (v.) 努力，奮鬥
procedure (n.) 程序，手續
referral (n.) 推薦

Heads in the Clouds: the Future of Skyscrapers
By R.W. DuBois and Andrea Simkins
371 pages, New York, Edge Trade Books

Editorial review:

There are skyscrapers in every major city, and there are usually more than one. However, DuBois and Simkins limit themselves to just 20, some of which are still under construction, for a thorough and surprisingly engaging review of modern structural engineering. Much of the text is a discussion of construction principles, which architecture and engineering buffs will appreciate. But, the text is supplemented by an incredible variety of colorful photos, architectural plans, and blueprints which will be enjoyed by nonprofessionals. Unfortunately behind the visual appeal, though, is the stilted and abstract language which is used throughout the book. Still, the book is worth a look for its technically sound and well-presented information.

Reader review:

DuBois and Simkins critique 20 notable new skyscrapers, including a ski jump in Tokyo and a spire-like tower in Dubai. The skyscrapers they've chosen have little in common, except in the chapter on the world's tallest building. But, the diverse collection allows the authors to analyze each building's unique features, and comment on how well the buildings fit into their respective neighborhoods. For me, the highlight of the book was the variety of photos. I was especially impressed with the Wing Tower in Glasgow, Scotland, which pivots like a weathervane. The elegant new Swiss Re London Headquarters is another beauty, which the author has compared to a gemstone. On a lighter note is the Stratosphere Tower in Las Vegas, which has a roller coaster on its top deck. Architectural fans will enjoy this book, and professionals will find the discussion useful.

1. Who would be most interested in this book?
   (A) Property developers
   (B) Architectural enthusiasts
   (C) Condominium customers
   (D) Electrical engineers

2. What information would you expect to find in this book?
   (A) The height of the world's tallest building
   (B) The basic principles of skyscraper construction and engineering
   (C) A discussion on the history of skyscraper building
   (D) A guide to the tallest buildings in Europe

3. What aspect of this book is criticized by the first review?
   (A) The language
   (B) The photos
   (C) The engineering ideas
   (D) The building designs

4. Where would one find a building with a moving structure?
   (A) Dubai
   (B) Scotland
   (C) London
   (D) Las Vegas

1 Ⓐ Ⓑ Ⓒ Ⓓ
2 Ⓐ Ⓑ Ⓒ Ⓓ
3 Ⓐ Ⓑ Ⓒ Ⓓ
4 Ⓐ Ⓑ Ⓒ Ⓓ

《直入雲端：摩天大樓的未來》
R.W. 杜布瓦與安德烈・希姆金斯　合著
371 頁，紐約市邊緣普及圖書

編輯書評：

每個大城市都有摩天大樓，通常還不只一棟。不過，杜布瓦與希姆金斯卻限制自己只能挑 20 棟，以深入且驚人的角度審視現代結構工程，其中有些還沒施工完畢。文章多在探討建築原理，這一點一定會受到建築與工程迷歡迎。但是文章裡也伴隨了各式各樣色彩豐富的照片、建築設計圖、藍圖，非專業人士看了也會很喜歡。然而遺憾的是，隱藏在這些視覺誘惑之下的卻是拗口又抽象的語言，貫穿整本書。不過，這本書可靠又精彩呈現的技術資訊仍然值得一看。

讀者書評：

杜布瓦與希姆金斯一同評論了 20 棟著名的新摩天大樓，包含東京的滑雪跳躍助跑道，以及杜拜的螺旋狀塔。除了世界上最高建築物的章節外，兩人所選的摩天大樓幾乎沒有相似處。但是如此多樣的組合，讓作者得以分析每棟建築物的獨特之處，並評論這些建築物適合當地環境的程度。對我來說，這本書最棒的是提供各式各樣的照片。我非常喜歡蘇格蘭格拉斯哥的翅膀之塔，就像風向計一樣地旋轉。倫敦瑞士再保險總部大廈則是另一美景，作者拿寶石來和這棟建築做比較。輕鬆一點的則有拉斯維加斯的同溫層賭場飯店，它的頂樓還有雲霄飛車。建築迷一定會很喜歡這本書，專業人士則會覺得裡面的討論很有幫助。

題目中譯

解題技巧

1. 誰會對這本書最有興趣？
   (A) 房地產開發者
   (B) 建築迷
   (C) 獨立產權公寓的客戶
   (D) 電子工程師

答案 (B)

找出題目中 interested 的對應內容，而在第一段第五行 ...which architecture and engineering buffs will appreciate 裡的 appreciate 就表示「有興趣」的意思；buff 是指「愛好者」。選出內容相同的選項就對了。

2. 你可以在這本書裡找到什麼樣的資料？
   (A) 世界最高建築物的高度
   (B) 摩天大樓建築與工程的基本原理
   (C) 摩天大樓建築歷史的討論
   (D) 歐洲最高建築物指南

答案 (B)

從編輯書評 (editorial review) 下面的第四行 review of modern structural engineering 可以推測出本書內容。接下來的 a discussion of construction principles 和選項 (B) 的 principles 一致。

3. 第一個評論批評這本書的哪一點？
   (A) 語言
   (B) 照片
   (C) 工程概念
   (D) 建築設計

答案 (A)

題目中的 criticizes 就是搜尋關鍵字。若知道第一段倒數第四行的 unfortunately 是相關字，就能直接從後面的 stilted and abstract language 得到正確答案。作答訣竅在於用 criticizes 搜尋時，找出帶有負面涵義的單字。

4. 在哪裡可以找到建築物上面有動態的建物？
   (A) 杜拜
   (B) 蘇格蘭
   (C) 倫敦
   (D) 拉斯維加斯

答案 (B)

用題目中的 moving 搜尋，在第二段倒數第五行能找到同義的 pivots。從 ...which pivots like a weathervane 可以直接找出答案。若不了解 pivots 或 weathervane 的字義，可先確認選項中的地名部分，再刪去不正確的選項。

註解

buff (n.) 愛好者
stilted (adj.)（寫作、講話風格等）做作的
spire (n.) 螺旋體，尖塔
pivot (v.) 以…為中心旋轉，在樞軸上轉動
weathervane (n.) 風向標
gemstone (n.) 寶石

Personal Time Management

There is so much stress in modern careers—finishing projects on time, managing your subordinates and pleasing your bosses, networking with others and, just as importantly, remembering their names—it's easy to feel overwhelmed. Oh, and don't forget to pick up the car from the garage before six! Panic is a natural condition, but it won't help. You need to get organized.

At one point or another, we all feel like there will be no light at the end of the tunnel. Busy at work, busy with the family, busy with friends and acquaintances—there just isn't enough time to do everything we feel we must do. But, you can manage your time more effectively by following a few simple guidelines.

First, sit down and make a list of items to put on your schedule. Don't leave anything out, especially personal time. Your goal here is to be realistic, so include time for your family and time for yourself, not just your work schedule.

After you have your list, prioritize it. Some projects will have deadlines that need to be met, and there is not much you can do about that kind of situation. Other activities, like hobbies and relaxation, are more flexible, but need to be on your schedule, too. Starting to think of the amount of time you should be spending on each activity will help you clarify how effectively you're using your time, and how you can improve in this area.

Once you have your priorities, evaluate them and decide which are most beneficial for you. Which mean the most to you? How much are you willing to sacrifice to accomplish them? Are you wasting time on projects of little importance? If so, you need to adjust your schedule. Other than that, though, you shouldn't change a schedule in the middle of a project unless it would save your time. When in doubt, it's usually best not to change a set schedule. And, just by going through this short exercise, you have set yourself on a course to improve your time management.

1. What is the purpose of this article?
   (A) To provide advice on time management
   (B) To introduce a new local garage
   (C) To explain how workers should organize their notes
   (D) To argue against the use of a general work schedule

2. What is NOT given as an example of something that makes life hectic?
   (A) Trying to finish a project
   (B) Studying for career enhancement
   (C) Spending time with the family
   (D) Keeping acquaintance with others

3. What does the author say a schedule should always include?
   (A) Ways of assessing the effectiveness of your team
   (B) Strategies for dealing with subordinates
   (C) Social engagements
   (D) Free time for yourself

4. When should you consider changing your schedule in the middle of a project?
   (A) When you are making little progress on your current task
   (B) When you find a short cut to your goal
   (C) When you are unable to set firm priorities
   (D) When you doubt the current course of action

1 Ⓐ Ⓑ Ⓒ Ⓓ
2 Ⓐ Ⓑ Ⓒ Ⓓ
3 Ⓐ Ⓑ Ⓒ Ⓓ
4 Ⓐ Ⓑ Ⓒ Ⓓ

個人時間管理

現代職業會帶來相當大的壓力——準時完成案子、管理屬下與討好上司、與別人建立關係，更要記得他們的名字——這很容易讓人感到不知所措。喔，還有，別忘了 6 點前去修車廠取車！有恐慌是正常的，但是一點幫助都沒有。你必須要有組織。

每個人都一定曾經在某個時刻，覺得繼續下去也不會有結果。忙工作、忙家庭、忙朋友、忙熟人——時間根本就不夠做所有我們覺得該做的事。但是照著以下幾點簡單的指示，就能更有效地管理時間。

首先，坐下來，把你要加入計畫表的事情都列成清單。不要遺漏任何事情，特別是你的私人時間。你的設定要非常實際，所以不僅是列出你的工作計畫表，還要列出陪家人的時間及給自己的時間。

列出清單後就按照優先順序排列。有一些案子有特定的截止期限，你一點辦法都沒有。其他的活動項目，如嗜好、休閒娛樂等，就比較有彈性，但一樣要排入計畫表中。思考每個活動應該要花多少時間，可以幫助你釐清是否有效運用自己的時間，以及可以如何改善這個問題。

一旦列出了優先順序，先衡量再決定哪件事對你最有益。哪件事對你最重要？你願意犧牲多少來完成它？你是否耗費時間在不太重要的案子上？如果是這樣，你就需要調整你的計畫表。不過，除此之外，你不該在案子進行到一半時改變你的計畫表，除非這樣能節省時間。不確定的時候，通常最好不要改變既定的計畫表。光是做完這個簡單的練習，你就已經踏上了改善時間管理之途。

題目中譯

1. 這篇文章的目的是什麼？

(A) **提供時間管理的建議**
(B) 介紹當地新的修車廠
(C) 說明員工應該如何整理他們的筆記
(D) 反對使用一般的工作計畫表

解題技巧

答案 (A)

這題問的是文章的目的，也就是主旨，因此先看第一段。(C) 的 notes、(D) 的 general work schedule 完全沒出現在第一段。(B) 的 garage 雖然出現在第一段，但讀過前面部分就能清楚了解 (B) 並非主旨。

2. 以下哪一項不是文中所列出會讓生活忙亂的例子？

(A) 試著完成案子
(B) **為了促進事業發展而唸書**
(C) 花時間和家人在一起
(D) 與別人保持往來

答案 (B)

搜尋關鍵字是題目中的 hectic。第一段的 stress 和第二段的 busy 都是相關字。在這兩段中沒有出現的是「學習」，因此要選 (B)。這一題不需要多花時間確認其他段落的內容。

3. 作者說計畫表永遠要包含什麼？

(A) 評估團隊效率的方法
(B) 應對下屬的策略
(C) 社交活動
(D) **自己的空閒時間**

答案 (D)

題目中的 a schedule should always include 就是搜尋的關鍵。這裡要注意的不是在各個段落中都出現的 schedule，而要特別注意 should 和 include，重點就在於發現第四段的 Other activities ... are more flexible, but need to be on... 中，need 的意思和 should 一樣。

4. 你什麼時候該要考慮在案子進行到一半時改變計畫表？

(A) 當你目前的工作沒有進展時
(B) **當你發現達成目標的捷徑時**
(C) 當你無法確定優先順序時
(D) 當你懷疑目前的做法時

答案 (B)

題目中的 changing your schedule in the middle of a project 和最後一段 you shouldn't change a schedule in the middle of a project unless it would save your time 的內容十分相近，可知這個部分就是對應內容。

註解

There is light at the end of the tunnel.
歷盡艱辛之後的成功，苦盡甘來。

prioritize (v.) 按優先順序列出
hectic (adj.) 手忙腳亂的

Segmenting Your Market

There are two basic ways to segment a market. The first is to focus on customers in a specific location. A local convenience store that places ads in its neighborhood would be a good example. The other is by focusing on customers who are more likely to be attracted to your products or services. When designing your own small business marketing plan, you need to keep in mind the following four aspects.

First, you need to make decisions about your products or services. You may want to focus on a highly specialized product or service, develop a niche market, or offer a broad range of products or services.

Second, you'll also need to make decisions about product promotion. Advertising is one of the oldest and most reliable ways of promoting a product, but good salesmanship is just as important for small businesses. Telephone directory advertising is also important, as many people turn to the yellow pages in a pinch. Also, direct mail advertising has been shown to be an effective and efficient way for small businesses to attract customers.

Third, pricing is important to ensure that your efforts are justly rewarded. Higher prices usually mean lower volume, and vice-versa. However, due to the high level of personalized services small businesses can provide, many can charge higher than market rates.

Finally, small businesses usually find it easiest to work with established local distributors. Those in the retail business need to consider cost and location when selecting a site. Keep in mind that the cheaper a space is to rent, the less customer traffic there is likely to be. A business with little customer traffic will need to spend more money on advertising.

The nature of business also plays a role. Impulse shoppers often look for a convenient location, so high visibility is a must if you sell, for example, hamburgers. But, if the product has a narrow niche, and if customers are willing to travel to find it, location is less important.

1. What is the purpose of this article?
   (A) To report a new marketing policy
   (B) To show how large retailers can increase their market share
   (C) To explain how businesses can reduce costs
   (D) To help small businesses in their marketing efforts

2. What is NOT mentioned as valuable for product promotion?
   (A) Salesmanship
   (B) Newspaper coupons
   (C) Phonebook advertisement
   (D) Direct mail

3. Why does the author say small businesses can often charge higher prices than other businesses?
   (A) They work with established distributors.
   (B) They offer personalized services.
   (C) They tend to be in convenient neighborhoods.
   (D) They seldom deal directly with manufacturers.

4. When is location especially important to small businesses?
   (A) When customers often make unplanned purchases
   (B) When there is a lot of local competition
   (C) When larger retailers enter a local market
   (D) When they offer a wide selection of products and services

1 Ⓐ Ⓑ Ⓒ Ⓓ
2 Ⓐ Ⓑ Ⓒ Ⓓ
3 Ⓐ Ⓑ Ⓒ Ⓓ
4 Ⓐ Ⓑ Ⓒ Ⓓ

切割市場

切割市場有兩種基本的方式。第一種是鎖定特定地點的顧客。在社區內張貼廣告的當地便利商店就是個很好的例子。再來則是鎖定有可能被你的產品或服務所吸引的顧客。設計你自己的小型企業行銷計畫時，要謹記以下四點。

第一點，必須決定你的產品或服務。你或許會想專注於非常專門的產品或服務，開創利基市場，或提供廣泛的產品或服務。

第二點，你也必須決定產品要如何宣傳。廣告是最古老，也是最可靠的產品宣傳方式，但是良好的銷售能力對小型企業也同樣重要。電話號碼簿的廣告也很重要，因為許多人必要時常常會去翻電話號碼簿。廣告信也證明是小型企業吸引顧客的有效方法。

第三點，定價非常重要，這樣才能確保你的努力獲得應有的回報。較高價通常代表較低量，反過來說也是一樣。不過，由於小型企業可以提供高度個人化的服務，多數要價都能高於市場價格。

最後，小型企業通常會覺得，與當地既有的經銷商合作最為容易。零售業者選擇據點時，必須考慮成本與地點。別忘了，空間出租價格愈便宜，客流量可能就愈少。客流量少的企業，就得要多花錢做廣告。

企業的特性也占有一席之地。衝動型的購物者常常尋找方便的地點購物，所以，舉例來說，如果你賣的東西是漢堡，能見度高就是個必要條件。但是如果產品的市場很小衆，而且如果顧客願意跑到比較遠的地方去購買，那麼地點就沒那麼重要。

題目中譯

解題技巧

1. 這篇文章的目的是什麼？

(A) 報告新的行銷策略
(B) 顯示大型零售業者如何增加他們的市場占有率
(C) 說明企業要如何降低成本
(D) **幫助小型企業進行行銷**

答案 (D)

在第一段的 When designing your own small business marketing plan... 中，small business 很顯然地就是主旨。此外，you need to keep in mind the following four aspects 之後的內容就是 small business 必備的四項要件。

2. 以下哪一項對產品宣傳不重要？

(A) 銷售能力
(B) **報紙折價券**
(C) 電話號碼簿廣告
(D) 廣告信

答案 (B)

找尋題目中 promotion 的對應部分，第三段的第一句出現了 promotion。依序確認選項後知道，除了 (B) 以外其他都在文章中出現過。

3. 作者為什麼說小型企業通常要價可以高於其他企業？

(A) 他們與既有的經銷商合作。
(B) **他們提供個人化服務**。
(C) 他們往往位在方便的社區內。
(D) 他們很少直接和製造商接觸。

答案 (B)

先確定題目中 higher prices 的對應部分出現在第四段。higher 在這一段出現了兩次。訂高價的原因是 personalized services，所以和這個內容相同的選項就是正確答案。

4. 對小型企業來說，地點在什麼時候會特別重要？

(A) **如果顧客常常未經計畫就購物**
(B) 如果當地競爭很激烈
(C) 如果大型零售業者進入當地市場
(D) 如果他們提供廣泛的產品與服務

答案 (A)

以題目中的 location 作為搜尋關鍵字，在最後一段的第二行可以找到這個字，這個部分也就是對應的內容。從 Impulse shoppers often look for a convenient location... 可以導出正確答案。impulse 和 (A) 的 unplanned 的意思相同。

註解

salesmanship (n.) 推銷術
in a pinch 在緊急時，必要時
vice-versa 反之亦然
personalized (adj.) 個人化的
distributor (n.) 經銷商，批發商
impulse (n.) 衝動，刺激
retailer (n.) 零售商

Life Expectancy

I get a lot of letters about people who are worried about outliving their savings. Most readers are worried that they are not saving enough. But, there is another side to this issue, and that is life expectancy, also called average life span, and it estimates how long you should plan to live. Men at age 60 live an average of 17.5 more years, so, for example, the life expectancy of men at age 60 is 17.5.

Statistics on mortality (e.g. death rate) are collected and analyzed by actuaries, professionals who use mathematical techniques to compute insurance premiums. To estimate the probability of death at any given age, actuaries use tables like the one below.

Notice that there are separate tables for men and women. At any given age, actuaries can estimate the number of deaths per 1,000 people. So, a man at 65 has a 0.025 probability of dying (25/1,000), and the average life expectancy of a man who has made it to 65 will be 14 years.

You'll notice that women live longer than men, on average. This is because men generally engage in riskier behavior and jobs (speeding, hunting, coal mining, military service, etc.) and are not as vigilant about their health. Men are far more likely to eat poorly, smoke, and drink excessively.

Of course, you must keep in mind that such tables are averages, which means that some people never even make it to 60 years of age, while others will make it to 100. So, in formulating a budget, it's better to be safe than sorry and plan on outliving your life expectancy.

Mortality Tables

	Male		Female	
Age	No. of Death	Per 1,000 Expectancy	No. of Death	Per 1,000 Expectancy
60	16	17.5	9.5	21
65	25	14	14.5	17
70	39.5	11	22	13.5
75	64	8	38	10
80	99	6	66	7.5
85	153	4.5	116	5
90	222	3	191	3.5
95	393	2	317	2

* Statistics provided by the American Association of Actuaries. See their homepage, www.aaa.com for more details and research.

1. What is the purpose of this article?
   (A) To describe the uses of census data
   (B) To explain why insurance rates are higher for men
   (C) To argue that men should take better care of themselves
   (D) To respond to reader concerns

2. What is the average life expectancy of an 85 year old man?
   (A) 153
   (B) 4.5
   (C) 116
   (D) 5

3. What kind of professional would most likely use the information in the table?
   (A) A journalist
   (B) An actuary
   (C) Coal miners
   (D) Military leaders

4. What should readers who want more information about life expectancy do?
   (A) Contact the writer
   (B) Visit a local insurance agent
   (C) Check an Internet site
   (D) Take a course in mathematics

5. What advice does the columnist provide to readers?
   (A) Men should stop participating in dangerous activities.
   (B) They should plan for living longer than average.
   (C) People over the age of 60 need to be more careful about their habits.
   (D) Women save more to compensate for their longer average life spans.

1 Ⓐ Ⓑ Ⓒ Ⓓ
2 Ⓐ Ⓑ Ⓒ Ⓓ
3 Ⓐ Ⓑ Ⓒ Ⓓ
4 Ⓐ Ⓑ Ⓒ Ⓓ
5 Ⓐ Ⓑ Ⓒ Ⓓ

預期壽命

我常收到很多信，這些人很擔心活太久而存款不夠。大多數的讀者都擔心自己的存款不夠。不過這個議題還有另外一面，那就是預期壽命，又稱作平均壽命，用來預估你可以準備活多久。舉例來說，60 歲的男性平均可以再活 17.5 年，所以 60 歲男性的預期壽命就是 17.5。

死亡率的統計數據由精算師進行蒐集和分析，他們是專業人士，運用數學技巧來計算保險金。要計算任何年齡可能什麼時候死亡，精算師會使用類似下面的表格。

要注意，男性和女性有不同的表格。對於任何年齡，精算師都能預測出每 1000 人中有多少人會死亡。因此，一個 65 歲的男性，其死亡率可能是 0.025 (25/1000)，而活到 65 歲的男性，平均預期壽命大概是 14 年。

你會發現，平均來說，女性活得比男性久。這是因為男性通常會從事比較冒險的行為與工作（如飆車、打獵、挖礦、從軍等），而且對自己的健康也沒那麼小心。男性更有可能亂吃、抽菸、酗酒。

當然，你也要記得這些表格只不過是平均數，也就是說，有些人根本活不到 60 歲，但是有些人卻能活到 100 歲。所以，列預算的時候，寧願多算也不要少算，先假設自己會活超過預期壽命。

死亡人數表

	男性		女性	
年齡	死亡人數	每千人預期壽命	死亡人數	每千人預期壽命
60	16	17.5	9.5	21
65	25	14	14.5	17
70	39.5	11	22	13.5
75	64	8	38	10
80	99	6	66	7.5
85	153	4.5	116	5
90	222	3	191	3.5
95	393	2	317	2

* 數據由美國精算師協會提供。詳細資料與研究請見網頁 www.aaa.com。

題目中譯

解題技巧

1. 這篇文章的目的是什麼？

   (A) 描述調查資料的用途
   (B) 解釋為什麼男性的保險費率比較高
   (C) 強調男性應該要更加照顧自己
   (D) **回應讀者的憂慮**

答案 (D)

這一題問的是報導的目的。由一開頭的 I get a lot of letters about people who are worried about... 及下一句的 Most readers...，可以知道這篇文章在回答來自讀者的詢問。

2. 85 歲男性的預期壽命是多少？

   (A) 153
   (B) **4.5**
   (C) 116
   (D) 5

答案 (B)

題目問 85 歲男性的預期壽命，從死亡人數表中就能找出正確答案。

3. 哪一種職業最可能用到表格裡的資訊？

   (A) 記者
   (B) **精算師**
   (C) 煤礦工
   (D) 軍事領袖

答案 (B)

在文章中搜尋題目裡的 professional 和 use，可以確定第二段的 Statistics on mortality ... are collected and analyzed by actuaries, professionals who use... 就是對應的部分。

4. 想要知道更多關於預期壽命資訊的讀者該怎麼做？

   (A) 聯絡作家
   (B) 造訪當地保險業者
   (C) **點閱網站**
   (D) 修數學課

答案 (C)

用題目裡的 more information 去搜尋，就能在表格下方發現幾乎和 information 同義的 more details and research。這個對應部分在敘述獲得資訊的方法。

5. 專欄作家提供什麼訊息給讀者？

   (A) 男性應該要停止從事危險的活動。
   (B) **他們應該計畫活得比平均壽命還久。**
   (C) 超過 60 歲的人要更小心他們的習慣。
   (D) 女性要存多一點錢，因為她們的平均壽命比較長。

答案 (B)

用題目裡的 advice 搜尋，從表格上面一段的 it's better to be safe... 可以知道這個部分就是建議。內容指出必須以長壽的觀念來計畫，以免後悔。

註解

outlive (v.) 活得比…長久
mortality (n.) 死亡率，死亡數目
actuary (n.) 精算人員，保險統計師
probability (n.) 機率，或然性
vigilant (adj.) 警惕的，注意的
better to be safe than sorry 寧可求穩，以免事後後悔

Classified Ad

趙御筌 TOEIC 字彙資優班——一次學會字彙、聽力、口語

MP3

作者：趙御筌

定價：480 元

本書從歷屆考古題中嚴選 TOEIC 複考率最高的 900 個核心字彙及其必考同義字，以獨創的「聽說雙併」學習法，幫助考生聽懂 TOEIC 字彙的連音、變音等快速發音，並搭配「考古題應用」和「口試練習題」，讓讀者一次學會字彙、聽力、口語！

商務英文分類字彙

MP3

作者：田中宏昌・石山昭彥・滝井寛

定價：480 元

本書收錄職場上最頻繁使用的 3000 個英文字彙，主題完整涵蓋商務職場各種情境：從基礎的辦公室溝通，到進階的協商談判。對於職場上班族來說，熟練本書的字彙及對話，不但是提升職場競爭力的最佳利器；對於要準備 TOEIC 的考生，更是不可錯過的工具書！

商務英文核心字彙

MP3

作者：味園真紀

定價：380 元

本書推薦給想提升商務英文程度和準備 TOEIC 的職場專業人士！針對進入職場 1~5 年的上班族，精選最低限度應熟記的 1600 個核心字彙，並搭配各式商業例句，幫助讀者了解用法，培養語感。隨書 MP3，幫助讀者用聽的背單字、唸例句，高效精進英文語感！

英文字根活用詞典

MP3

作者：白安竹 Andrew E. Bennett

定價：400 元

「字源分析法」是最科學、最速效的字彙記憶法！再複雜的字，也能透過字首、字根、字尾等字源的組合，推斷出大概的字義。對於要準備 TOEFL、TOEIC、IELTS 及英檢中級以上等考生，更可利用此方法來應付閱讀及字彙的測驗，是對付茫茫字海的最佳利器！

Classified Ad

美國老師教你寫出好英文

作者：Scott Dreyer・廖柏森

定價：320 元

本書由美國老師 Scott 以及台北大學廖柏森教授攜手合作，其豐富的英文寫作教學經驗，使本書成為專為台灣學生打造的英文寫作專書。Scott 老師透過寫作 7 大文體以及獨家 12 步驟寫作技巧，並藉由批改台灣學生的英文作文，教導讀者從無到有寫出好英文！

英文寫作正誤範例

作者：James T. Keating

定價：350 元

多寫沒用，要準才行！本書要教你如何寫出簡潔的英文文體。作者具有 35 年豐富的校正經驗，深知讀者在書寫時常犯的錯誤，整理出百餘條錯誤或語意薄弱的用例，並提供正確用法，讓讀者一目了然。全書用例以英文字母的順序編排，是一本寫作的自修書，也是一本實用的工具書。

商務英文書信寫作

作者：有元美津世

定價：350 元

不論是剛進職場的新人，或是想自我提升的資深職員，從推銷產品、寄送人事信函，到編寫合約、處理智慧財產權糾紛，各種職場領域所需的英文書信祕訣，本書提供即查即用、簡潔切要的中英對照範例，教你一次就把商務英文書信寫完、寫對、寫好！

讀出好英文—用美國中學課本學閱讀

MP3 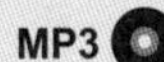

作者：林功

定價：350 元

大量閱讀，是增進英文能力的最佳方法！本書從美國中學課本取材，文章內容涵蓋數理文史，讀者在做主題性閱讀時，廣泛接觸日常、課堂使用詞彙，無形中內化成自然語法，豐富相關背景知識，英文也可以和美國學生一樣好！適合各種英文能力檢定的準備教材。

Classified Ad

一看就會唸的英語發音法

MP3

作者：足立惠子

定價：320 元

本書介紹英語系國家的人，從小就開始學習的發音法：利用 Phonics 練習發音，再透過 Rhyme 練習語感！不需背複雜的 KK 音標，每單元皆有大量的簡易字彙及押韻例句做練習，搭配活潑逗趣的插圖及 MP3。扎實易懂的內容，讓本書一上市，即盤踞各書店排行榜長達數月之久。

和英文系學生一起上英語聽說課

2CD

作者：黃玟君

定價：280 元

作者黃玟君老師於國立台科大教授英語多年，首次公開英文系學生的課堂訓練方式－「懶人聽說法」，幫助讀者從基礎的發音和語調練習起，對於外國人日常使用的「連音」、「削弱音」及「彈舌音」，提供易懂易記的口訣以達到事半功倍的效果。用對方法，英文也能比本科系學生還要好！

英式英語的 32 堂聽力課

MP3

作者：Christopher Belton

定價：350 元

要學好英式英語，就從了解英國人的文化特性開始。全書 32 篇文章，從英國的飲食、體育、到聞名全球的文學名著、電影人物等，皆以中級程度的英文詞彙所編寫。除了可以提升「聽力」，也是增進「讀寫」及「口說」的最佳教材。同步提升英語聽力及閱讀力，讓你學習英式英語零障礙！

聽見英國

1CD

作者：上田真理砂・Iain Davey

定價：320 元

本書所有對話內容皆與英國當地生活息息相關。CD 以純正英式發音及實況背景收音，彷彿置身倫敦街頭。每單元並附生動的練習，選擇、填空、排序、問答及改錯等多樣題型，赴英留學、旅行、短期居住者必讀！

國家圖書館出版品預行編目（CIP）資料

NEW TOEIC® TEST 金色證書：閱讀 / Institute of Foreign Study 編；柯乃瑜, 葉韋利譯.
-- 初版 . -- 臺北市：眾文圖書, 民 98.04. 面；公分
ISBN 978-957-532-355-4（平裝） 1. 多益測驗 2. 試題
805.1895 97013560

TC008

NEW TOEIC® TEST 金色證書：閱讀

定價 250 元
2014 年 7 月 初版 11 刷

編者	Institute of Foreign Study
譯者	柯乃瑜．葉韋利
英文校閱	D. Corey Sanderson
責任編輯	黃琬婷
主編	陳瑠琍
副主編	黃炯睿
資深編輯	黃琬婷．蔡易伶
美術設計	嚴國綸
行銷企劃	李皖萍．吳思瑩
發行人	黃建和
發行所	眾文圖書股份有限公司 台北市 10088 羅斯福路三段 100 號 12 樓之 2
網路書店	www.jwbooks.com.tw
電話	02-2311-8168
傳真	02-2311-9683
郵撥帳號	01048805

"SHUTSUDAI ITO GA MIERU! TOEIC® TEST 990-TEN SOKKAI READING" edited by Institute of Foreign Study. Copyright © Institute of Foreign Study, 2006. All rights reserved. Original Japanese edition published by The Japan Times, Ltd. This Complex Chinese edition published by arrangement with The Japan Times, Ltd., Tokyo, in care of Tuttle-Mori Agency, Inc., Tokyo, through Keio Cultural Enterprise Co., Ltd., Sanchong District, New Taipei City, Taiwan.

The Traditional Chinese edition copyright © 2014 by Jong Wen Books Co., Ltd. All rights reserved. No part of this publication may be reproduced, stored in a retrieval system, or transmitted in any form or by any means, electronic, mechanical, photocopying, recording, or otherwise, without the prior written permission of the publisher.

ISBN 978-957-532-355-4 Printed in Taiwan

本書任何部分之文字及圖片，非經本公司書面同意，不得以任何形式抄襲、節錄或翻印。本書如有缺頁、破損或裝訂錯誤，請寄回下列地址更換：新北市 23145 新店區寶橋路 235 巷 6 弄 2 號 4 樓